THE
BATTERED

THE BATTERED

ANNO INITIUM 3

DINKO SKOPLJAK

Podium

For my uprooted brethren

Translation from German edited by Sarah Rimmington

Cover design by Marcus Dorau

ISBN: 978-1-0394-2811-9

Published in 2023 by Podium Publishing, ULC
www.podiumaudio.com

THE
BATTERED

CHAPTER 1

SHKODËR

Lucas Morel emerged silently through the water's surface, took off his diving mask, and looked around in the darkness. The sky above him was clear but moonless, and it was only by the light of the stars that he was able to see the gray strip of the coast twenty meters away. Behind it rose a hill that, in the gloom, looked like a long wall of obsidian. Cold water rushed down his neck into his wet suit, expelling some of the liquid his body had already warmed. The sea temperature was low this early in March, but Lucas put up with it stoically. Bubbles gurgled to the surface as he spat his mouthpiece into the water. Carefully, he flipped down his night vision goggles. He switched on the image intensifier, and his surroundings instantly glowed green.

Other silhouettes appeared to his left and right at short distances. He recognized Ramona immediately, towering unmistakably above the others. Matteo wiped the salt water from his full beard and nodded at him, his eyes glowing in the intensified display. Angela and Argiris swam onward. Lucas glanced at his wristwatch. He waited, glancing left and right. Fourteen seconds later, he heard staccato rifle volleys two kilometers away. Angry shouts from an unseen coastal patrol rang out, quickly disappearing in the direction of the fighting.

Thinking about the task ahead of him, Lucas felt his pulse quicken. He took a tighter grip on his foil-wrapped rapid-fire weapon. His index finger wandered automatically to the trigger, which he could feel through the thin material.

He suppressed the impulse to remove the cover. The rifles needed to remain dry for the time being, in case the group was spotted and forced back into the water. He took three deep, steady breaths and managed to calm himself a little. At this distance, muzzle flashes seemed like dim sheet lightning to the northwest and southeast of the coast. Now he was fully focused again on what was happening on the beach at Rrjolli.

Lucas peeled himself out of the harness, whose attached pressurized oxygen cylinders took it swiftly to the bottom of the Adriatic Sea. Lastly, he stripped off his fins and swam toward the shore. With the company behind him, he stepped onto the fine sand, adjusted his waterproof shoulder bag, and set off at a run. He took care to avoid the low bushes, hoping not to get bogged down in one of the swampy hollows, which despite his night vision equipment was no easy feat.

In order not to expose the strength of their troop, his people would follow him in a line. After five hundred meters, he had them stop and form up all around, ready for battle. Kneeling, he listened. Beside him, Argiris stared into the darkness. Angela stretched her muscular neck until her vertebrae cracked. The noise of the fake battle had not abated. No alarms had gone off. Everything was going according to plan.

Once his breathing had settled, he had the team sprint the rest of the way to the hill. Under cover of a pitiful pine grove, they unwrapped their weapons and put silencers on them. They traded their diving suits for clothes steeped in the smell of decay, which they had transported in their shoulder bags. Where they were headed, that would be the only camouflage they had.

Underneath, each of them wore a vest that held spare ammunition, bandages, and three days' rations. Their mission would not be allowed to last longer than that in any case. The familiar doubts nagged at him, but he dispelled them with a shake of his head. The rapid-fire weapon in his hand gave him confidence.

Lucas was once again grateful that they had been able to take advantage of the pre-pandemic overproduction and consumption. At the time, he had been too young to understand the negative societal and environmental consequences. But since the human population had shrunk to less than four percent of its former size and was no longer in need of massive industries to support itself, nature had been able to recover—wherever there wasn't contamination from radioactivity or chemicals.

A large proportion of the goods produced at that time were, therefore, still in warehouses, stores, or in containers on abandoned freight trains and ships. The sources that had not burned down or sunk provided survivors with vast choices whenever scavenging for useful items. Lucas and his troop had found their diving equipment and several other useful items in sporting goods stores. They had also procured clothing, shoes, and medicines, though the drugs, for the most part, were past their expiration dates.

Getting ahold of weapons was a more serious problem. Firearms and ammunition could only be procured—if they could be found at all—on military bases, where they were usually stored behind impenetrable security systems. So a new era of cold weapons had dawned, but these weapons were ineffective against the hordes of the undead. Nonetheless, Lucas's sworn band of followers had managed to stockpile an exclusive supply of firearms for missions like this one.

Lucas himself had fought on the front lines for three years. The unit had been formed to track down the last of the survivors and liberate those who were besieged by zombies. It numbered just eighty souls drawn from all over Europe. Together they had already fought dozens of battles.

He and his team worked their way from enclave to enclave, freeing the entrapped and eliminating the undead. But the number of people living in the liberated areas was stagnating. It had been clear for years that humanity had no future under these conditions. They needed more people, who were nowhere to be found nine years after the outbreak. Six months ago, however, they had heard rumors that raised their fading hopes. And the young Frenchman was about to get to the bottom of the gossip.

Under cover of the pine grove, Lucas retrieved the radio and binoculars from his shoulder bag. Before stowing them in the vest, he turned on the device and selected the frequency they had agreed upon. Since most of the group understood English, that was the language they used.

"Wet rat is dry. Repeat: Wet rat is dry. Over," he said softly and released the PTT button.

The line hissed and crackled, and then he heard Lena's voice. "Roger, dry rat. Over and out."

"Over and out," Lucas replied, turning off the radio and stashing it under his dirty shirt.

He surveyed his team as they stuffed their protective wraps and wet suits into their waterproof shoulder bags before stowing them in the bushes. He noted with satisfaction—and disgust—that he exuded a zombie-like smell of decay. Last of all, he knelt and tied the laces of his running shoes.

As if on cue, the mock fighting fell silent.

"Are you ready?" he whispered to the group. No one answered, and he took this as confirmation. "Right then, follow me," he said, leading them up the hill. They had five hours of hard marching to reach the rendezvous point, and they hoped to get there before sunrise.

Taking care not to kick any rocks loose, they trotted off. After a few minutes, they approached the ridge but kept a few meters below it on the coastal side so that they could not be spotted against the stars. The brisk pace kept them warm. Lucas kept reminding himself what this mission was all about. Determinedly, he focused on the insubstantial path at his feet.

Twenty minutes later, the terrain sloped gently downward. They braked along a dry creek bed, took their hydration bladders out of the pockets of their cargo pants, and drank. From here, they would be heading straight north, through an area that was flatter but also more frequented by the undead, and better guarded. The Albanian scouting parties had provided them with all the necessary information, and this formed the basis for the meticulously planned operation. Lucas looked at his watch, consulted his compass, and told the group to prepare to move on. Then they headed for the valley.

They covered the eight and a half kilometers north to the old SH27 federal highway in three hours, which wasn't exactly a record. But in order not to attract attention, they were moving at a zombie-like pace, avoiding settlements and giving the isolated buildings a wide berth. And they already made it more than halfway without being detected. Lucas hoped that it would stay that way.

The second stage took them to Masmalaj, over an asphalt road pock-marked with potholes. Outside the deserted village, they swung east onto dirt tracks. They found a hiding place in the low bushes on the hill between Bërdicë and Mllojë, which gave them a clear view of the road to Shkodër to the north and to the fields to the south. The sky to the east glowed red as they finished the stage for the day. The team stationed themselves around Lucas so they could keep watch in all directions. They wrapped themselves in thin camouflage sheets lined with rescue blankets. Despite the sun's early rays, the Balkan mountains were ice-cold in the morning. Now the task was to gather enough information about enemy movements within a maximum of three days.

Lucas pulled out his radio and transmitted, "Dry rat is in the rathole. Repeat: Dry rat is in the rathole. Over."

He could hear relief in Lena's voice as she replied, "Roger, dry rat. Over and out."

"Over and out." He turned the device off. They would have no further contact until morning unless there was an emergency. Deep inside enemy territory, it was futile to call for help. But he figured it wouldn't come to that. He rummaged in his vest pocket for his binoculars. In the light of the rising sun, he monitored the bridge, two kilometers to the north. It had been a long time since any vehicles had crossed it.

All being well, they would intercept the contact there tomorrow morning, and she would give them more information on the situation in Shkodër. All very cumbersome compared to how things had been before the pandemic. Lucas longed for the time when it had been easy to scout an area from space with cameras attached to satellites, without the people being shadowed having the slightest idea. His father had often told him about it. That kind of knowledge had protected national security, he claimed. But for all its technological advances, humanity had failed to repel a zombie invasion.

Lucas took a deep breath. He thought about the early days of the apocalypse. As happened so often lately, former classmates, people he hadn't seen in years, came into his mind. What had become of them? How many of them were still alive? Who, if anyone, had made it? When this was over, he would be hard pressed not to make his way to Paris to . . . what? To search for them would seem hopeless. Hardly anyone still lived in the capital, as far as he knew.

He pushed these gloomy thoughts aside. If the mission succeeded, he would have more than enough time for them. But right now, he was in the Balkans, thousands of kilometers from the city of his birth, and he had a job to do. He still had a clear memory of the day a year ago when someone had first told him about the grievances in Shkodër. At first, he had paid little attention to the rumors. But the reports piled up until he couldn't ignore them any longer.

* * *

Over the last few months, he had invested almost his entire fortune in putting together a crew to help him undertake the mission. As soon as the weather had improved, they loaded the weapons onto the three-master and sailed from Marseille toward the Adriatic.

In Corfu, where a colony of Albanian, Greek, and Macedonian survivors had settled, they learned that the rumors were bitter reality. Lucas's initial hopes that he could quickly bring the nightmare to an end were quickly dashed. His team was far too small to take on the Shkodër zombie population, which controlled the whole of the plain around Lake Skudari. So they scrapped the first plan and came up with a new, more realistic one: They would obtain tangible evidence about what was happening, in the hope that this would mobilize broader support. But the means of obtaining such information were limited, and the geographical location of the target area didn't make it any easier—to say nothing of the innumerable undead moving in and around it. The plain to the south of the city, which had once been agricultural land and had supplied Albania with food, was sealed off from the rest of the country to the northeast by the high and craggy Albanian Alps. Scouting parties from the area had provided some very useful information, but Lucas did not consider it shocking enough for a major mobilization of the kind he thought necessary. It was sufficient, however, to enable them to plan their little mission. Someone had even suggested using old-fashioned drones for reconnaissance. But their batteries were so low on power after all these years that most of the devices could barely stay in the air for more than ten minutes. That wasn't nearly enough time to fly them in and out of the city, let alone provide usable images over a long period.

Finally, it was agreed that they would install small video cameras deep in enemy territory and hide there for a few days while the recordings were made. It was unnecessary even to mention the enormous risks associated with this tactic. No one in his team was under the illusion that they would survive if they were discovered.

But Lucas was convinced the mission would go well. His customary optimism, and also the thought of their new friend Nesha in the city beyond the bridge, filled him with confidence.

"Nesha should have the cameras in place now," he said. He directed his words partly to the team and partly to himself, as if to assuage his concern for the young woman.

Nesha was one of the few escapees who had spent almost her entire childhood in the city. Much of Lucas's hope in the mission was because of her support. She had been picked up last winter in an exhausted state on the beach at Dubrava and taken to Sidari on Corfu, where she recovered for the most part. They consulted with her on how to reconnoiter Shkodër as they put the plan together. Nesha had suggested she go back to the city in person to get them the information they needed. All they had to do in return was promise to get her out alive. After two weeks of meticulous planning, most of the concerns about putting the plan into action had been eliminated.

Lucas had befriended Nesha during the training—to the extent that this was possible. The sixteen-year-old had been reticent, probably a result of her long stay in the Enclave from Hell. Like him, she was ruthless in her determination to play a part in the liberation of Shkodër. He often wondered where she got her motivation from, especially after she escaped. It was not often that someone succeeded. The punishments meted out for failed escapes were too brutal. No one except Nesha had been willing to go back—which was not surprising, given her stories.

But she seemed different. She quickly agreed to infiltrate the city and provide reconnaissance. Lucas's mission, on the other hand, was to scout the southern plains and escort Nesha out the next day with the recordings intact.

A light breeze rose, rustling the leaves of the bushes around him. He looked to the east. The minute the sun rose above the horizon, he fished out his radio. This was the time Nesha he made contact each day. She had entered Shkodër four days ago under cover of darkness on a camouflaged raft, via the icy rapids of the Kir, which carried vast quantities of melted snow from the Accursed Mountains into the River Drin. She would currently be waiting for his call in her shelter, about six kilometers north-northwest of his position.

Lucas radioed her, hoping to hear her voice in the next few seconds. He took a deep breath to control his anxiety.

Deep in the gorge, fifteen kilometers east of Shkodër, the entire area was overshadowed by the high cliffs. Even on clear days, the sun made only a brief appearance as it traversed the narrow sliver of sky between the peaks. But now the relative brightness of midday had passed, and the shadows had returned.

Nesha watched curiously as Blerim rummaged in his backpack. He pulled out his hand and held out a roll about the length of his forearm.

"Wrap yourself tightly in that. The plastic wrap goes under the neoprene," he said over the roar of the nearby river. He pointed at the dilapidated cabin in front of which they had tied the raft together. "In there." Then he turned his attention back to the misshapen pile of logs, branches, and brush at his feet.

Nesha looked at the plastic wrap, nonplussed, and then gave the forty-year-old a skeptical look. "And what good is that going to do?"

"I saw it in a movie once, a long time ago," he replied, panting. He braced his foot against the structure, which was sitting on top of some plastic barrels. He tugged at the strap holding it all together until the construction groaned. "Two men broke out of a prison in the middle of winter," he continued, "and this is what they did. Not sure it really helps. But it made sense to me at the time. If you don't want to, you don't have to."

"Can't hurt," she replied, and made her way into the hand-carved limestone ruins. Just a sliver of light shafted in through the demolished roof. Nesha undressed.

After laboriously loosening the beginning of the roll, she wrapped the film several times around her left foot. She worked her way up to her hip, then down her right leg, tearing off the transparent plastic below the sole of her right foot. Her torso and arms were next, and finally she wrapped her neck and head before pulling on the wet suit Lucas had given her. The film actually made the suit feel warmer than she'd expected. She put on the green-and-brown plastic helmet and pulled the black protective vest over it. Someone had even taken the trouble to wrap tendrils of fresh ivy around it for extra camouflage.

"It seems to be working," she called from the doorway to Blerim, who was lowering the raft into the rushing mountain stream. "I'm sweating already."

Visibly satisfied, he smiled and adjusted his colorful mintan jacket with his free hand. "I've put your gear in the blue barrel," he explained. "If the raft comes apart, just cling onto that. You can ignore the white ones. But it should hold until we get to Shkodër."

It'll be difficult to tell the difference at night, Nesha thought. Instead she said only, "Looks stable."

The girl approached the raft. A fine mist sprayed her. She felt Blerim's gaze on her back as she checked everything.

"Are you sure you want to do this?" he asked.

She looked him in the eye. "Yes, of course." She was unabashed as he scrutinized her. He nodded at her and gave a sharp whistle. A similar whistle sounded from a nearby bush. Several guards in old army uniforms and carrying AK-47s immediately emerged from it.

Blerim handed Nesha a long black knife in a sheath. "Tie this to your forearm. In case you get stuck somewhere or have to cut the ropes," he explained. Then he ordered the guards, "Help her onto the raft!"

Nesha rejected the offers of help, climbing onto the wobbly craft unassisted while Blerim held on to the rope and tried to control it. She lied down immediately, clinging to the loops provided. She had attached the knife to her left forearm with Velcro. Then she looked up at him and nodded.

"Good luck, my daughter," he called over the roar of the rapids.

Her chest tightened at that final word, but she had no chance to figure out where the sensation was coming from. Blerim had let go. The current whirled her and the raft she was on around with such ferocity that she almost let go of the loops. Suddenly, icy water was swirling all around her. She screamed in fear but could not hear her own voice. The cold crept into the wet suit, which immediately felt like icy armor. Her heart skipped a beat, her body stiffening. She forced herself to breathe, but the current swirled around her, pulling her under again and again as she shot downstream. Each time the raft hit one of the many lurking boulders, it shook her mercilessly. Nesha frantically tried to hook her feet around something, but they kept slipping. The journey had only just begun and already the strain was making her whole body ache. Would she be able to endure it for the next ten kilometers? She doubted it. She'd already lost the feeling in her toes and fingertips.

It wouldn't be long before her strength was gone. Nesha traversed one set of rapids after the next. She went under as the raft rolled sideways, but the buoyancy righted it again. She spat out water and almost lost her grip for good but realized at the last moment that the river had widened. The current was no longer raging so wildly. Seconds later, her craft settled. Now that she had left the rapids of the gorge behind and was floating on the plain, the day's last rays of sunlight hit her. Exhausted, she rested one cheek on the rough wood and tried to relax.

Soon she felt warmth slowly returning to her body. Ten minutes later, she was able to move her fingers and toes again. Every now and then she bumped into other flotsam, including some tree trunks that had probably been uprooted by a storm. She was glad not to be the only object floating in the River Kir; she was less conspicuous that way. If she managed to remain undetected until she reached the Mesit Bridge, she could claim a partial victory. But there were a few kilometers to go yet.

Motionless, she scanned the banks to the right and left as the current turned the raft. From here on she was in enemy territory. She caught sight of figures walking sluggishly up and down the embankments. Nesha hardly dared move. An icy cold tingle crept up her spine, and it wasn't because of the water temperature this time. She tried not to let her fear of the zombies distract her and concentrated on the rest of her journey. At last, a stone arch came into view downstream. Nesha breathed a sigh of relief.

Around half a kilometer ahead of the ancient structure, where the Kir was just under two hundred meters in width, the first part of her journey ended. She slid into the water. After the anticipated cold shock, she swam toward the eastern shore, dragging the raft behind her. The spot—where the shore was lined by dense woodland—had been carefully chosen. She quickly tied the craft to one of the branches that was overhanging the river and crawled onto dry land. Water ran out of her suit onto her hands and feet. Lying on her front, she felt her heart drumming in her chest. She used the knife Blerim had given her to cut the blue barrel free. She had to give it a good shake to extract it from the tangle. Making a huge effort, she tugged and rolled the barrel and finally got it to shore. Pausing to catch her breath, she watched the remains of the raft drifting slowly downstream until she remembered why she was there. She immediately berated herself for not first checking her surroundings. She looked around her. On the street in front of the former cement factory and barely thirty meters away, five or six of the undead were staggering toward Shkodër. Nesha wondered if they were the ones she had spotted from the raft earlier. Her heart in her mouth, she identified from their posture and agility that they weren't weakened zombies; they were untainted and could only be a few days old. They were young men, some who were still teenagers.

Fear and disgust rose in her. She buried her face in the grass to avoid having to look at them. Suppressing her anger at the fate that had befallen the earth, she tried to focus on the plan. Now was not the time to let her emotions take the wheel. Nesha reminded herself of the preparations of the past few weeks, of the physical and mental drills she had voluntarily put herself through. The success of the mission depended on how well she was able to apply what she had learned. The lives of nearly three thousand people were in her hands. And one of those people was more important to her than anything.

She waited a long time until the figures disappeared. Then she took a deep breath and opened the blue barrel. She took out ski socks, sturdy hiking pants, a lined expedition jacket, and a towel. Nesha laid out the clothes, stripped off her clothes, and got rid of the plastic wrap. She had been sweating hugely into it for the past hour. Under the cover of darkness, she immersed herself in the river to eliminate the smell. She scrubbed herself with sand, shivering, her breath catching in the excruciating cold. She dressed quickly, barely drying herself. She shouldered the ultralight backpack with the day's rations before pulling on her jacket. At the bottom of the barrel was a plastic bag containing a shrink-wrapped poncho made of two layers, camouflage fabric on the outside and a rescue blanket on the inside. Her stomach turned at the stench emanating from the contents of the bag. A familiar smell, evoking fear and hatred. Nesha fought rising panic but threw the blanket over herself and stuck her head through the hole that had been cut into it. The weight of the Glock, which was the last thing she retrieved from the barrel, gave her renewed courage. She got a grip on herself, hid the barrel in the bushes, and ventured into the city.

The night was cold, but her outfit kept her warm. Under cover of near total darkness, she ran, crawled, and crept along the paths. She figured she'd be reasonably safe since the enemy was unlikely to be expecting an incursion. But if they were, she was happy to take the risk in any case. She had no choice. Her stubborn sense of duty stemmed from more than the promise she had made to her mother on her deathbed.

She crawled the last few meters to the city limits. Arriving at the fence of the first camp, she sought out the hole that she and her friends had dug secretly long ago, well before they had been recruited and taken away.

Reaching the chosen spot, she began to enlarge the opening. She used the knife to loosen the ground they had firmly trodden down, stabbing the blade into it repeatedly and shoveling away endless handfuls of earth until she had an entrance large enough to crawl through. Covered in dirt, she crept toward the production hall, ready at any minute to run away or thrust with the knife. The Glock was in its holster on her right hip. Nesha would resort to using it only in an emergency; it would take only a single shot to alert the undead and ruin all their plans. The factory building, which had been used for textiles production pre-pandemic, was directly ahead of her. She looked for the wall that included the remains of a two-meter air conditioning unit, climbed it, and peered in through one of the windows. Fear caught her breath again as a familiar scene came into view. In the flickering light of a couple of oil lamps, she saw dozens of beds standing close to one another. Among them, sundry mattresses had been thrown onto the floor. A number of heavily pregnant women tossed and turned restlessly in their sleep. Smaller figures lay between them.

Nesha suppressed the feelings that rose inside her. This was where she would position the first camera. She pulled one out and began to feel with her fingers for a suitable place to attach the clamp.

She froze. She could hear footsteps approaching. A patrol walked by beneath her. Nesha couldn't tell if they were undead or collabs. She took a tighter grip on the knife handle, waiting breathlessly to see how the guards would react. She braced herself for them to raise the alarm and attack her. But nothing happened. The footsteps moved away and disappeared into the night. Nesha exhaled and set to work.

She mounted the camera on the grille outside the window to allow the wide-angle lens to film part of the exterior of the hall as well the interior. Her hands shook, and she needed two attempts to tighten the screws. The camcorder would take one infrared picture every minute through the night. Its flashing red light was covered by a thick layer of adhesive tape.

As the night wore on, she managed to install four more cameras. One of them monitored the area where the children were being held. She had to force herself not to stay there for longer and look for her brother. If she saw him, she probably wouldn't be able to leave without him—and that would jeopardize the entire mission. The third camera covered the hall where recruits and the undead were fed. Here, the smell of blood and decay was so strong that it easily masked her own scent.

She completed this part of her task just as the sky grew lighter in the east. It was time to hide. Satisfied with her work, she listened for approaching sentries. Having detected no signs of danger, she jumped down and left the site. She covered the hole she had dug with rubble.

By sunrise, she was lying on the flat roof of a skyscraper, which could only be reached by a risky ascent of its exterior wall. Inside the building, the stairs had partially collapsed and were crammed with debris in many places. Nesha knew this because she had scrambled over it count-less times. When her mother was alive, she and the other children had snuck out of the dormitory to play outside and test their courage in life-threatening situations. Once again, she felt rage, luring her blindly into action. It could almost have led her to climb back down and rescue her brother from the camp. To take him and flee Shkodër without having accomplished anything. That would be the wrong thing to do, so she forced herself to remain calm. The way to give them both the best chance was to deliver the recordings. Exhausted from the stress and strains of the night, Nesha holed up on the western corner of the roof, wrapped herself in her camouflage cloak, and watched the sun rise over Prokletije.

Someone was shaking his leg.

"Lucas, wake up."

"Hmm?" he grunted sleepily. It took him some time to remember that he was lying on a hill between two Albanian villages, from which they had been monitoring the area since the day before.

"Yeah, I'm awake." He yawned. His wristwatch showed that it was a few minutes to nine. Lucas picked out the others at their posts. "Have you seen Nesha yet?" he whispered.

"Negative. She's probably still waiting for the zombies to get off the bridge," Angela replied without taking her eye from the scope.

"Zombies? Where?" Lucas looked through his binoculars at the bridge two kilometers to the north. "Have they been there long?"

"Mm-hmm, an hour or so. I thought they'd move on eventually. But they don't seem to be going."

"Then Nesha can't get past them."

"Seems like it. So what do we do?"

Lucas thought. "Three of us will work our way there and cover her as she crosses the bridge. Two will stay here in case she takes a different route from the one we agreed upon."

"Who's going?" asked Angela.

Lucas knew that she was keen to do more than just watch. He felt the same way himself after days of inactivity.

"You, Matteo, Ramona?" he suggested.

All three agreed.

"Good. Turn on channel fourteen; I'll guide you there. The street is empty, but there's a good chance there'll be stinkers between the houses."

Angela, Matteo, and Ramona nodded in unison. Then they crawled down into a hollow, where they stopped, adjusted their radios, put their earphones in, and activated the throat microphones.

Lucas turned his radio on and sent a test transmission.

"Loud and clear," the three responses reverberated back.

"Descend northward. Then keep to the field until you reach the crossroads. Seven hundred meters in total."

He watched as they obeyed the order, moving through the deserted landscape with tactical skill.

Angela led the group across the intersection, and they climbed down into the ditch at the side of the road. They followed it north for two hundred meters until it went into a tunnel at a ruined hotel. They didn't dare go below ground, so they climbed back up.

"Enemy movement fifty meters north, right side of the road," Lucas warned calmly. The unit paused. Tension electrified the air. Almost welcoming the change of activity, Angela saw three undead emerge from the gate to a courtyard, lifted her gun, and waited to see if any more would appear.

"How many?" she whispered.

"Three," Lucas replied. "They're coming your way."

She remained still until they were close by. Then she fired three shots. Muffled by the silencer, the gun made only a soft *chu-chu-chu* sound. The wandering corpses toppled over. Angela, Matteo, and Ramona ran over to the carcasses. They dragged them by the feet behind an ancient red Zastava 128, which was almost entirely composed of rust, and covered them with trash that was lying around.

"The road's clear now," Lucas reported. The trio darted north again. Around a hundred meters before the bridge, they took the fork to the right that would take them to a disused railroad bridge. The entrance to the site itself was barricaded, so Angela had to lead the squad around to the left through an overgrown vegetable garden.

Peeking around the corner at the other side of the river, she immediately spotted the zombies, which were still standing by the bridge.

"Any sign of the contact?" she asked.

"Negative," replied the Frenchman.

"Then we'll hole up here and wait."

"Okay, you got it."

Angela told Matteo and Ramona to take up their positions, and they awaited Nesha's arrival.

After what felt like an eternity had passed, Angela cursed, "Oh shit. I see Nesha."

Lucas asked, surprised, "Where is she?" The girl was more than two hours late.

"Around two hundred meters away from the railroad bridge."

"Can't see it from here. What are the zombies doing?"

"They're staying put. Some of them are still blocking her way."

"Can't you take them out?"

"Hmm," Angela said. "The ones in front of the bridge, yes. But all the ones around it? I don't think so."

Lucas sounded impatient. "Is there any way of making contact?"

It was a few seconds before Angela finally said, "I'm just going to try something."

He couldn't help asking, "What?"

"I'll aim the laser on the sight at her. Maybe she'll notice me."

"Hmm, not a bad idea. Go for it."

An agonizingly long minute later, Angela reported back. "Okay, she's spotted us. What now?"

Lucas seemed to think feverishly. "Is she in imminent danger?"

"Negative."

"How many of them are there between Nesha and the bridge?"

"Ten or twelve, I'd say. And a total of about forty in the area. If they discover her, she'll be in trouble. But so far no one's noticed her," Angela reported.

"Okay, shoot a way through for her. And as soon as she gets close to the bridge, take out the rest of them, too."

"Aye, aye, Captain," the Spaniard confirmed. "Ramona, you cover Nesha. Matteo and I will take care of the route to the bridge."

"All right," the other two agreed.

"Now!" she commanded quietly.

Muffled shots rang out. The first wandering corpses toppled over. Matteo and Angela quickly decimated them.

"The contact is on her way to bridge. She's carrying a large bundle," Ramona reported, continuing to fire.

Watchfully, Angela tried to make out Nesha. *What kind of bundle?*

"Nesha will be with us soon," Ramona went on. "I'll be able to intercept her any minute!"

There was only a handful of zombies staggering around now; they seemed to be searching for the cause of the thinning in their ranks.

"I see seven of the undead in front of the bridge on your side of the river," Lucas relayed.

"We'll deal with them later," Angela replied.

"Will you be able to cover your tracks?"

"Pshaw, that's not on my list of priorities. I'll only be able to decide when we get back to the road. But probably not, with the number of zombies on the bridge."

"Okay, then do it that way. How far away is Nesha?"

Ramona spoke again, "I'm almost with her." Five seconds later, she called out, "Hey, over here." And then to everyone, "We have contact."

Angela wiped her sweaty palms on her pants. "Does she have it?"

Ramona relayed the question. "Yes, it seems to have worked," she answered briefly.

Then Angela heard Ramona inquire, surprised, "Who's okay?"

Nesha had waited on the roof for three nights and had only weakened once. Under the cover of darkness, she had climbed down and ventured over to the recruit camp. She'd had to kill a zombie along the way and hide its emaciated body in the trunk of a car. She'd decided not to enter the area directly in front of the warehouse. Arriving at the surrounding fence, she'd squeezed herself into a crevice between rubble and splintered wooden pallets and waited.

Despite her agitation and the cold, she'd fallen asleep. She dreamed of playing with Nedim on the beach and swimming in the sea. In the dream she taught him to swim, as her mother had once taught her. They'd built drip castles with sand and lounged in the sun until she was woken by children's voices. Nesha lifted her head and bumped it against the pallet, but she didn't register the pain. Her heart was racing. Beneath a burned-out truck three meters away, she could see the grounds through the chain-link fence; children dressed in rags had just stepped out of one of the halls. That was all she could make out. She crept closer, moving underneath the wrecked truck. The view was better there, but the scene she saw was not. The distressed-looking tots were carrying tiny bowls and spoons in their filthy hands. Many of their faces were swollen, and each had at least one bruise. Nesha knew where these came from. When the boys weren't fighting among themselves, the collabs would be only too happy to take over.

"How many times do I have to tell you?" a man's voice bellowed. The boys flinched. "If you want to eat, get in line," Afrim, the collab, shouted with contemptuous satisfaction. Startled, the little ones lined up one behind the other. "Yes, that's much better."

She couldn't see Nedim anywhere. She looked fearfully to right and left without spotting him. Her life had no meaning without him. Where had he gone? It had been a long time since anyone had come out of the hall. Nesha felt as if her heart were going to shatter into a million pieces. She still couldn't see him. Fear gripped her mind; paralyzed, she thought it might suffocate her. Slowly, the world darkened before her eyes. Just before her senses left her, Nedim emerged. Tears of relief rose in her, and she let out a loud sigh. The children looked abruptly in her direction. Her breath caught in fright. But a few seconds later, Afrim appeared with a bucket, its contents steaming. The boys seemed to forget her immediately. They turned their attention to the collab.

Nesha watched Nedim, who joined the end of the line. She hoped there'd be enough food left for him. The very sight of him made her euphoric. Tears ran down her cheeks. Nedim stood before Afrim, who filled the boy's bowl to the brim. Porridge dripped through his tiny hands. She almost laughed out loud as he licked his little fingers with relish. Sitting cross-legged in the dirt, he ate. Nesha watched him until he had finished the bowl. She saw him join some other boys playing soccer and judged that this was the right moment to leave.

This time, the first thing she did was climb up floor by floor. Her silhouette could potentially be spotted against the crumbling facade. She waited a minute or two behind some smashed-in windows to make sure no one had seen her. But nothing happened. Back on the roof, she began making plans to rescue Nedim. That hadn't been part of the deal, but she would not leave him there. He had to get out. Because she couldn't survive losing him forever.

There weren't many options, so Nesha didn't dither around. She decided that on the final evening, after she had collected the cameras, she would break into the boys' dormitory and get him out of there. All they'd have to do after that was cross the bridge over the Drin, and their chances of survival would be better. That was four kilometers away. Nesha was confident she'd be able to cover the distance with Nedim at night. She'd carry him in her arms if necessary. She did not allow herself to think for a second about what would happen if the interception team was not waiting for them as agreed.

Instead, she tried to think of her mother. Of the circumstances that had forced her to flee from the mountains to Shkodër. Back then, Nesha had been five years old.

Most of her memories from that time were blurred; even her mother's facial features had long since lost their sharpness. Not even the feeling of being safe had remained with her. Three years after her mother's disappearance, Nesha still longed for her touch. Only Nedim's presence had helped in part to satisfy this longing.

She had never known her father. All she knew was that he had left the country before she was born, out of fear of a blood feud with her mother's clan. The two families had carried on a vendetta for over a century. Nesha had never understood this, and her mother had never been able to give her a plausible explanation. The factions had lived in permanent fear of each other and had avoided any kind of contact. Against all odds, the two teenagers had found each other—and fallen in love. Nesha's mother fell pregnant and was disowned as soon as the family found out. For six years, she and her daughter had fended for themselves in women's shelters—until the epidemic hit the Balkans. For the first year after the outbreak, they had to live in a small, abandoned apartment without any modern conveniences. And the pandemic had also changed the balance of the population. In Shkodër, people on the run from all over the Balkans came together. Soon they were sharing their living space with a Macedonian family. Nesha did not remember their names—she knew only that they kept to themselves and avoided all outside contact. She had a vague recollection of how at one time everyone had expected the afflicted to be finished off by the cold. Although Lake Scutari's proximity to the Adriatic Sea meant that the climate to the southeast was mild, they had put their hopes in the brutal Balkan winters. No one could imagine that the undead could withstand them. So the survivors barricaded themselves in around the fertile areas of the lake, stockpiling agricultural produce from the fields and gardens between the Kir and Drin Rivers. Families supported each other, and even centuries-old blood feuds were put aside. People quickly began to work together, making plans for the postapocalyptic world. Everyone was geared toward making a clean start in the coming spring.

But the next year, the snow had thawed. The undead, who had converged on the city from all directions, as if gathered in by some invisible force, seemed unaffected by the weather and had even increased in number by March.

Meanwhile, the survivors ran out of food. They also ran out of medicine, which they had to divide among themselves during the winter.

During the summer that followed, the neighbors watched over Nesha whenever her mother stole out of the surrounded city behind enemy lines, gathering at least some food. It was difficult for the besieged to put up any active resistance because the number of zombies did not decrease, no matter what they did to reduce their ranks.

And yet they continued to try to break the siege, regardless of the countless casualties they incurred in the process. The alternative—starvation—did not hold much appeal.

Eventually, their resistance was broken down. The city was overrun by zombies. Over the years, Nesha had managed to piece together what happened next. As they pored over the plan, she told Lucas a story he would probably never have bought from anyone else. A third person interpreted whenever the language barrier became too difficult.

"The undead seemed to be crowding around one person," she had told him. She often checked to make sure he was understanding what she was saying. Lucas nodded if he was. "She seemed to be able to communicate with them. As if she herself were undead. From a distance, she looked quite normal. She came from the north, and people said that in some places her skin was as gray as the zombies.'"

Lucas opened his eyes wide, but he let her continue.

"And people who were bitten by her became zombies. Some of the people she hadn't bitten became collabs."

Lucas frowned at the last word, which she interpreted as a question.

"Col-la-bo-ra-tors," she said slowly, emphasizing each syllable. She waited for him to nod again, then continued, "The job of the collabs is to look after children, women, and girls, right? To send them into the fields to harvest crops. Collabs are not recruited, and they're not used as food for zombies, either."

Lucas continued to nod. She noticed that the more she told him about life with her mother, the tighter he clenched his jaws. After the city had been taken, they'd had to stay hidden for a long time. They were often hungry for days on end. Sometimes Nesha stayed in their hideout alone for a whole night and the following day until her mother returned with food. Each time, her mother seemed more confused than she had been before. Soon she brought a pair of scissors back with her and cut off Nesha's hair. Nesha cried bitter tears at this, but her mother would not be swayed. She procured new clothes for her, like the ones the boys in town wore. Soon she began to call Nesha her son and address her as boy. At first, Nesha found this strange, and her mother's reluctance to explain didn't make it any easier. Whispering, she implored Nesha not to let anyone know she was a girl. To always behave like a boy. Not wanting to cause trouble, Nesha didn't question the request. She gave her word a hundred, no, a thousand times. She promised so many times that at some point she herself began to believe she was a boy. But as the hunger and cold increased, the collabs tracked down their hiding place. They were crammed into an old, poorly heated machine hall with other women and children, where they were allowed to share a pallet.

She had tried to placate herself at first. *At least there's something to eat here.* But it wasn't long before the collabs began showing up at night and taking her mother with them. The following mornings, she often had bumps and bruises on her face. Weeks later, when she began vomiting regularly before breakfast, the nightly visits stopped. Her mother became more and more tight-lipped, spending the whole night lying on the mattress holding Nesha in her arms.

In the months that followed, her mother's belly grew bigger and bigger. When Nesha wasn't lying next to her during the day or bringing her water and food, she played with the children in the hall. She was careful to avoid the company of other girls. Soon she got firsthand experience of how harsh the tone of conversation had become. The boys often fought, spurred on by the cheers of the collabs, who enjoyed it when the little ones scuffled with each other.

Nesha, who took a lot of beatings in the early days, learned from brawl to brawl how to hold her own, even against bigger adversaries. She made up for her lack of body weight with skill and speed. Identifying her male opponents' weak spots, she capitalized mercilessly on the knowledge whenever she got into a fight.

For many years, it did not occur to her to question the life she had led.

It was only when she saw Lucas's outraged expression that she suspected that her upbringing wasn't the usual way the world worked.

In spring, she was ordered to work in the fields, where she toiled from dawn to dusk alongside other young people and one or two women and learned to grow crops. Operations were supervised by the collabs while the undead patrolled, their mere presence nipping all thoughts of escape in the bud. On the few days off that seemed to be allocated at random, she secretly left the area to play with the other children in the ruins of the city. Soon she was spending fewer and fewer nights with her mother. The ridicule heaped on her by the boys for "going to Mom's to sleep" made her furious. She lashed out at anyone who made fun of her—although it regularly earned her a bloody nose, a split lip, and a black eye.

Every time this happened, her mother was distressed anew. Nesha soon grew tired of it and sought out a place to sleep in the boys' quarters. But when one day Nedim was born, it ignited something in her that she had been unaware of before. In the evenings, when work was done, she could hardly wait to see him.

She spent every free minute she had with him, looking after him. Having a little brother was a legitimate reason to give the boys for wanting to return to her family.

The birth must have met some unknown criteria, because the collabs left the three of them alone for a while. Nesha's mother seemed to have come through the delivery well, and her spirits revived. She nursed the baby whenever he cried for food and taught her daughter how to care for him.

Two months later, however, she was forced back to work. Nesha watched every day as she tied the baby to her back and obeyed the order. Life in Shkodër was hard, but they were given food, at least, and they didn't get too cold in winter. After the first harvest, their rations were increased, and people got a little more meat on their bones again. She was to learn the reason for this much later, but not before the collabs once more began to come for her mother at night. Wordlessly, her mother left her cot, leaving Nedim in Nesha's care. Hours later she would return with a blank look on her face. Once again, she seemed to lose her good spirits. Nesha said nothing and tried to comfort her as much as a ten-year-old could. As they had the first time, the visits ended when her mother began to feel ill in the mornings. Soon her belly began to swell again.

Meanwhile, Nesha became the most important person for Nedim. Their mother became more and more withdrawn. Her health deteriorated until, shortly before she gave birth for the second time, she was barely able to stand up. She was emaciated and refused to eat.

One day while giving her mother a hurried wash, Nesha came across open pressure sores on her hip and back. She cleaned and bandaged them as best she could.

"My daughter," her mother croaked, her eyes closed. It was the first time she had called Nesha that in three years. "Nesha, my child." Her lips barely moved. "I'm sorry I . . . couldn't be there for you both."

"Oh, Mama!" Tears ran down Nesha's cheeks. "There's nothing to be sorry for."

But her mother didn't seem to hear her. "Please . . . look after Nedim," she said, "better than I looked after you. Please. Promise me, my daughter. Take good care of . . . both of you. Please." Her head tilted limply to one side.

Veiled in tears, Nesha gave her word, but her mother had already drifted away. Nesha spent the rest of the night beside her, holding her in her arms, while Nedim slumbered fitfully between them.

The next morning, Nesha said good-bye and went to the field with Nedim on her back. With an indefinable sense of distress, she worked until evening. When she returned, she found the berth empty. Panicking, she ran to the collabs. When she asked where her mother was, she was met with a hard slap in the face. This incensed her even more. She went at the two men with her child's fists, although she didn't stand a chance against two adults. By the time they grabbed her by the ankle that night and moved her and Nedim to new quarters, she was covered in blood and half conscious.

From then on, they lived in the boys' camp. The absence of her mother created such a deep sadness in her that she had to constantly fight not to choke on the lump in her throat. Caring for Nedim was the one and only thing that kept her sane.

Over time, she learned to suppress the despair. She took on the role of mother and fulfilled the promise she had made. Another four winters passed, but day-to-day life was as bleak as it had always been. However, her body began to grow and change. At the age of fourteen, her periods started. Once she had reassured herself it wouldn't kill her, she had to learn to conceal it. She secretly hoarded scraps of clothing, which she cleaned meticulously and used as pads. Every four weeks, she provoked a fight and let someone beat her up, providing an explanation for the smell of blood and the bloody scraps of cloth she was washing.

She continued to guard Nedim like a lioness. She would not permit the bigger boys to harm him. All was well for a year or so until one night she had to go to the bathroom. Carefully, she stole out from under the covers and went to the bathrooms of the former factory. Moonlight was slanting in through the broken windows. Nesha disappeared into the single cubicle. She locked the door and squatted over the bowl.

As she was doing her business, she heard footsteps in the hallway. She finished hurriedly, swilled her hands quickly with the measuring cup hanging from a bucket of water, and pulled up her pants. When she opened the door, she saw Almir, who three years older. The duty collab had chosen him to keep the night watch in case anyone tried to escape. Now he was leaning against the opposite wall. Without looking at her, he cleaned his fingernails with a splinter of wood the length of a finger.

She ignored him and strode past. In Malbulru, a mixture of Macedonian, Albanian, Bulgarian, and Romanian, he called after her, "What were you doing in there?"

Nesha faltered. "Huh? Are you stupid? Shitting. What else would I be doing?"

He snorted arrogantly. "You know, I've been wondering for a long time why Vladimir never calls you into his office when he's on the night shift."

It was true. The collab had never shown any interest in her. She turned and looked at Almir, unimpressed. "I don't know. Because he likes you better?"

"Oh no." Almir laughed. "I don't think so. He weeded me out years ago. I'm probably too old for him now. You probably are, too. But—come to think of it—I don't remember ever seeing you with Vlado." He put the little stick between his lips. Took a step closer. "Besides, I've never seen you take a piss, Neshi. Not here at the urinals, not against the wall outside, not under a tree. Never. Never with the other guys. And then I figured out why."

She suppressed the reflex to swallow and looked him straight in the eye. "Well?"

He grinned smugly and stood directly in front of her. Out of the corner of her eye, she saw the bulge appear in his crotch. She had an idea what would happen next. Almir was breathing heavily.

"I may be wrong, Neshi, but I think . . . you're . . . not a boy at all."

In that moment, she shot her hand upward, slamming the piece of wood deep into his mouth. It was neither big nor solid enough to do any damage, but the maneuver gave her a moment that she used to her advantage.

Almir tried to back away, but his back was against the wall. With all her might, she rammed the heel of her hand right into his face, and shortly afterward, a knee between his legs. A stream of blood shot out of his nose. He doubled up in front of her, but she grabbed him by the hair, preventing him from falling over. Noisily, he tried to suck air past all the blood into his lungs. Nesha opened the cubicle she had just left and pushed him inside, smashing his head into the toilet bowl. The excruciating impact on the rim of the bowl destroyed his larynx. She stamped on him a few times with her heel until he stopped moving.

Inhaling and exhaling deeply, she tried to get over the shock. It had only been a matter of time before they found out what she was. She'd long been expecting it. But she hadn't expected it to happen so soon. If Almir could put two and two together, it wouldn't be long before others did, too. They'd put her in with the women. But the worst of it was that they'd take Nedim away from her.

She went over to the bucket by the sink and splashed a handful of water onto her face. She washed her hands quickly before someone came and discovered her next to the corpse. Trembling, she climbed the stairs.

What if someone had realized that the two of them had been down there? That would draw too much attention to her. Attention she didn't want. And if they held her responsible for the death of a night guard, there might even be consequences for Nedim. She had to get out of here as soon as possible.

But not without her brother. If she went in to get him, though, she might miss her only chance to escape. She'd never come across an unguarded door again. She had to do it now. Right now. But if she did, she'd be breaking the promise she'd made to her mother.

If she could find a way to get Nedim out of here later, though, she'd be keeping it again. Rumors of people living free outside of Shkodër came to her mind. If she managed to escape, she could get help and come back. Save Nedim from this hell. But where could she flee? Where would she find other survivors? She had no idea, but she had to try. For as long as it took to find someone who was willing to help.

Before she could admit it to herself, her decision was made. The door was unguarded. Nesha opened it just enough to slip through the crack. Her old hoodie wouldn't be much good against the bitter cold, but she had no choice. Tears burned her eyes as she scurried across the compound. In the darkness, she felt her way along the fence to the spot where she and some friends had secretly dug a hole. The opening wasn't large enough for the boys to crawl through. But Nesha was thinner and wirier than most. And she'd still have to undress to get through. The hole was concealed by a layer of corrugated roofing felt. She squeezed under it, careful not to make any noise. Lying on her back, she wriggled her way to freedom. On the other side, she quickly got dressed again. If she tried to escape into the mountains, she'd certainly die before the night was through. Either the cold or the wild animals would kill her. So she took the path toward the sea. With each step, her desire to return to Nedim increased. But she knew that there was no future for the two of them in this. She had to get help, and not only for their sakes.

It was a windless night, and there was little danger of her body odor being carried far. She hoped there were no undead in the immediate area. But she couldn't do anything about that in any case. At a crouch, her heart hammering and her hood pulled down deep over her forehead, she stole from corner to corner along the street. The few patrols she came across did not spot her. Fate was kind to her all the way to the Buna River. Nesha hoped the old footbridge over it would be unguarded; given its dire condition, this was a reasonable possibility. She took her time, observing the bridge from a distance. Only when she was sure there was no imminent danger did she creep cautiously onto it.

Some of the beams were so rotted that they gave way at the slightest pressure. Some were missing altogether. Nesha positioned her feet right at the edge, directly above one of the steel beams. Squatting down and keeping her head below the railing, she gradually worked her way across.

Throughout the rest of the night, she ran through deserted towns and along icy tracks, through dark pine woods toward the west, where she suspected the sea was. Where she hoped to find help, someone who would rescue them from this nightmare. Her and Nedim.

Long after sunrise, she stepped onto the beach of Veliki Pijesak, completely exhausted. The village behind her was in ruins. There was no one there she could ask for help.

Nesha was tired, hungry, and thirsty. She dropped to her knees. Her eyelids drooped and a pleasant warmth spread through her body. She surrendered to the feeling, closing her eyes. Her limbs went limp, and she hit the sand, face first.

More than a year later, Nesha was back in the city again. Her prayers seemed to have been answered. Well rested, she waited for the hour before midnight, carefully stealing back to all the sites where she had hidden the cameras. Before entering each one, she took the time to observe it closely. Once she was satisfied she wasn't walking into a trap, she took down each recording device, removed the memory card, and packed it away, ensuring it was waterproof and protected, even though she was itching to get to Nedim. But she forced herself to do what she had come to do.

Arriving at the children's camp, she immediately began to dig a hole with the knife. She had chosen the spot by the wrecked car. The earth was incredibly hard due to the nighttime cold, but larger chunks came loose. Now and again, she stopped and listened to see if the guards were approaching. Whenever they appeared, she let them pass and then continued jabbing away. Once on the other side of the fence, she got to her feet and took a tighter grip on the knife handle. She ran toward the building where she thought the entrance was. Millimeter by millimeter, she pulled the door open, fearful that the hinges would squeak. Fortunately, they didn't. She was greeted by absolute blackness. The air was warm, and she heard fire crackling in one of the stoves. Beds creaked as people shifted around in them. Nesha entered, pulled the door shut behind her—and faltered. How was she going to locate Nedim? She hadn't thought about that until now. Again, she felt panic rising inside her. The feeling of being so close to him and yet so helpless was clouding her senses. She took a step to the side and collided with a bed. The metal frame rattled. Nesha held her breath. The knife almost slipped from her hand, but she didn't let go of it.

She heard footsteps. A flashlight came on directly ahead of her, barely five meters away. The beam blinded her.

"Damn it, who are you?" asked the person behind the light. She recognized Afrim's voice, and her panic left her for a moment. Hatred ignited in her, stronger than the fear that had paralyzed her before. "Wait, I know you," said the surprised collab. "You're . . . you're Nesha! You little shit! We thought you'd frozen to death when you escaped in the middle of winter. How did you survive? Hmm, you won't get away from me this time."

The beam of light and the tramp of Afrim's footsteps moved toward her. He shot out his hand and grabbed Nesha by the neck. She lost her footing and felt an abrupt pain as he gripped her below the ears. He pulled her toward him; she smelled his foul breath. He grinned. Instinctively, she closed her fist around the handle of the blade and thrust upward with all her might. For an infinitesimal moment, the knife tip paused under his chin as the skin held firm. But the tissue immediately gave way and the blade buried itself up to the hilt in Afrim's oral cavity. Warm blood trickled down her fist. She gave the knife a jerk and pulled it out. At the same time, he let go of her and grabbed the wound, gasping.

Nesha landed on the floor, gasped for air in her turn, and crawled to the flashlight, which had rolled under a bed, clattering. She got ahold of it and shone it around frantically. The boys had sat up in their beds and were staring with blank eyes at the writhing collab. The first of them went over to the man, who had sunk to his knees, and began kicking and punching him. Those behind them pressed forward. Nesha averted her eyes, desperately searching for Nedim in the crowd. Silently she called his name over and over again as she made her way between the beds. And there he was, still asleep, untouched by the racket in the hall. Lovingly, she shook him by the shoulder.

"No, let me sleep," he moaned, burrowing into the frayed blanket.

"You sleep," she said, crying and smiling at the same time, "and I'll get you out of here." She grabbed the pitiful bundle—dear heaven, it was light—and hurried out the door, ignoring the children beating the last breath of life out of their tormentor.

On the alert to avoid stumbling into a patrol, she ran through the zombie-infested city. Nesha tried to find her way in the darkness. What could she use to help her? Panting, she stopped at a rusty street sign and quickly shone her flashlight on it. The paint had partially peeled off, but she recognized where she was. Now she knew where they could stay overnight. They would hide out in the remains of the Lead Mosque, which was just a few hundred meters away from the bridge. The ruin was far enough from the camp not to be searched but close enough to the river to enable them to reach it on foot in a couple of minutes. At dawn they would cross the Drin. Her heart was hammering with joy at the thought that she would soon have freed Nedim. His weight did not bother her as she ran down street after street. In the rubble of the mosque, she placed him on her lap and covered them both with the camouflage cloak, which kept them warm within the dusty gray walls.

Nedim was quiet. He probably couldn't believe that Nesha had come back. He probably didn't realize what that meant at all. But at least he had recognized her. To have him curled up in a ball in her lap filled her with such elation that it made the world spin. Nedim put his arms around her neck and gave her a squeeze. Her heart whooped with joy. She kissed his forehead. All she wanted was to survive one more day so she could take him to freedom. She rocked back and forth, the bundle in her arms, remembering again how they had played on the beach. Soon she fell into an exhausted sleep.

They rested until just before dawn, eating the last of the bars and drinking some of the water in Nesha's backpack. Quietly, they relieved themselves in one of the corners. Then it was time to head for the bridge. Mllojë was going to meet her beyond the bridge, and if they got out, she could finally live in peace with Nedim. Full of joy, she thought of her dream of the sea. How she would love to build sandcastles with her brother once more. Her bundle under her arm, she walked around the ruins toward the bridge, creeping carefully past abandoned family homes.

Her happy thoughts evaporated the instant she saw the undead standing by the bridge. She quickly hid behind a house near the riverbank. She held the gun in her free hand, but with the number of zombies she was facing, it would be hopeless to try and shoot her way through. She couldn't go back, either. She'd rather try her luck in the ice-cold river than lose her little brother again.

Nesha walked around the house, hoping for a direct route from the backyard to the water. She peeked around the corner and noticed that the bank was also crowded with zombies. She almost gave a loud shout but remembered the precious cargo in her arms.

For two unending hours, she waited for the wandering corpses to move away. But they stayed where they were, as if rooted to the spot. It wouldn't do Nesha much good to attack them. There were just too many of them. Her arms grew heavy. At least Nedim was quiet. In her mind, she heaped praises on him for his patience. *All we need to do is survive today.* Suddenly, she was blinded by a beam of red light. She blinked in surprise and drew back. Then she peered around the corner again. The reddish dot danced repeatedly on her face. She followed it to its origin on the opposite bank, where someone was giving hand signals. Nesha recognized Ramona, with whom she had been training for the past few weeks, and waved back. Ramona signaled to her to back off and wait. Nesha did as instructed, holstering her pistol and flinging an arm around Nedim's shoulders. Shortly afterward, she heard dozens of silenced gunshots. When these died down, she looked over. The zombies lay in the ankle-deep grass, scattered like dolls by a child. The bridge, however, was still teeming with them.

Ramona beckoned her onward, straight across the stream. What was that going to achieve? Was she supposed to swim? Nesha inspected the river once again. Suddenly she saw what Ramona was up to. An old railroad bridge, completely overgrown on the banks and only visible when given a closer look, led across the river not far from the road bridge. If she could just make it there . . .

Ramona was signaling her constantly to start moving. Nesha took a deep breath, hugged Nedim tightly to her chest, and ran. Soft gunshots sounded again from the other shore. Everywhere she looked, the undead were falling. She stepped over a segment of barbed wire at knee height, then scaled a crumbling wall before stepping onto the rusty steel beams. With her free hand, she held on to the cross struts. Meter by meter, she fought her way forward, pressing Nedim against her.

Nesha trod only on the sections that had not been eaten away by rust. With every step she felt freer, lighter. She didn't care that the rough metal was rubbing her palm raw.

Then she was over. Ramona came up to her and helped her the last few meters. She seemed to be talking to someone Nesha couldn't see. Suddenly she was sure that today would end well.

"You see, Mama. See, I did it. I did it," she whispered. Tears of joy came into her eyes. She hugged the bundle more tightly to her.

Ramona took ahold of her arm. "Did you get it all? Collect all the cameras back in?" she asked.

Nesha smiled exhaustedly and nodded. "Yes, I have everything. I have . . . kept my promise. He's all right. He's fine."

The tension in Nesha's body suddenly gave way to fatigue. Her knees buckled.

Ramona's look betrayed confusion. "Who's okay?" She pulled Nesha roughly to her feet. "Come on, we have to get out of here. You can't sit down now." Then she reached for the blanket Nesha had wrapped her brother in.

"Nedim," she said, overcome by happiness. "Nedim. I rescued my brother. My little brother." All at once she felt weak. She held out the bundle to Ramona. "Take him . . . I can't . . . hold any more . . ."

"What's this?" asked Ramona.

"My little brother, Nedim. In here," Nesha replied, nodding toward the blanket. Ramona obviously hadn't realized he was wrapped in it. But she frowned and rolled up the holey blanket, which was suddenly dangling loosely from her hands.

"There's . . . nothing here," she said. Alarmed, Nesha reached for the blanket.

"My brother! Give it here! I rescued him!" She wrapped the cloth into a bundle again, pressing it tightly to her chest.

Ramona was getting more and more nervous. Impatiently, she tried to take the blanket away from Nesha again. "It's empty, Nesha. There's nothing there. Your brother's not here! Stop it! Come on, we have to get out of here!"

Nesha clutched at the fabric frantically. With all her remaining strength, she fought against Ramona's tugs. "No! I saved him! Give him to me!"

In obvious desperation, Ramona hit Nesha in the face with the flat of her hand. Nesha staggered, fell backward, and landed heavily on the ground. The empty blanket lay half on top of her. She stared at it in disbelief. She inhaled, but no air seemed to reach her lungs. On all fours, she groped around on the blanket. She felt as if she were suffocating. Realizing the truth, she stopped, staring aghast at Ramona. "He . . . he's . . . not there," she whispered.

Nedim wasn't there anymore. Nesha shook her head. There'd be no summer's day at the beach with her brother. She had failed. Nesha smiled tiredly. She reached for her pistol, placed the muzzle under her chin— and pulled the trigger.

"No! Don't!" cried Ramona, reaching for Nesha's gun. But it was too late. The shot rang out, soiling her with drops of warm blood.

"What was that?" came Lucas's voice in her ear. "You're supposed to be using silencers, damn it!"

"That wasn't us," Ramona replied, paralyzed by shock. She gazed at the lifeless body for a moment until the rattling of the approaching zombies brought her back to the present. Coming to from the shock, she grabbed Nesha's backpack, hoping it did actually contain the footage. She turned and ran. Angela and Matteo were right behind her.

"Nesha . . . She put a bullet in her head," she announced, loud enough for everyone to hear.

"What?" Lucas sounded horrified.

"If I understood her correctly . . . then . . . she somehow thought she had her little brother with her. But there was nothing there."

"Couldn't you have stopped her?"

She ignored the implied reprimand. "Negative. All happened too fast."

"And the recordings?"

"I have them. We'll be back. How does the road look?"

"Fine for now," he replied, audibly struggling for composure. "But the gunshot startled the zombies on the bridge." Five seconds later, just after they turned onto the main road, he spoke again, "I can see you . . . and the first stinkers, too. You've got a good five hundred meters on them. Argiris and I will leave our position and come to meet you. Rendezvous at the crossroads in five minutes."

"You got it," Ramona replied. The other two had just passed her. She looked around and sighted the undead leaving the bridge. It was unlikely they would catch up with them. Arriving at the intersection, they waited a full minute before Lucas and Argiris joined them.

"We have to assume that more undead are on the way," the French-man said. "We can't wait till tonight to set off for the beach. We'll move on right away." When no one objected, he ran off westward. The others followed, Ramona jogging silently behind.

Seven kilometers later, Lucas called a breather before the final stage. The team used the five minutes to check their magazines and reload. They all drank their remaining water, then marched on.

Lucas led the unit over the crest of the dune where they had landed on the beach two nights earlier. He was sweating in the heat of the spring sun. He had long since removed his zombie camouflage. In a few min-utes, their mission would be over in any case. His concentration had waned. In his mind, he was already in the shower.

Suddenly, a knee-high shrub five meters ahead of him shifted, extend-ing into the air in seconds. Lucas almost stumbled in surprise. His unit immediately moved into a defensive position, training their rifles on the bushes. Other bushes around them also stretched up rapidly. They could see guns among the foliage. Another tendriled form approached him from the side, and Lucas realized it was a human in a camouflage suit. He looked at the place he thought his counterpart's eyes were likely to be. The other figure shouldered a Kalashnikov and peeled the suit off its head. It was a tall woman, barely three years older than himself, Lucas guessed. She looked at him, waiting.

"Who are you?" he asked in English. *How did they know we would pass by here? Were they waiting for us?*

"We intercepted your message," the woman replied, as if that were explanation enough. She nodded toward the beach. "Your people are waiting down by the boats."

Lucas nodded, though a thousand questions were racing through his mind.

"Was it a success?" she inquired.

Despite their weapons, they didn't seem threatening. He decided to act accordingly and nodded. "I think so. We haven't been able to evaluate the footage yet, but I assume it's usable."

"Good," the woman said. Then she shouted something in a language he didn't understand. Her tone was rough, and her volume was high. The camouflaged combat squad formed up behind her. Its presumed leader pushed her hood back down over her head and led the unit at a run down the dune to the beach.

Lucas hung back slightly, wanting to take a closer look. The rear guard was dressed as a gigantic bush. He bared his head, which had been hidden under a tangle of vines and branches draped over a camouflage net. A ferocious face emerged. The man was bald, but he had a thick, silver-flecked beard. In the crook of his arm, he held what looked like a .50-caliber sniper rifle. Like the marksman himself, it was elaborately draped with ivy, pieces of bark, and moss. It looked like a branch from the forest that had lain for years in the undergrowth and had been over-grown by plants.

Although the weapon had to weigh almost ten kilograms, the man with the beard held it like a toy. He jutted out his chin and told Lucas to follow the woman. Lucas obeyed and instructed his people to do the same.

Down on the beach, he spotted three large rowboats and, about five hundred meters offshore, a two-master. The slope under his feet became steeper. At his side, the giant with the sniper rifle ran downhill, taking enormous strides. When they reached the water, they all set to pushing the boats into the sea.

Lucas threw his gun into one of the massive craft, planted his feet in the soft sand, called on his last reserves of strength, and pushed as hard as he could. The boats slid into the water, ponderously at first, but once they got enough buoyancy, they rapidly floated westward.

The troops helped each other aboard. Several of them grabbed paddles and rowed toward the schooner. Lucas was too perplexed by the unexpected appearance of the strange escort to assist, so he sat back and finally allowed himself to relax a little.

CHAPTER 2

ZADAR

The rhythmic rise and fall of the rowboats gave Lucas such a sense of security that he almost fell asleep. He had to pull himself together and stay awake. This was not a trip down the canals of pre-pandemic Venice. It would be disrespectful to surrender to fatigue while others rowed, even if every muscle in his body was burning. He splashed his hands and face with salt water, which refreshed him a little. He closed his eyes and thought about the mission they had just completed. Nesha's suicide felt like a defeat. At the very least, it threw doubt on whether they could claim to have succeeded. Even if the footage turned out to be usable, did that justify Nesha's death? Why had the young woman done it?

And who were the people who had been waiting for them in camouflage suits?

The small convoy docked at the two-master, whose dark blue hull impassively awaited their arrival. The crews climbed up the rope ladders past two rows of solar panels attached to the railing. Lucas was assigned a spot at the bow, where he and his team could stay out of the way while the sails were set. The light breeze that was blowing despite the sunshine lifted his spirits. All the same, now that it was spring, it was a good ten degrees warmer out at sea than it was inland. He sat down on the wooden deck and set his weapon down beside him. Leaning against the railing, he watched as canvases were unfurled. The mate yelled orders in the unfamiliar language, and squeaking loudly, the lifeboats were hoisted out of the water by powerful pulleys.

No sooner had they picked up speed than they were joined by the company commander, who had now introduced herself as Lejla from Newgoslavia, joined them. She had divested herself of her camouflage suit and was wearing an ocher tank top. Olive-colored linen pants fluttered around her muscular legs. She distributed water and warm flatbreads.

"Welcome to the *Sinji Galeb*," she said as Lucas and his team divided the food between them. "Sorry we caught you guys off guard like that. But there was no time to communicate in more detail. We can answer your questions now, though."

"How did you even find us?" asked Ramona between bites.

"Two weeks ago, we received news that a ship flying the French ensign had been spotted off Corfu. We wanted to see who else was sailing in the Adriatic. This morning we spotted your mother ship and contacted the crew. At first, they were skeptical. But, as a sign of good will, we offered to intercept you and bring you back. After tough negotiations, they agreed, on condition that some of them be allowed to come along."

"Oh dear, that will have been my sister. I'm amazed she responded to you at all." Lucas grinned. "She can be very distrustful."

Lejla returned his grin. "Indeed. We came close to giving up, but then she realized that it would make more sense to have us on your side."

"This new alliance could prove helpful," Argiris said, squinting thoughtfully in the direction of Shkodër.

Lejla's curiosity seemed to have been piqued. "So—what were you doing there?" In the hour that followed, Lucas and his team told why they were here. They explained about Corfu and the idea of getting to the bottom of the rumors about Shkodër. The Newgoslavian listened patiently. Afterward she said, "We thought about that too, but we were too busy putting our own house in order. Until recently, I thought the rumors were absurd. But I guess I was wrong about that. What are you going to do with the recordings?"

"As soon as we get back to the *Jacques Cousteau*, we'll analyze the data," Lucas replied.

"Can I come?"

"Of course. We're allies now," Lucas joked. "And you have to meet my sister."

Lejla nodded, grinning. The lookout called out. Lejla rose, looked over the railing toward the bow, and said, "Oh, we're there already."

One of the lifeboats had been launched. Lucas's unit waved good-bye and then left the *Sinji Galeb*. Lucas climbed down second to last, followed by Lejla.

His sister, Lena, was waiting at the railing of the sturdy *Cousteau* and watched as the team climbed the rope ladder. Lucas had barely got to the top before he found himself in his sister's embrace. She was obviously relieved he had returned from the mission unharmed. She held out her hand to Lejla and laughed out loud when she was greeted by the question, "Permission to come aboard?"

"Granted," she said, grabbing Lejla's forearm. Angela, Ramona, Argiris, and Matteo took the opportunity to sneak past them without attracting attention.

"Is there somewhere we can talk?" inquired Lejla.

"Sure. Let's go aft. There's no one at the helm right now," the Frenchwoman replied.

Lucas watched them for a moment before going to his cabin. Once inside, he undressed and cleaned his body with a rag, which he rinsed in salt water. He dampened the dirt that was crusted on his neck and throat for a moment before gently rubbing it off. Then he dried himself and put on clean clothes. Just as he was about to turn his attention to his rifle, there was a knock at the door.

"Yes, what is it?" he asked.

"Lena wants to talk to you," said one of the young sailors under her command. "Aloft, at the stern."

"Tell her I'll be there in a few . . . No, wait! Is she still talking to the Balkan woman?"

"Yes."

"Forget it. I'll go right away," he said, yanking open the door and stomping barefoot past the surprised sailor. Once on deck, Lucas slowed his pace. The smoothly polished and freshly scrubbed planks felt cool under the soles of his feet. He climbed the six wooden steps to the stern as nonchalantly as he could. He waited a few heartbeats to see if the women would notice he was there. Since they didn't, he cleared his throat, whereupon they interrupted their conversation and turned to him.

Lena said, "We're curious to know if the recordings are usable. Can we look at them now?"

"Of course. Is there any particular reason for the rush?"

"We'll explain later. First, show us what you brought back."

"The memory cards are in my cabin. Start up your computer while I go get them."

Three minutes later, they were huddled around Lena's computer. The captain's sparsely furnished cabin was illuminated by the light from two portholes. In the low room, there was scarcely enough space to sit next to each other without touching.

Lucas sat down at the table, took out one of the memory cards and slid it into the designated slot. With a few clicks, he called up the folder and opened the first image. Using the arrow keys, he switched to the next one every two seconds. The more photos they viewed, the less he felt like saying anything. Whenever it became too much for him, he switched memory cards.

The result was always the same.

"I guess the rumors are true then," Lena whispered.

"Or worse," Lejla added.

"I need some fresh air," Lucas said.

"Let's go back upstairs," his sister suggested.

It was only after a few minutes on deck that he felt like himself again. He had not really taken in that the two women were still talking. When Lena said, "Lucas, how long would it be before we could come back with more troops? And how much resistance would you expect?" he looked at them, stunned.

She'd caught him unawares. In the shadow of the mainsail, he looked up at the sky and mused, "If we could contact potential crew immediately by radio, it would take three or four weeks. But I'm afraid not many will volunteer without seeing the pictures of Shkodër with their own eyes. If they don't, no one will believe that intervention is necessary. Remember how long it took us to get our little expedition up and running. And to even consider launching a tactical mission to liberate Shkodër, we'd need more than our little team." Lucas paused and thought further. The women waited silently.

"It won't take long to get Argiris and Ramona back to Corfu and drop Matteo in Bari," he continued. "But Silvia and we have to get to Montpellier. That alone will take us a good four weeks. And when we could round up enough volunteers by is hard to say. Three to six more weeks, if we're lucky? And then we all have to get back here. Add three weeks if the others can organize transport to Shkodër without us having to pick them up—otherwise five. And longer if there are any unforeseeable events."

"What do you mean by *unforeseeable*?"

"Bad weather, the wind being against us, catching a cold, I don't know. There are a hundred things that can go wrong. But to answer your question, if I've done my math right, we'll need at least fifteen, sixteen weeks. Minimum. What I can't estimate at all, though, is how many people we'll be able to convince and mobilize. At an optimistic guess, I reckon fifty per country."

"Four months for just a hundred and fifty people willing to fight," Lena said, glancing at the Newgoslavian. "That's not many. And it's a long time."

"What are you getting at?" Lucas felt Lejla looking at him. He swallowed and avoided her gaze.

"Lejla's just made a proposal. We could be outside Shkodër in four to five weeks with three hundred armed men."

"In just five weeks? How's that going to work?"

Now Lejla put in, "I'd ask my father for support. He has hundreds of Newgos who are loyal to him. It wouldn't take long to mobilize some of them. If we sail right away and go via Zadar, we'll reach Bihać in six or seven days. We take two more weeks to round up volunteers, arm them, and prepare them for the mission. In the meantime, we get boats ready to bring the forces here. All in four to five weeks. Roughly."

"Hmm, off the top of my head I can't think of any argument against it," Lucas said. "I was admiring your equipment earlier. You guys didn't skimp on the ammo, either. How come?"

"Ha," said Lejla, "we have the criminal machinations of my fellow Balkans to thank for that, in the period before the outbreak."

"What do you mean?" he asked.

The fighter took a deep breath. "After the Yugoslav civil war in the 1990s, the arms-smuggling gangs that had established themselves during that time simply continued their business. Tools of war of all kinds came into the Balkans from Russia and Ukraine. Croatia made the perfect temporary storage facility, especially since it had direct access to the sea. It was a piece of cake to bribe the underpaid officials' guild of one of the poorest states in Europe. But the outbreak of the epidemic put an end to the goings-on. A few years later, we came across the smugglers' warehouses and overseas containers, which were not as well secured as the official military depots. And now, well, we have firearms in abundance. Not to mention ammunition."

"That explains a lot," Lucas said, impressed. "And what does my opinion matter? After all, there's every reason to do it the way Lejla suggested."

"Well," Lena continued, "we'd like to use the Shkodër footage to convince Lejla's people of our plan."

Now it was his turn to look back and forth questioningly.

"Many follow my father blindly. But he's not an easy person; he won't agree just like that. Your live pictures could back up our demands, though, and prevent unnecessary discussion, and that would get us back here faster. And maybe even mobilize more fighters."

He nodded. "Okay. I'll copy the data and give it to you, then. No problem."

"There's just one more thing," Lena added.

As if the two of them had practiced this speech, Lejla continued, "If you come along as a representative of western Europe, my father would hardly dare refuse to help. Besides, you've been on the ground in Shkodër and can give a firsthand account of what's going on there."

"You want me to represent western Europe?" It seemed a strange idea. But at the hopeful way she was looking at him, his resistance subsided. He chewed thoughtfully on his lower lip. Finally, he said, "Why not?" Then he turned to his sister, "And what will you be doing?"

Lena replied, "We'll return to Corfu and get everything else ready. I'll contact our people in Marseille. Maybe we can mobilize additional volunteers without having to sail there. And there may be other ways to get help."

"I don't know if our command will be happy about it. Have you talked to them yet?" He turned to Lena.

"No, I wanted to talk to you first."

"Actually, there's only one answer to that." He looked at Lejla. "But how certain are you that your proposal will work?"

"More certain than about your original plan. Mine would be faster, too. And our people are better armed than yours."

He nodded. "And when do you want to set off?" The women looked at him silently, and he gave a deep sigh. "Oh man. All right, I'll get my stuff together and bring the data. Won't be long."

"Great," Lejla said, "I'll radio Sanel."

Lucas nodded and headed for his cabin.

Barely an hour later, he was back in the rowboat. The sun was slowly approaching the horizon, and a strong evening breeze was freshening the air. Lucas pulled the zipper of his olive green jacket up to his chin. This time he had packed hiking boots, which lay in the backpack at his bare feet, next to his rifle.

Lejla sat across from him, looking up at the schooner's fluttering sails. "The wind seems favorable, but we shouldn't get too comfortable. In spring, the weather can often change suddenly."

He nodded, knowing that a bora could easily take you by surprise in the Adriatic. One moment the sun was shining down from a cloudless sky and the next a brutal storm could be raging. "I'm used to rough seas. But what I really want to know is your zombie status. Is it true that you've wiped them out completely? All I've heard are rumors, but hearsay . . ."

"Can't be relied on," she added with a grin. "The question is, who do you mean by *you*?"

"I meant Newgoslavia. How are national borders demarcated, if there are any? Like in the old Yugoslavia?"

"No, not quite. We had to give up territory because of the zombies. Today we consider Newgoslavia to be everything south of the Sava River, west of the Danube, north of the Drin, and as far as the Adriatic Sea. The rivers form the official border. They make a good barrier, especially since most of the bridges have either been blocked or blown up. With a few exceptions, the country is safe. The Newgoslavian people worked together for many years to cleanse it of zombies, and our brigade was a big part of that. Smaller bands of undead occasionally manage to invade the safe areas."

"How long have you been involved?"

"Seven years ago, when I turned sixteen, my father put a rifle in my hand, taught me how to shoot, and took me with him from then on. Uncle Sanel taught me hand-to-hand combat. You saw him, too, earlier on the dune."

"Oh, the sniper? That's your uncle? Is he the one standing at the railing right now, waiting for us?"

Lejla nodded, smiling.

She reached for the rope ladder that dropped down from the schooner and climbed up nimbly.

Meanwhile, Lucas shouldered his backpack. He then put his head through the strap of his gun before scrambling after her.

Sanel hoisted him effortlessly up the last few rungs, placing his mighty paw on Lucas's shoulder.

"So you're coming with us to Bihać?" he asked.

Lucas grinned. "Yes, and to be honest, I'm looking forward to it. You're Lejla's uncle, I hear. Are you her father's or her mother's brother?"

"Neither." Sanel laughed. "We are related, but not in the way you might think. I am the son of Lejla's paternal grandmother's niece."

"Huh, what?" Lucas gave it some thought, irritated. "Then you're . . . her . . . great uncle."

"You're splitting hairs. Here in the Balkans, besides parents and grandparents, we only have aunts and uncles."

"And cousins?"

"Nah, they're all brothers and sisters. And then we have relatives. But those are mostly families-in-law."

"It sounds much more complicated than the system we have in France."

Sanel laughed—a sound like an avalanche of boulders. "It's good that you're coming. You'll soon see it all at firsthand. Have you got the recordings?"

Lucas tapped his breast pocket. "Is there a computer on board where we can back it up?"

Nodding, Lejla said, "In the officer's cabin, right next to yours. Come on, I'll show you." She turned and trudged away. He followed her down a flight of stairs. In the twilight of the lower deck, she held a door open for him. The tiny room beyond, where he deposited his belongings, was lit by a single porthole.

"Here's your place. It's a bit cramped, but it'll do for a few days. The cabin next door belongs to the captain. During the day, we can access the computer in there," she said and led him inside.

"Then let's transfer the data right away. I feel much more comfortable with a backup."

Lucas reached into his pocket, pulled out the SD cards, and handed them to Lejla, who had already sat down at the computer. She switched it on and inserted the first card. Lucas watched on the monitor as she downloaded the images.

"Was that all of them?" she asked, after the last card had been read.

"Yes. Nesha had five cameras."

"I'll copy the folder to an external hard drive, then we'll head to the galley. I don't know about you, but I'm starving," she said.

"Something to eat would be really good right now. I haven't eaten since the morning."

"My sentiments exactly," she responded, shutting down the computer. "Let's go. We have potatoes and polenta to attend to. We've done enough work for one day."

Driven by hunger, they went into the galley, where they had to duck their heads under thick wooden beams. Fresh air was streaming in through the open portholes. They took two large plates from a pile and filled them with unseasoned fried potatoes and polenta. On deck, they sat down next to each other on a bench. They ate without speaking, watching the sun set.

Over the next few days, when he wasn't sitting at the computer with Lejla analyzing data, Lucas greedily soaked up life on the *Sinji Galeb*. For breakfast, he drank tea and ate flatbreads. There was an abundance of jams and protein-rich plant milks, made on the mainland from peas and oats. In the mornings, they mixed oat and pea flour with finely chopped onions and garlic and made talers—finger-length rolls—and fried them using solar power. They caught the sun's rays using a kind of magnifying glass and focused them on the center of the pan to heat it. Then they arranged the patties in concentric circles and turned them until they were dark brown. To cook potatoes and vegetables, they placed a steel plate on top of the pan. They had a wood-burning stove, but they only used it on cloudy days.

Between meals, Lejla and Lucas sorted out the weapons or worked in the captain's cabin.

Not all cameras had functioned as expected—some of the shots were blurry, underexposed, or overexposed. They immediately deleted the defective images. But they managed to gather enough intelligence that clearly showed what was going on in Shkodër.

"I've seen a lot of sick shit, but this . . ." he said on the second day, after they had finished sifting through the contents of the last folder.

Lejla stared past the screen with a blank look, shook her head, and didn't reply for a long time. Then she said, "I had no idea of the scale of it. Not even in my most terrible dreams did I think anything like this was possible."

Lucas nodded. "I just hope we can get enough fighters together to overcome this horde."

He looked thoughtfully out the window. "Give me some distraction, please. Tell me more about . . . Newgoslavia."

"Whoa," she said, "what can I tell you about such a young country without first telling you the story of its past? How familiar are you with Yugoslav history before the apocalypse?"

"My father was a political scientist and used to work as a consultant for the French government. When no one had any use for his expertise any longer, he bombarded me with his knowledge of the politics and history of the West. But I don't know very much about Yugoslavia. And I know even less about Newgoslavia."

"Good, so I can tell you whatever comes into my head, and you'll just have to believe it." She grinned. "Don't look like that; I'm just kidding. So," she began, her gaze drifting skyward as if she were searching for the information there. "About a hundred years ago, there was the kingdom of Yugoslavia. Probably in order to be able to control the population better, it was split up on the basis of religious affiliation—a classic case of divide and rule. People with Serbian roots were officially Orthodox, people from Croatia were supposed to be Catholic, and people in Bosnia, Kosovo, and Sandžak were mostly followers of Islam. There were also lots of other people who didn't fit this pattern: people of the Jewish faith, Sinti and Roma, people with no religion. But also people from the border areas with neighboring states."

Lucas blew out, to give himself a little time to process what he had heard, at least superficially. "Sorry, a bit too much input this early in the day. Go on."

She gave him a tongue-in-cheek stern look before continuing. "That was the theory, anyway. But people didn't want to stay in one place all their lives. Many moved around within Yugoslavia. Families and tribes intermingled, as they always have—until the beginning of the Second World War, when the royal family fled to England. The entire nation was left to the mercy of the fascists from Germany and Italy. Suddenly there were Nazis everywhere. And they had their supporters in Yugoslavia, too. Just like in other countries, nonconformists were persecuted, and concentration camps were built that rivaled Auschwitz and Treblinka. The Yugoslav Nazis—the Domobrani, Ustasha, and Chetniks—enjoyed friendly relations with the Vatican and Constantinople."

"But as I remember, there were insurgents in Yugoslavia, too, who stood up to them," Lucas said.

"Yes, there was the antifascist guerrilla resistance, led by Tito. After five years of bitter fighting, the right-wingers were defeated and driven out. Tito was proclaimed president. The new socialist-communist government enforced a strict separation between church and state. As a result, religious pseudopatriotism quickly lost importance. Unfortunately, it couldn't be completely eradicated."

"I can guess what came next," Lucas interjected. "The civil war in the '90s?"

Lejla nodded. "Yep. After Tito's death in the early 1980s, nationalism flared up again. Subtly at first, but it succeeded in turning the Yugoslav people against each other so that nine years later, they were on opposite sides of a civil war. Families were torn apart; friends became enemies. Good neighborhoods disintegrated and often ended in bloodshed. The resulting mutual hatred was burned deeper into the collective consciousness over the next six years than it had been in the preceding world war. Well, that's how it was until the outbreak of the zombie plague. Hardly anything had changed. How could it have? The religious leaders continued to use their influence on politics to stoke prejudice, and that damaged the economy. Many people couldn't bear the hopelessness any longer and emigrated to the West, which proved to be the worst possible choice in view of the pandemic. But the people who stayed—the ones who survived the apocalypse—had to join forces. It was the only way to survive the catastrophe in the long run. And so, out of necessity, the proverbial hatchet was buried, and a new society was formed, which managed to defeat the zombies in its territory in the years that followed. Working together like this also made religious beliefs seem less important. But now that the infected aren't a real threat anymore, voices are being raised again, calling for separation. *Religious identity* is what they're calling it today. They come up with some nasty shit to make themselves heard. Some preachers are saying the apocalypse happened because people turned away from God. But the really bad thing is that desperate people keep falling for it. For many of the country's elders, the wounds of the civil war haven't healed yet. That's fertile ground for the discord the faithful are looking to sow. Meanwhile, there's a growing fear that the old hostilities could be rekindled."

Lejla looked tired and sad as she spoke these words. He was about to ask her what role her father had played in the whole political merry-go-round when there was a knock at the cabin door. Without waiting for an answer, Sanel stuck his head in and said, "Dinner's being served. Are you hungry?" Lucas looked at Lejla. They both nodded.

"We'll be approaching the Kornati Islands soon," Sanel continued. "I don't want Lucas to miss them. So I'll get some food brought up on deck for you both."

They accepted the offer, and he left. Lejla stood up and stretched her back. "Whoa, sitting around for hours like this is getting on my nerves," she said, closing the laptop. "Come on, let's get some fresh air."

Lucas followed her willingly. The wind was almost chilly, but the spring sunshine, which was beaming down from the sky broken only by a few scattered clouds, drove them into the shade of the mainsail. Above them, crew members were clambering around in the rigging, capturing loose ropes and sails. The keel cut through the dark blue sea, trailing a wide wake behind them.

"There! Look!" exclaimed Lejla excitedly, pointing toward the bow.

Lucas leaned over the railing and caught sight of the foothills of the archipelago. "Are these the hundred and fifty pebbles scattered by the Creator—the sight of which he afterward found so beautiful that he would not change them?"

She looked at him in surprise. "Then you are not as ignorant as I thought. Ah, the Kornati Islands . . . Beautiful to look at, but unfortunately completely unfit for habitation."

"Look pretty bleak, don't they?"

"On most of the islands, it's almost impossible to find drinking water, let alone grow anything. The landscape is mercilessly dry. Before the epidemic, they had a few seawater treatment operations, but the filtration systems stopped working a long time ago. The few people who live there today make their living from fishing. They also distill seawater and trade the salt and bycatch for the things they need. That reminds me—If we're lucky, we'll catch the market in Zadar. It's spectacular! Merchants from all over northern and western Yugoslavia, even Italy, sail there once a month just to sell their wares for a week. You just have to see it. As well as food and clothing, they have pre-Initium-era objects; some of them are of no practical use. But they trade for astronomical sums on the off chance that they'll strike a sentimental chord with someone." She fell silent, looking thoughtful as they sailed past the first of the islands.

Lucas regarded the pitifully overgrown mounds rising from the sea. From a distance, he could only see sparse bushes and gray lichen. He could not imagine anyone being able to live there. The flat hills offered no protection from the sun or wind. All the corners and edges of the white limestone had been ground away by the elements.

"I have a question," he said casually. "What did Zadar use to be called?"

"Uh, what? Why would it have had a different name?"

"Well, you know . . . At the beginning of the pandemic, people wanted to associate everything with the zombies and came up with new terms for everything. Like everything had to start or end with the letter Z, or zombie, even. Like Day Z. Or Barzelona and Zeville. You're not saying you didn't know about it!?"

She grinned and wrinkled her nose. "Just wait till you find out how my father got his name." But then she said, seriously, "No, Zadar has always been called Zadar. And of course I knew that people were distorting words and combining them arbitrarily with *zombie*—I live in the Balkans, not on the dark side of the moon."

Now he was grinning. "Okay, okay, I didn't mean it."

"Well then. Shall we pack our things and clean the weapons? We're gradually approaching the finish line."

He nodded.

"We're not allowed to take weapons into Zadar's old town. And it's best we put on civilian clothes," she continued. "We'll all stay on board until Sanel has arranged transportation. We should be ready to go in case we have to leave early."

"Are we going to spend the night on the ship?"

"Yes, but we're off duty till midnight." She sounded pleased.

"Great. I'm really excited to see what's going on."

A few minutes later, they were sitting across from each other at the table under the main mast, which was soon full of springs, pipes, and other components from dismantled rapid-fire weapons. Concentrating intently, they cleaned and brushed all the individual parts. Where necessary, they smeared them with oil.

After Lejla had put her AK together, she slid three cartridge magazines and a pouch full of ammunition across the tabletop to Lucas. "Try these out and see if they fit your gun. They should be the right caliber."

He inserted one of the magazines, which clicked into place. "Perfect, thank you." Then, looking at the bag, he asked, "Is this really all for me?"

"Sure. There's so much, I don't know how we're ever going to shoot it all."

"Maybe we can buy some of it from you?"

"Don't worry about it. I'm sure we can come to an agreement," she said, winking at him.

He smiled back gratefully.

The schooner glided northwestward through a wide passage. They encountered more and more other watercraft. People in fishing boats and sailors coiling ropes briefly interrupted their activities to wave at the *Sinji Galeb*. Cheerfully, the crew returned each greeting. They sailed past a town three hundred meters away whose houses seemed to be made of white limestone.

"This is Biograd," said Lejla, "which means *White City*. Until recently it was uninhabited, but slowly its streets and houses are filling up again. We're not far from Zadar now."

Two hours later, Lejla's entire brigade had gathered at the bow. The sailors maneuvered the ship into the harbor. Having sailed in a wide arc around the old town, which was on an elongated headland, they docked on the port side. The city walls and the buildings behind them were made of the same material as the buildings in Biograd—with the difference that here, there were countless people bustling about. The din of voices, haggling and arguing, droned over from the pier. Cargo was being unloaded by wooden cranes and piled onto handcarts. Instantaneously, they disappeared into the crowd that was gathered in the harbor. A number of people without any obvious job to do were gawking at the hustle and bustle.

Ropes the diameter of arms flew toward the land from the two-master, which was then moored to black bollards rubbed smooth with use. The mate shouted at a group of men who were probably in the way, but who shouted back indignantly in their turn before finally making way for a two-meter-wide plank that was lowered with a crash.

"Looks like it's market week," Lejla rejoiced. She followed Sanel, who left the ship with the brigade in tow. "He and the team will sort out the transport to Bihać now. Then they'll be off duty, too," she said over her shoulder.

Lucas had to raise his voice in the general confusion. "How far is it to your house?"

"About a hundred and fifty kilometers along the old freeway and several highways," she called over her shoulder. "If Sanel can get a pedal bus organized, we'll be there in five or six hours. But you'll have to make a big effort if we go via Velebit and Plješavica."

"Don't worry about it," he said, anxious not to step on anyone's toes. He had no idea what a pedal bus was, or what Velebit or Plješavica were. The chaos, which grew more intense the closer they got to the entrance of the historic town center, prevented him from thinking about it. Just before the city gate, Lejla put a hand up in the air and beckoned him forward. He followed her. Now he had to call on all his strength to make headway in the crush. At the old wall beneath the archway, a white sign read *dobrodošli u njugoslaviju*; next to it was written *welcome to newgoslavia*. Each of the statements was written over three lines. The upper words were colored dark blue, the lower ones deep red. In the middle, two red stars hung resplendent with white text inside them. Below that, he spotted graffiti framed by fresh flowers. He had no idea how to pronounce it, or what it even meant, but he memorized the words *Živio drug Tiz*. He would ask Lejla about it when he got the opportunity.

The pavement inside the city walls was polished smooth. He slid over it as if it were a patch of ice. Lejla had stopped on the left twenty meters farther on, under a staircase. She was talking with Sanel, who glanced at his wristwatch and swayed his head back and forth, thinking. After around a minute, the meeting was over. The older man waved to him and disappeared up the stairs with the rest of the team. Lejla turned to Lucas and spoke directly into his ear, drowning out the noise. "We need to be back on the ship shortly after sunset. That'll give us time to get the most important stuff."

"Can we grab something to eat, too? I'm starting to get hungry again."

"That's mostly why we're here." She grinned. "Have you ever had South Indian food? They have the best snack bar in Europe here."

"Sounds good. Let's go; I'll follow you."

She nodded, crossed the street, and led him down a narrow alley where a different kind of chaos seemed to be reigning. Two streams of people were moving toward each other between the market stalls, driving those caught between them ahead. He looked down over the shoulders of the hagglers at the tables, which were piled with clothing, spices, grains, and pickled fruits and vegetables. Early potatoes and onions were stacked in pyramids. One or two of the merchants were trading around five- or ten-liter bottles covered in rattan. Wine and home brew, Lucas guessed.

Two market stalls farther on, a trader was selling small signs with logos and remote control keys for car brands that had been popular before the apocalypse. Blue-and-white shields and three-pointed stars, which had apparently been stolen from car hoods, lay next to yellow badges containing horse silhouettes. In between were smartphones, silver-gray laptops, and stylish wireless headphones under which someone had written *Original Beats slušalice* on a yellowing scrap of paper.

"These are selling like hotcakes," she called, pointing at the computers. "I know people who can get these kinds of devices to work. They hack into them and set you up with a new password. But you can't do much with them. Create spreadsheets, edit pictures, and watch movies—if they have a DVD drive. Or play computer games. Since the internet's down, people can't think of what to do with them."

Lucas nodded and turned his attention to a stand that had books, magazines, and newspapers, seemingly from all over Europe. Fiction, nonfiction, *TIME* magazines in German, French, and English all piled up any which way.

"How do you pay for things?"

"Mostly people barter; otherwise they use the old Euros. Their value has increased to many times their original rate. You can buy a mountain bike for a few cents. And a house for a hundred Euros—although hardly anyone does that, since so many are standing empty. A loaf of bread costs two cents, and ten kilograms of grain is eleven cents. Lunch at Sweet Chili is ten cents."

"Is that the Indian takeout place you were telling me about?"

"Yeah—it's right over there," Lejla said, pointing to a nondescript door between two arms dealers, who were loudly advertising their rapid-fire rifles and handguns. Ammunition was apparently being sold somewhere else because Lucas couldn't see any.

The window was adorned with an oversize hand-painted chili pepper. The logo with the name of the snack bar was modeled on Indian script, with an almost continuous upper line and squiggly letters below it. They entered the crowded store. It was at most six meters square, Lucas calculated, suppressing a surge of claustrophobia. The space even included the kitchen, which was giving off a pungent smell of curry, garlic, and onions. Oil was sizzling in a couple of pans. A bald South Asian man was at the stove. On either side of the room were three tables with benches designed to seat four people each. Some of them had as many as nine people crowded onto them, eating with their fingers.

It seems like a popular place, Lucas was about to say, but a shrill exclamation suddenly put him on alert. All conversation ceased. An Indian woman in her forties, dressed in a purple and green sari, stormed out from behind the counter. Her long straight black hair fell down her back. She clapped her hands together delightedly and came toward Lejla, who was a head taller. The Newgoslavian grinned and embraced the woman. The guests resumed their discussions while the women began talking animatedly.

Lejla pointed at one of the occupied tables. The Indian woman moved away, looked around the room, and spoke to a group of guests who had finished eating. Inexplicably, a heated debate flared up. The woman—who Lucas assumed was the boss of the establishment—shouted at the burly men and gestured toward the door.

When they shook their heads and showed no sign of moving, she raised her voice almost to a scream. She yelled roughly, something that sounded like *Hajde mrš, odjebite odavde*. When the other guests weighed in to support the Indian woman, the men she had been addressing gave in and reluctantly left the table. Lejla grinned at the displaced diners as she passed them, and they suddenly responded with a smile as if they recognized her.

One of the men tossed a handful of copper coins to the woman in the sari before they left the store.

Meanwhile, the cook had also appeared. He happily pressed Lejla to his smeared white jacket, while the Indian woman tidied up the dishes the men had left. She handed him the plates and sent him back behind his counter.

"Come on, let's wash our hands." Lejla prompted Lucas, leading him to a corner with a tiny sink. They then took a seat at the table, which had just been wiped clean. "Shanti, this is Lucas. Lucas—Shanti," Lejla said in English. Lucas greeted the woman.

Shanti looked him up and down. Then she looked at Lejla and grinned conspiratorially. "What can I get you?" she asked politely.

"Do you still have idli and masala dosa?" the Newgoslavian inquired before Shanti could speculate about how the two of them knew each other.

"For you—always, my child."

"Then I'll have an idli and a masala dosa." She then looked at Lucas. "What do you want?"

"Can I maybe get a Punjabi thali?"

Shanti beamed and called over the chatter of the guests, "Anand, can you do idli and masala dosa for Lejla and a Punjabi thali for her boyfriend!?"

"Punjabi thali?" said the cook, suddenly glowing with pride. "Yassir. Consider it done."

"He's from Chandigarh," Shanti explained, nodding her head happily. "It's not often that white people specifically order Punjabi food."

"Do you have sheera, too?" inquired Lucas with a smile.

"Sheera I will cook for you myself," she declared ceremonially.

Shanti moved away toward the kitchen. Lucas called after her, "And two ginger lemon teas, please."

He looked at the pictures on the wall. They were digital photos that had been printed on old color printers and placed in simple wooden frames. Some showed the Taj Mahal in Agra, one the Gateway of India in Mumbai, and three featured the Golden Temple in Amritsar. Another showed two people who were clearly of European descent, and between them was an Indian-looking couple holding up a child for the camera. The photo had been taken on a hill. In the background was a city and a meandering river. On the wall below, in cursive script, was written: *Živio drug Tiz*. Surprised, Lucas exclaimed, "That's Shanti and Anand, isn't it? They were much younger then. How long ago was that?" He looked more closely at the scene. "That's . . . *you!*" he said, dumbfounded. "How old are you there? Ten? Eleven? And who are the others?"

Shanti appeared, smiling, placed the drinks in front of them, and turned her attention to the guests at the table opposite. Lejla grinned, slightly embarrassed. "Yes, that's me, with Shanti and Anand. And my parents. The photo was taken a long time ago, in Bihać. Two years before the outbreak."

"You all look happy. And where are your parents now?" Too late, he wondered if the question was too personal, but she chattered happily on.

"My mother now lives in Sarajevo; my father stayed in Bihać. He wasn't very good at controlling his urges—so he didn't make the best husband, I guess. After a certain point, my mother couldn't take it any-more, so she left him in the middle of the pandemic. Since he was always away and busy with zombie cleanups—and probably with other women, too—it was no great loss to her. She has remarried. He, on the other hand, has . . . changed. Or rather, he's become . . . more authentic, if you know what I mean."

Lucas shook his head.

She sighed and seemed to search for the right words. "He's become more introverted, which he always was underneath. I didn't notice it as a kid, but the older I got, the more clearly I could see that side of him. There was something melancholy about him, as if a certain part of him were missing. Something that came out more and more the older I got. Or the more independent I grew. I guess being a father distracted him from it for a while. Now he seems to be in crisis; his child has left home and the zombies are far away."

"Are you guys close?" asked Lucas.

"Very! Don't get me wrong, he's a good father, as far as he's able. But his longing is not something that I or anyone else can satisfy. Maybe it's itchy feet, maybe it's something else . . . He's been through a lot since the civil war. Very little of it good. Back then, he planned to leave the country with an uncle who lived in Austria, only hours before Bosnia's borders were closed because of the war. They were close to getting out when his uncle took a risk overtaking another vehicle." She shook her head. "It didn't go well for him. My father, for his part, ended up in the hospital and was in a coma for weeks. After six months, he was transported back to Bihać. He served the last three years of the war. He was just eighteen years old."

Lucas exhaled.

The voice of the Indian woman made them raise their heads. "Children, make way, here comes your food!" Shanti placed two round stainless steel trays on the table and pushed their orders toward them. "Thali for the young gentleman, masala dosa and idli for the lady."

"Yes! Garlic naan!" Lucas exclaimed gleefully, seeing two thin flatbreads studded with bits of garlic. It had been a long time since he had eaten anything well seasoned. The sight alone made his mouth water. Next to a large rice bowl, he counted four other small bowls, each filled with something different: one had yellow lentil soup, another potatoes and okra garnished with parsley and a red chili pepper. The third contained a kind of stew of tomato sauce, mashed pumpkin, peas, and roughly chopped cubes of tofu. Everything was steaming and giving off a delicious smell. In the fourth small bowl, freshly sliced tomatoes and cucumbers lay alongside rings of onion.

"Bon appétit," Lejla said. She was already holding a neat piece of crêpe made of rice and lentil flour and filled with a paste of eggplant and mashed potatoes. Before shoving it into her mouth, she dipped it into the bowl of spicy tomato sauce. As she chewed, she announced, "Wow, this is delicious." She immediately took another bite.

Lucas tore off a piece of pita bread and picked up some of the rice and dal with it. Two seconds later, his mouth was burning like fire. He inhaled noisily. "Whoa, that's hot!"

"Mega, isn't it?" said Lejla enthusiastically, the first drops of sweat shining on her forehead. She then grabbed one of the white patties made of fermented rice and urad dal, stirred it in the sauce, and bit off half. "Indian food is the best, man!"

"Mm-hmm," Lucas confirmed. He washed the food down with a sip of lemon ginger tea, which intensified the burning sensation.

"Want to trade?" she offered when they got to the halfway point.

"Sure," he replied.

They rotated the trays. The paper-thin crêpe was crispy. Just like the soft idli, it went perfectly with the spicy sambar stew. "This is awesome," he said, looking at the patty he had bitten into.

They ate their portions, then sat back.

"You just can't stop there, even if you feel like you're about to burst," Lejla said, belching.

"I'll be full for the rest of my life." Lucas moaned, wiping his hands on a damp kitchen towel. "I'm never going to eat again."

They both groaned loudly as Shanti placed two small bowls containing the dessert in front of them.

"I totally forgot about the sheera," he lamented. "I can't eat it right now. I need a break."

"Can we sit here for a few more minutes?" Lejla asked the Indian woman. In answer, she received a kiss on the forehead. Shanti carried away the empty dishes.

Lucas sipped his tea and looked at the pictures on the wall again. "What does it say?" He pointed to the sentence underneath them. "I've seen that in a few places around town."

She took a deep breath. "You asked earlier if Zadar had been given a new name."

He nodded.

"Of course, during the apocalypse, they used the letter Z everywhere, even here in our country, and that's also the case with the graffiti. But to understand what it means, we have to go back to World War II. Are you ready?"

Lucas, eager to hear the story, nodded emphatically.

"So, during the National Liberation War, which in the original language is Narodnooslobodilačka borba—or NOB for short—there was a figure who led the guerrilla war against the German occupation. His name was Tito, and he later became president for life. He gained his experience in the Spanish Civil War of the 1930s, where he also got his nickname. Back in Yugoslavia, shortly after the occupation, he gathered a guerrilla army around him, which he led in the struggle against fascism between 1940 and 1945."

Lucas nodded.

"Tito's followers saw no point in maintaining the old social structures, especially as far as religions and ethnicities were concerned. From then on, they saw themselves as Yugoslavs. The new society was characterized by atheism, communism, and socialist thinking as propounded by Marx and Lenin and—where was I going with this? I've totally lost the thread."

Lucas pointed at the phrase on the wall.

"Oh, that's right. So, Tito united and liberated the people of Yugoslavia during the NOB. But they were divided and threatened again a half century later by the zombie apocalypse. This is where my father comes in; he rounded up survivors without caring about their origins or religion. After long years of struggle, they threw the zombies out beyond the Yugoslavian borders I was talking about. Since there were certain undeniable parallels with NOB and Tito, he was given the nickname Titwo—*Ti* paired with the English *two*. The second Tito, so to speak."

Lucas laughed and shook his head. "And when you write *two* as a number, it looks like a *Z*. That's why it's Tiz."

"Correctomundo. *Živio drug Tiz* means *Long live Comrade Tito the Second*. And the NOB 2 is called . . . ?"

"NOB Z?"

"Welcome to Newgoslavia, Frenchie," she replied patronizingly, spreading her arms and grinning. "But now let's finish dessert. And then I'll show you the world-famous Zadar sea organ."

When Lejla asked for the bill, Shanti feigned indignation and hit her with a tea towel. Laughing, they said good-bye to each other, which seemed to Lucas to take an eternity. He had to hug the Indian woman and her husband four times before they allowed them to move on. How many times he had to assure them that he would come back, he could not remember.

"Anand and Shanti are like family to me," Lejla explained superfluously as they made their way into the crowd again. "They moved here from Bihać three years ago and opened the café. That was always their European dream, in any case."

The Newgoslavian stopped at a stand advertising bluish plastic cases with pictures on them. Lucas stood next to her and watched her dig through the Blu-Ray movie collection. She selected four cases and haggled loudly with the salesman, both gesturing wildly. Eventually, they seemed to come to an agreement, which put a broad smile on both of their faces. Lejla fished out some copper coins and pressed them into the merchant's hand.

"What a cutthroat," she lamented after they had gone barely two meters. "I could have fed myself for a year for that. But I can sell them again, anyway." She stowed her purchases in the pockets of her cargo pants and led him to the right, away from the worst of the hubbub. Side by side, they walked through alleys barely two meters wide. The noise of the market receded behind them. Clotheslines stretched above their heads. The laundry hanging from them looked black against the dark blue sky of the late afternoon. A gaggle of screaming children chased after a soccer ball and disappeared into the next alley. The closer they got to the sea, the stronger the salty smell of drying seaweed became.

Lejla led Lucas past white church spires. Around one more bend, they stepped out into a large semicircular area full of people. Soft noises that sounded like an oversize glockenspiel echoed in his ears. Puzzled, he looked around. The source of the sounds, which synchronized with the rise and fall of the surf, could have been beyond the horizon, or at his feet. They made his whole body vibrate. The noises had an intense, disconcerting effect on him. "What the hell is that?" he asked.

Lejla laughed. "Beneath this square is an installation made up of over thirty tubes. Each tube is a different size and set at a different angle. The waves and currents create the tidal music that you're hearing now." She motioned for him to follow her. Near a stairway around a hundred meters wide that led directly into the sea, he saw a row of holes that had been made in the ground.

"This is where the sounds come out," she explained.

"It's bewitching," he said reverently. The music triggered an inner peace in him, and he looked around at the people sitting on the steps and watching the sun set over the island on the horizon. He took in the general bustle with a clarity he had previously only known in combat, but without the adrenaline spike that came with it. He was in harmony with the world. His heartbeat seemed to have aligned with the rhythm of the music. Couples walked by holding hands. The sun was coloring the western sky red.

Three men approached Lejla, smiling. One waved in a friendly manner. The Newgoslavian returned the gesture. Lucas recognized one of the men who had been asked to make way for them at Sweet Chili. The other two were walking a step behind him, their eyes fixed on Lejla. Suddenly, alarm bells rang in Lucas's head. Time seemed to slow down. The close combat sequences that were second nature after years of practice took control of his body. He leapt to Lejla's side and kicked the man's wrist, which had been flashing toward her stomach. Only now did he see the knife that the man had jabbed through her clothes. Lejla made a sound of surprise. Lucas's kick stopped the weapon before it could stab deeper. The knife flew away and bounced off a woman's bag before falling to the ground with a clink, barely two meters away.

The attacker used the force of Lucas's kick to generate momentum in his torso. Skillfully, he rocketed his other hand, clenched into a fist, toward Lejla. Lucas instinctively shifted up a gear. Countering the movement, he used his forearm to ward off the mighty blow that would have knocked the Newgoslavian down if it had connected. Then he in turn struck with his parrying hand. The force he generated from a slight turn of his hip was enough to break the man's nose with one straight punch. The man staggered back a couple of steps, forcing one of his henchmen to dodge, while the third assessed the situation. Hardly anyone around them had noticed what had happened in the two seconds that had lapsed.

The attackers obviously hadn't expected such aggressive resistance. They took a moment to collect themselves. And that was all Lejla needed to get over the shock and prepare for the second wave. She stepped to the side, picked up the knife, and adopted a combat stance. Her feet shoulder-width apart and slightly offset, she bent her upper body forward and pointed the blade forward.

Lucas also planted his feed firmly and let his arms dangle loosely like a street fighter waiting for the best opportunity to throw a punch.

One of the three jerked his head curtly, and the trio turned and ran off. They quickly disappeared into the crowd.

Lucas heard the tidal music again. He looked over at Lejla. She was holding the place where the blade had gone into her belly. Her fingertips were red with blood. "How bad is it?" he asked.

"Not at all. Barely scratched the skin. As long as the edge wasn't poisoned, I'll survive."

The idea that she could have been seriously hurt sent shivers down his spine. "Let me see!" he urged her and knelt. Without wincing, she lifted her shirt. She was right, the wound wasn't deep. The tissue around it appeared normal. He waited a few seconds to see if it would begin to go gray. "Looks okay," he said when nothing else happened. "Who were those guys?"

"How would I know? But it can't have been a coincidence that they were at Sweet Chili."

"Were they waiting for you?"

Lejla shrugged. "Quite possibly. Let's hurry back to the ship before they set another trap for us in one of the alleys." She started to move off but turned back to him and said, "Hey, Lucas—thanks!"

CHAPTER 3

LIKA

Making their way through the hustle and bustle cost them more in nervous tension than any antizombie mission in recent years. Out in the postapocalyptic wilderness, the line between good and evil, friend and foe, was clearly defined. But in a city full of living people, Lejla suddenly couldn't rely on the old familiar categories. The lively pulsating crowds around her had lost all appeal in one fell swoop. Anyone who smiled at her also presented a potential danger.

She held one hand protectively over her wound. The exposed ends of the separated nerves burned. Blood oozed between her fingers and dripped onto the ground. It wasn't much, but the mere fact that she had been attacked sent her into a panic. *At least the knife wasn't contaminated,* she reasoned. Otherwise, Lucas, who was running close behind her and covering her back, would have been forced to kill her to prevent an outbreak in the middle of Zadar.

But who on earth wanted them dead? And why? Lejla also wondered how many of the people wandering through the alleyways were illegally armed—something she had not given any thought until ten minutes ago. Illicitly—not illegally—she corrected herself. There were no laws in Newgoslavia like there had been pre-apocalypse, and in any case, hardly anyone in the Balkans had obeyed them back then, either. Things were going better with the code they had now, despite the initial skepticism about such a liberal concept. Over time, however, people had realized that the freedom that came with taking responsibility for themselves was far more empowering in contrast to the spoon-feeding that had gone on under the laws of the previous culture.

People didn't need laws, certainly, or authorities in order to live in peace or to develop. They needed attitudes and cohesion that cut across ethnic groups and were not related to individuals' social position. Her father had used to say something like that when he was defending the new social order.

The thing the Balkans need first and foremost is a good education, she would have added, if it hadn't sounded so cynical.

In Lejla's shattered world, education had been a scarce resource long before the pandemic. Despite the collapse of civilization, Tiz had done everything he could to make sure she had access to knowledge. And he vehemently insisted that she use it.

She suppressed that stream of thought and focused on not running headlong into another blade. In the fading light, it was hard to spot a fist with a weapon in it, and right now she was surrounded by dozens of people.

Once they had left the old town behind and could see the *Sinji Galeb*'s lamps, Lejla's knees began to shake. She mustered all her willpower to avoid letting anything show. Wordlessly, she marched past the guard, who eyed her questioningly. Lucas would tell the crew about the incident while she tended to the wound in her cabin. At least that's what she hoped.

She had scarcely reached the stairs to the lower deck when she heard him telling the guards about the attack, alerting them. Lejla climbed down to the floor below, propping herself against the corridor wall with her free hand. She went into her cabin and pushed the door shut behind her. From the upper deck she heard scrambling footsteps, which probably meant that the number of guards was being increased. *They might be sending someone out to find Sanel, too, if he hasn't come back yet.* With her clean hand, she groped for the light switch in the doorway that connected the 12-volt battery under her bunk to the LED light. A cold bluish light flickered into life above her.

The tension wouldn't ease up. She strained to calm her pounding heart. Inhaling and exhaling deeply, she leaned back against the door. Fear was not a new experience for her. But to have looked death in the face in a protected area shook her to the core. Who was responsible for this? Who wanted her dead?

Lejla clenched her jaws as hard as she could. She had to force herself to think clearly. Her fear gradually turned into anger. An anger that was even harder to contain than panic. She had inherited this trait from her father, though she wasn't quite as hot-tempered as him.

An angry dragging feeling just above her belly button moved upward, constricting her throat. She exhaled jerkily and clutched at her blood-soaked shirt with her fists. With control, she unbuttoned it. Under the cool light, she took a closer look at the injury. A tiny trickle of blood flowed out in time with her beating heart.

The stab had caused more than superficial injury to the tissue over a length of about five centimeters; this was probably due to the forcible removal of the blade as Lucas defended her.

Lejla turned to the sink, soaked the tip of a towel with water and washed away the encrusted blood. She rolled up the terry cloth and tucked it into the waistband of her pants below the wound. In the mirrored cabinet, she found a first aid kit and a bottle containing two hundred milliliters of rakija brandy. Lejla uncorked it, rubbed her hands with a little of it, placed the lip of the bottle above the wound—*Someone will pay for this*, she promised herself—and poured the alcohol over it. She groaned. The towel turned dark with blood.

After most of the pain had passed, she fished out a sterile needle threaded with one of her long hairs. It was not the first time she had needed stitches. After years of fighting, minor wounds had become almost a given. She had suffered a broken bone or two as well, which had been taken care of by someone with medical experience. But this time, Lejla patched herself up with eighteen stitches. Normally a knotted section of hair yarn didn't hold very well, but the sticky, encrusted blood would hold it in place until she taped a bandage over it. Once she was done, Lejla poured some more liquor over the wound. She clenched her teeth so tightly she feared the enamel might crack.

Next, she proceeded to puncture a piece of gaffer tape, about ten centimeters long, over and over again with a needle. She then fished out a gauze cloth the size of her palm from the first aid bag, folded it twice, and placed it over the injury. She covered it with the now breathable tape. Relieved, she exhaled—and shuddered. The abrupt drop in her stress hormones left a void that was seamlessly filled by a state of shock. Lejla groped her way to the bunk and lay down. Her head was spinning, but she had the presence of mind to raise her legs up on her pillow and a winter jacket that was hanging on the hook next to the porthole. With an effort, she covered herself and then allowed her body to shut down.

The roaring in her ears merged with the lapping of the waves against the ship's hull. The outlines of the objects around her blurred and she plunged into the welcoming darkness.

The sounds seemed to be coming from a long way away. "*Mala*, are you okay?" With each repetition, they became clearer. Closer. Louder. Something warm touched her cheeks. And immediately after that, something damp and cool was placed on her forehead.

"What?" Lejla slowly opened her eyes and saw Sanel's worried face above hers. He stroked her face with his powerful paw. "Oh, hi. What's up?" she said.

"Are you okay? What happened?" His dark voice betrayed uneasiness.

"My head is spinning." It took her a few moments to remember. "Some *šupak* tried to stab me." She pushed the blanket aside and showed him the taped-off spot. "Didn't get in deep enough, though. Just a scratch. I've already stitched it," she affirmed.

Anger crept into his voice. "Who? Where?"

"I don't know. Lucas and I went to Shanti's for dinner. Some guy with two buddies in tow was there, too. An hour later, he tried to take out my appendix on the sea organ without any anesthetic. But I think he might not have been a doctor."

"Cut the stupid talk! What did he look like?"

"How should I know what he looked like? Just a Newgo. You'd better ask the Frenchie. He broke his nose. He may have got a closer look at the rest of his face in the process."

Sanel turned around. The young Frenchman was standing behind him. Lejla smiled at him and said dreamily, "Bordoure."

"Bonjour," Lucas replied suspiciously. "Is she on drugs?" he said a little more quietly to the older man, who had just discovered the half-empty liquor bottle on the edge of the sink.

Sanel leaned forward and smelled her breath. "No," he announced, audibly relieved, "just in a state of shock. Do you remember the guy who attacked her?"

"Not really," Lucas replied, shaking his head. "It all went way too fast. And suddenly they were gone."

"Ubiću ih, majke mi," Sanel said through gritted teeth. He called out to one of the two sailors waiting in the doorway, "Bring her something to drink! And sugar!"

After draining a heavily sweetened glass of water, Lejla's spirits gradually returned. She tried to sit up, but the freshly stitched wound pinched and discouraged her from doing so.

"No, you lie down for the moment," Sanel ordered. "It's best you sleep now until I figure something out."

Lejla let her head sink deeper into the pillow he had placed under her neck. "You already have an idea who it might have been, don't you?" she whispered.

There was an unease in his voice that revealed more than the knowledge of an unspecified danger. "Does it have something to do with my father?"

"You shouldn't think so much. Like I said, you need to recover!" he told her. Again, the concern for her, poorly hidden behind a veil of threatening gestures. He glanced at his wristwatch. "It's three hours to midnight. At dawn we want to move on, so shut up now and try to sleep," he growled, kissing her forehead. "Zdravko and Siniša are outside. If you need anything, call me."

She nodded.

Sanel asked Lucas to come with him. He turned out the light, and they both left the tiny cabin. Lejla heard him talking to the guards outside the door, instructing the two young men not to let anyone in except him. Then his footsteps moved away. In the darkness, it took less than five minutes for her to fall asleep.

Lejla was woken by a commotion on the upper deck. She shook off her drowsiness. Her wound hurt less and was only pinching. Feeling her abdomen, she checked the bandage before moving carefully. It wasn't oozing or bleeding. Lejla sat up and slid her feet into her boots. She looked through the porthole into the harbor but saw nothing in the darkness. Outside the door, she heard Sanel's heavy footsteps approaching. He entered the cabin without knocking. He left the light off.

"Ah, good, you're already awake. Grab your jacket and your gun and come with me. How's the injury?"

"It's all good, just pulling a little. What's the plan?"

"We don't have time for long explanations. You and Lucas are leaving right now. He can tell you the rest on the way. I've already launched the dinghy. A pedal quad with provisions and ammunition is waiting for you on the other side of the harbor. I've also had your rucksack packed. Standard survival rations for a week."

Was the situation so serious that she had to leave Zadar under the cover of darkness? Sanel did not give her the chance to think about it and marched out again. Hastily, she laced up her boots and took her AK-47 and the Blu-Ray discs she had bought at the market out of the closet. Her winter jacket under her arm, she hurried along the corridors through the dark ship. On the upper deck, she saw Sanel at the railing, waiting with Lucas and three other figures. The minute she joined them, the Frenchman swung himself over the railing. He disappeared downward on a rope the diameter of a fist. With a jerk of his head, Sanel told her to follow Lucas. Wordlessly, she obeyed.

"See you in Bihać," he whispered after her. She looked up at him and nodded. But in the darkness, she couldn't tell if he had noticed.

Lucas had sat down in the rubber dinghy, which was being held in place by a sailor hanging onto the rope. Lejla recognized Mirela, who nodded her head, indicating that she should sit down. When Lejla had settled herself, Mirela let go of the rope and grabbed the two oars. Smoothly, she turned the bow eastward, away from the ship. The gentle dip of the oar blades was barely distinguishable from the lapping of the ocean. In the flickering light of the stars, she could only guess where the deserted part of Zadar was. The closer they came, the clearer the contours of former hotels and high-rise buildings became. They docked silently and Lejla and Lucas carried their weapons and backpacks onto the pier. Carefully, they climbed up a rusty ladder embedded in concrete. Behind them, Mirela turned her boat around. Lejla looked at her watch. They had three hours until sunrise.

"What's the plan?" she asked quietly as they shouldered their backpacks.

Lucas looked around. "I can't see much. But there should be a vehicle around here somewhere."

Lejla blinked and pointed past a palm tree. "There's a pedal quad." Behind the tree stood a box-shaped cage on four wheels. Crouching, they made their way the few meters over to it, keeping their eyes on their surroundings. The rear door on Lejla's side opened effortlessly. "We didn't even have to put the backpacks on," she grumbled, rolling her eyes. She tossed hers onto the single seat, securing it with a seat belt. Then she pulled open the front door. She placed her gun in the holder provided next to the steering wheel. Out of the corner of her eye, she could see Lucas copying her every move. Two black helmets lay on the seats. She fished thick ski gloves out of them and a pair of ski goggles to replace the missing visor. Since her helmet was loose, Lejla considered putting up her hood first, but she was too comfortable and let it go. Tightening the chin strap should be enough. She locked both doors on her side and felt for the switch that controlled the circuit. Once she found it, she pressed it. A gray LED indicator flickered in front of them. The lighting icon was crossed out. Tonight, she'd have done without them anyway. The display read ninety-seven percent in big numbers on the following line. Lejla pressed a button next to the number. The display light went out. Only a tiny green glowing dot indicated that the vehicle was active. "Nearly done!" she announced, pulling on her gloves. Lucas had put his on long ago. "You pedal like you're riding a bike," she instructed him. "We can both steer, at the same time if we have to. The electric motors do the rest. Getting up hills is child's play. On the flats, we can go seventy kilometers an hour, maybe. In theory, we could even go faster, but a pedal quad is, unfortunately, about as aerodynamic as a pre-pandemic SUV."

Lucas laughed—a little too loudly for her taste—then looked around nervously.

"It's as streamlined as a parachute," she went on. "Because of the grille all around it. There's a flywheel in the big box between the back seats, which helps generate the electricity. It's stored in the batteries underneath us."

"Will this get us to Bihać?" He pronounced the name without the H.

"Sure. Once we're past Velebit, it's almost all downhill. As we roll downhill, the batteries are recharged. For the tailwind—if we get any— there's an extra feature. But I'll show you that later. Are you ready?"

"Can't wait," he replied.

"Let's roll," she said, starting to pedal. She ignored the tug of her wound and went flat out. A moment later, the electric drive came to life and reduced the resistance. The vehicle began to move sluggishly. "Let me get us out of town. After that, we can talk more."

Lucas nodded.

She fixed her gaze straight ahead.

The vehicle gained momentum. Just a few seconds later, they were moving so fast that the headwind took their breath away. The outlines of the ruins around them were pale shadows in the approaching dawn. Lejla pulled the zipper of her winter jacket up under her chin. She maneuvered the pedal quad onto a multilane road, where she accelerated away. The road led steadily uphill. Half a kilometer later, she turned left. After ten minutes, they had left the city behind. The salty scent of the sea had given way to the resinous aroma of pine groves.

A cool breeze was blowing down from Velebit. Soon she was shivering. Her wound pinched incessantly but did not prevent her from driving. On the side of the road, they saw squat buildings that had used to belong to a restaurant. "Now we're out of town," she called over the breeze. With the push of a button, she activated the display. They were going at forty kilometers per hour and had used eleven percent of their power. "Can you tell me Sanel's plan now?"

Lucas thought for a few seconds before he spoke. "He reckons we can't believe we're safe for a moment. Not even in Bihać."

"I got that far myself."

Lucas passed over the remark. "That's why you needed to leave unnoticed before they could set another trap for you."

"Good, what about Sanel and the others?"

"They're leaving at sunrise. Our places will be taken by a female and a male sailor, so it shouldn't be immediately apparent that we're not on board."

"Hmm," said Lejla. She ruminated for a while. "I keep wondering how they could have known we were in Zadar. It can't have been a coincidence that they were at Shanti's."

"Maybe they've been listening to your radio communications. Or maybe you have a mole in your ranks."

A mole in our ranks! What the hell was going on? Who would want to plant an informer and why? Was the failed attack just a message? To get to her father, maybe? To force him to take political action—or to render him harmless?

It was pointless racking her brains over it. She didn't have enough clues to draw any concrete conclusions. She would have to wait until they were in Bihać.

Not wanting to work herself into a paranoia, she steered the conversation into safer waters. "What do you say to our vehicle?"

"I'm impressed," Lucas said. "Where did you get it?"

"Tourists used to drive around in it before everything fell apart. A few years ago, some survivors broke into a garage in Zadar. There were dozens of these multiseat bikes stored inside. So they reinforced the chassis and welded grids over them to protect them from zombies. There are also larger vehicles, where you sit opposite each other. And then someone came up with the idea of cannibalizing old electric vehicles and incorporating their usable parts. I'll let you drive this one once we get to the other side of Velebit, okay?"

He grinned at her and nodded before his gaze drifted to the mountain peaks in the east, their black outlines contrasting with the pale sky.

"We're about to start climbing. At the top, we have to go through a tunnel."

"I'm guessing it'll be darker than the night around us."

"It sure will. But don't worry, the pedal quad has lights. There's the first access road to the freeway up ahead. I'll take the next one, though."

"Why?"

"I just like the area," she replied with a shrug.

They drove past the ruins of a village that had been built on the bank of an estuary to their right. The rugged, barren landscape blended seamlessly with the postapocalyptic scenery. Except for a few cats and hares that took flight on the other side of the road, nothing moved. A few kilometers after the village, they crossed the Maslenički Most, the seventy-meter-high bridge that connected the mainland with the northern Zadar peninsula. Lejla had to countersteer strongly as the crosswinds caught the pedal quad. Battery power had dropped to seventy-six percent and was falling by one point every ten kilometers. A few minutes later, they switched from the country road to the freeway, where one of the two lanes was always clear. To left and right, the remains of demolished vehicles were piled up.

"In the first year after the outbreak, the main arterial roads were plowed by military clearance vehicles. This was a time when it was still believed that the zombies could be kept at bay or even defeated. Maintaining infrastructure was the top priority. Without it, people feared the economy would grind to a halt," she called out to him over the rush of the wind.

His helmet nodded.

The road wound farther and farther upward. The steeper it got, the louder the electric motors attached to the axles hummed. Sometimes they went only fifteen kilometers per hour. The number on the percentage display dropped and dropped. At the tunnel entrance, it had reached thirty-six.

"Are you sure that's enough?" asked Lucas, pointing at it skeptically.

"Sure. We just have to get through the tunnel. We'll recharge on the other side." Lejla leaned forward and turned on the lights. The LED lights effortlessly illuminated the first fifty meters ahead of them.

"How long is it?"

"It tells you there," she replied, pointing to a green sign with a gloved fist.

"Right. Almost six kilometers."

Without the headwind coming down the mountain, the pedal quad was much more stable—and quicker—as it rolled into the tunnel.

"Get ready, Frenchie," she warned, pulling out her gun and taking the safety off.

"Ready for what?"

"For the unlikely event that we come across the undead."

"I thought everywhere had been zombie-proofed here?"

"It has, but you never know." His helmet prevented her from seeing his reaction. Lejla stuck the barrel through the grating. "It may not necessarily be the undead trying to get in our pants. The tunnel would be the perfect place for a trap."

He nodded and pointed his machine gun ahead of them.

As always, Lejla found the tunnel unimpressive. She tried to remember how many times she had taken the road before and concluded that it was a good dozen times. The first time, her heart had been in her mouth. Back then, they had dared to go to the sea on foot. However, the undead hadn't been interested in the tunnel or the surroundings area, probably because there were hardly any human settlements. You could pass through unhindered. And things were no different today. In the middle of the tunnel, it turned downhill. After a few hundred meters, the pedal quad easily reached maximum speed.

Fifteen minutes later, they emerged from the tunnel. They had barely passed underneath a long-extinguished speed display when Lejla stopped the vehicle. An angry wind rattled the caged chassis.

"Come with me," she urged Lucas, leaving the pedal quad. Wordlessly, he followed her. She made her way to the front of the vehicle, where a winch emerged from behind a sheet metal panel. Lejla pulled out a flat bag that was connected to the coiled rope. Running backward, she rolled out ten meters. At the same time, she unraveled the contents of the bag. "Take this," she called to the Frenchman, who was watching as if spellbound, and handed him a corner of the exposed fabric. He reached for it carefully. Lejla moved away from him. A paraglider made of ultralight nylon materialized between them, connected to the rope by dozens of thin threads. "This is our power now. You have to hold it in the wind, farther ahead of us. As if you're flying a kite," she said, pointing in the direction of travel. "I'd do it myself, but as you know, I'm injured." Too late, it occurred to her that he couldn't see her mischievous grin. "I'll pick you up in a minute, I promise." Lejla saw him shake his head in disbelief. Then he did as she asked.

She hurried to the pedal quad, got in, and fastened the seat belt. In one fluid motion, she released the handbrake. Lucas, meanwhile, had unwound the entire rope. It looked to her as if he were wondering what to do next. But before he could react, a gust of wind tore the sail out of his hand. The Frenchman lost his balance and fell backward onto the asphalt. With a jerk, the rope tightened. The heavy vehicle leapt forward, almost tipped over, stabilized—and rolled off ponderously.

"*Get in!*" yelled Lejla over the roar of the wind. She almost hit him, but Lucas dodged expertly. Running at full tilt, he caught up with her, yanked open the door, and jumped into his seat.

"Now the fun really begins, Frenchie."

Frantically, he strapped himself in. "What happens to the sail when we go under signs or through underpasses?"

"I'll show you when the time comes."

With the wind tugging furiously at them, they accelerated away. After half a minute, she said, "You don't need to pedal any more. We're sailing now." The pull became more constant as they got farther from the tunnel. The parachute hung above them, forty meters ahead. Near the viaducts, there were side gusts, which Lejla deftly countered. After a while, the terrain started to rise. Not wanting to lose momentum, they pedaled again until an overpass came into view two kilometers later. Lejla pressed a toggle switch next to the display. At the same time, the winch gave a grinding sound. The pedal quad picked up speed, and the sail began to descend. "I'll haul it in until we're through the overpass. After that, the wind will pull it out again. So we'll be below the maximum height of the four-and-a-half-meter-limit for the trucks of yesteryear."

"Smart," he exclaimed, impressed.

After the obstacle, Lejla released the sail.

"Now it'll be more relaxed. Nothing much will happen for the next hour. Sit back and enjoy the view. And if you want, you can drive, too."

"I'd like to try that."

"The wind's from the south today, which is good." She pulled a lever behind her control unit. "Now you're at the helm."

She let him drive all the way to the Gospić exit, only intervening a couple of times to keep the vehicle on track. But the wind was favorable. Barely half an hour later, his fun was over. "We're going to leave the freeway in a minute," she told him. "Then I'll take over again."

"Are we already there?" The disappointment in his voice was unmistakable.

Lejla laughed. "No, we're about halfway. But we won't be able to move so fast on the country roads. They're very twisty in places."

"The batteries are at almost eighty percent again, at least. It's great fun driving with this. I'd be happy if the route was even longer. The landscape is beautiful, too, despite how barren it is."

"Lika," she said.

"What?"

"Lika. That's the name of this area."

"Are people living here again?"

"Yes. Some villages have always held their own against the undead, mostly because they were off the beaten track and not discovered. Unfortunately, none of them are on our route."

Shortly before Gospić, they stopped and together furled the sail again. The battery gauge had reached eighty-five percent. They took advantage of the rest to eat some of the modest but nutritious ship's food and relieve themselves behind an abandoned electric vehicle. The interior of the latter bore witness to the fact that its gullwing doors had been open for almost a full decade. The seat covers had countless tears, and brambles had grown through them.

At Lički Osik, they turned east. From then on, they saw hardly any villages. Only a few buildings in the hilly area had resisted collapse, including a burned-out church that had been built in among the winding roads. There seemed to be no life for miles around. But the landscape, covered only with shaggy grass and leafless bushes, shone golden as soon as the sun rose over the horizon ahead of them. Only now did Lejla discover fresh wild boar tracks; the animals had been furrowing in the fields.

But they did not show themselves. Instead, an abandoned vehicle appeared behind a knoll. Under its brown-beige paint, the bodywork was extensively rusted. The many stickers on the rear bumper had faded and become illegible. Lejla slowed the pedal quad. Four skeletons sat in the small car, their heads leaning against the windows. The flesh and skin were nowhere to be seen after all these years.

"They've been here awhile, haven't they?" asked Lucas as they left the car behind.

"Yes, certainly from the beginning. This is the fourth time I've passed by. Each time the sight makes me unspeakably sad."

"They look peaceful. Like they positioned themselves there on purpose."

She nodded. "Now you have to tell a story about them."

"What kind of story?"

"Something nice. Who they were, why they picked that place of all places. That sort of thing . . ."

"Why?"

"It's become a ritual for my troop. Every time we come by here, some-one has to come up with a story."

"Hmm, I'll give it a try."

Lejla waited until he had his thoughts in order. Then he spoke. "They were four friends who were on the run together until one of them was bitten. The others didn't want to leave him alone to his fate. They went to a place where they loved to play as children. And they all took their own lives."

Lejla sighed. "Beautiful, Frenchie. Although extremely unlikely, it's still a wonderful story."

To the left and right of the road that wound down from the mountain range, they could see for miles over the plain. To the south, cloud forma-tions were gathering into a storm. But it was too far away to worry about.

To keep the conversation going and distract herself from her fatigue, Lejla asked her passenger, "Did you bring rain gear?"

"Yes. Sanel added your standard equipment to my backpack. A rain poncho, a tarp, a hammock, and a pack of bandages. Plus two days' rations. And the ammo you gave me. Why?"

"In case we get caught in the storm." She pointed southward. "But if the wind continues to be kind to us, we'll be there in two hours. No need to panic."

"Okay. Do you mind if I close my eyes for a moment? I didn't get any sleep last night."

"Go ahead," Lejla said generously.

He thanked her, crossed his arms, and leaned his helmeted head against the bars. *Great. Now I'll have to figure out how to keep myself awake.* She unbuttoned her jacket and took off her helmet. The cool breeze was invigorating, even if she was soon shivering again. She kept her eyes on the road and drove on. On the horizon, she spotted Plješevica, the mountain that lay between her and her hometown. It was so close. In a sudden rush of homesickness, her heart began to race. She swallowed hard and calculated how long it was since she had been home.

Half a year had passed since she had seen her family. Her stomach growled in anticipation as she thought of her grandmother's cooking. Lejla pedaled as hard as she could. The speed indicator jumped to sixty-two. The wind had shifted and was blowing northward, parallel to Plješevica. She had expected that, but it also meant the storm was getting closer. As long as they went at half this speed, though, it wouldn't catch them.

Shortly afterward, the landscape changed, albeit only slightly. More and more small patches of mixed woodland appeared. North of the small town of Korenica, they passed the ruins of inns and motels that had fed and housed innumerable guests in another era. Now they lay neglected, at the mercy of the elements.

Lejla remembered driving this way with her parents as a child to spend vacations by the sea. On many a Saturday, they would take day-trips to Pag or even go as far as Sveti Filip i Jakov and Biograd. Moving images, bursting with brightness and lightheartedness, flared up in her mind's eye. Beaches full of pebbles. Salty sea spray and the scent of pine. Camping in a cheap tent. Evening walks down the alleyways of lime-white old towns, her parents holding either hand. Strands of hair sticking to necks and shoulders from sweat. Pistachio ice cream and corn on the cob.

Before the memories drifted her into melancholy, she jabbed her elbow into the side of her passenger. Startled, he jerked awake, his hands automatically reaching for his gun. He looked around—and paused. Gradually, Lucas seemed to realize where he was. Yawning, he stretched. Following her example, he took off his helmet.

"What's wrong? Why did you wake me up?"

"Relax; nothing happened. I'm just bored," she reassured him.

"How long was I asleep?"

"An hour, at least!"

They drove up an incline that bent to the right and then led downhill. "Are we there yet?" he asked, yawning again, although they were in the middle of the forest and there was still no town in sight. He began to pedal, bringing his speed up to hers.

"Mm-hmm, just about. Another hour, tops," she replied, looking over at him. She pointed at the mountain range above his head to the right. "Bihać is right there, only on the other—"

"*Look out!*" he yelled abruptly. Lejla looked at the road ahead. A split second later, she braked violently. The rear wheels locked, the pedal quad drifted to the left as it rounded the bend only to crash five meters later into a spruce tree lying across the road. Lejla was thrown against her seat belt. The vehicle tipped onto its side, flinging its load around mercilessly. Finally, it rolled over three times before coming to rest on its roof in the ditch.

She hung upside down, held by the belt. The wound in her stomach hurt. A warm, viscous liquid was running down her chest. Backpacks, weapons, and helmets lay scattered all over the vehicle.

"Lucas, are you okay?" she moaned.

He made no sound. He hung there motionless, both arms above his head, as if he were about to push himself away. But he had no body tension.

Groaning, she shook his shoulder. "Damn it, Frenchie, wake up!" His upper body twisted back and forth. Blood was dripping from the ends of his hair. "Shit, man, don't do this to me." Making a huge effort, Lejla pushed open her door. The seat belt, under tension, wouldn't release. She reached for her backpack and rummaged inside. Seconds later, she was sawing in front of her chest with a close combat knife. To allow herself to control her fall, she braced herself with her forearm. Then she rolled out onto the shaggy grass. Ignoring her pain, she jumped up immediately. Before she ran to the other side, she scanned their surroundings for danger. Nothing moved. She had to shake Lucas's dented door hard, too. A long, vertical laceration gaped at his right temple. Lejla worked at his seat belt with the knife. He fell headlong onto one of the backpacks, giving a groan. "Moan all you want," she gasped, dragging him out by the wrists, "just don't die on me!" She leaned his upper body against the edge of the roadside ditch. His eyelids flickered. Lejla hurried back, got her things out of the vehicle, and fished a first aid kit out of her backpack. She cleaned her hands with some rakija and dabbed at his temple before carefully picking out individual hairs from the wound. *That could do with stitches.* But they didn't have time for that. A tight bandage that bound the edges of the wound as close together as possible would have to do for now. Whoever had cut down the tree might still be in the vicinity. She couldn't imagine they'd be up to any good. Lucas groaned again. She ignored him, put a sterile dressing on the cut, and began to wrap his head with a long bandage.

"Not so tight! My skull's about to burst anyway!" he complained.

"Shut up! You're bleeding like a pig." She put the little bottle to his lips. "Here, take a little slug."

"What the . . ." he gasped, eyes wide, barely choking down the liquor. "Are you trying to kill me?"

"Chill, it's only rakija," she defended. "See, you're already conscious again."

"At what price! My guts have just melted."

"Don't be like that." She unbuttoned her jacket all the way and looked at the bandage on her stomach, which was half undone.

Fortunately, the suture hadn't opened, but it was bleeding at the bottom. If she didn't move, the bleeding would stop in a few minutes. But she couldn't afford to stop yet. Lejla removed the blood-soaked dressing. She cleaned the wound with the alcohol and put a fresh gauze pad over it before wrapping a long bandage around her stomach.

Groaning, she handed Lucas his machine gun. "Don't move. I'm going to take a look around." She took the safety off her Kalashnikov and crept toward the road. Cautiously, she raised her head. In her olive camouflage gear, she could hardly be distinguished from her surroundings. Everywhere was empty, both the asphalt and the forest across the road.

There was no doubt that they had fallen into a trap. The spruce had been felled with well-aimed ax blows. Were these the same people as the ones behind the attack in Zadar? It was possible. Over her shoulder, she looked at the demolished pedal quad. Its front axle was broken. The left front wheel was missing. They wouldn't be able to go any farther in it, but that wasn't essential given where they were. All they had to do was go around the mountain. They'd be at their destination by evening. Lejla crept back.

"How's your skull?" she inquired in a whisper.

Lucas stretched his neck muscles. "I'll be all right. How does it look out there?"

"The tree across the road was cut down deliberately. I haven't seen anyone yet, but that doesn't mean there's no one there."

"It couldn't have been the zombies. They can do a lot of things, but cutting down trees . . . ? Surely not!"

"I have a theory. This might be linked to the attack last night."

Lucas nodded in agreement. "I have no doubt it is. What's your new plan? You have one, I hope?"

"Of course. We'll have to walk. Think you can make it?"

"Hmm, how far is it?"

"Thirty kilometers if we go by road."

"I can manage that. But why don't we go over the mountain?"

"Too dangerous. There are wild animals. Wolves, bears. The latter will just have woken from hibernation, and they'll be mighty hungry."

He sighed. "Let's have another sip of your disinfectant."

She grinned and handed him the bottle. Lucas sipped it, coughed, and then announced, "Good, we can go now." He stood up, shouldered his backpack, and tilted his head to left and right until the vertebrae in his neck cracked.

She let him take the lead. It made it easier to match his pace without constantly having to make sure he wasn't falling behind because of his head injury. But it didn't seem to affect him. They marched robustly northward through the woodland.

Following an impulse, Lejla came to an abrupt stop after three hundred meters.

Lucas glanced at her over his shoulder. "What are you waiting for?" A familiar stench was making her neck hairs stand on end. Irritated, she raised a fist to warn him, but he seemed to have noticed it now, too. They stared around silently. Nothing stirred. It was so quiet that she could hear every raindrop hitting the ground. And then she spotted a figure whose milky white eyes were staring at her from behind the young leaves.

The ice-cold patience radiating from the creature made Lejla catch her breath. At no more than ten meters away, it looked her straight in the eye. Demanded her full attention. Distracted her with its malice. She didn't dare breathe. "Lucas," she whispered, barely audibly.

Abruptly, the undergrowth around her exploded. Out of the corner of her eye, she saw two shadows rushing at her from either side at breakneck speed. The sudden shock helped her break free from paralysis. Her survival instinct took over. She turned to her left. Behind her, she heard

Lucas firing. Without knowing where she was aiming, she fired a long volley in her turn. The bark of the trees she hit burst in all directions. Amid the shrapnel of bark, a silhouette came inexorably closer. Like a wild animal, it leapt two meters into the air, claws curled and fangs bared. The Newgoslavian raised the barrel. Dropped onto her back. Fired again. The creature's head burst open. Its lifeless body hit the ground barely a meter from her feet. In a flash, she whirled around and fired the next salvo into the ribcage of the second undead, which had just shaken off a shot to its hip from Lucas and was attacking again. A single, well-aimed shot from her AK met its skull. Lejla jumped to her feet.

The third zombie was upon them. Instinctively, she moved out of its line of attack. At the same time, she raised the rifle and shot the magazine into the monster's neck. With a jerk, she directed its trajectory toward the foliage. The zombie rolled agilely over on its shoulder, turned around, and got ready to spring. Lucas's burst of fire sent it flying backward.

Backpack to backpack, Lejla and he stood panting, frantically searching for the next danger. Their eyes were wide with fear.

"Who let the fucking velozombiraptors out?" she panted.

"And I thought you'd cleared all the zombies out here!" he said reproachfully.

"I did, too. But what kind were they? Have you ever come across any like that?" Cautiously, they approached one of the bodies. "They're different from the ones I've seen before. Naked. Their sexual characteristics are atrophied. Look at the musculature. Every strand is defined," Lejla said.

"Do you think they go to the gym?"

"Dude, that was really close, and you're trying to be funny. We need to get the hell out of here." She turned and ran north through the thicket. Behind her, she heard Lucas's footsteps. A clearing opened in front of them, and she headed for it. If there were more undead in the area, and they had them in their sights, the forest wouldn't be able to hide them now, either. She kept her eyes on the road to the right. Lucas ran after her, a few paces behind. They drank from a crystal clear stream and then hiked on. Both of them were sweating. Lucas had unbuttoned his jacket even though the sun had disappeared behind the clouds, which now hung over them like a dark premonition.

"I feel like I'm being watched," Lucas said.

"This clearing is just made for an attack," she replied. "Get ready."

A light drizzle began to fall.

A handful of ruined houses appeared on the right-hand side of the road. Just a few seconds later, another wave of attackers burst out of the forest. Lejla counted seven Grays barely a hundred meters ahead of them. She estimated that the two rows behind them held twice as many again. "Over to those buildings there. That's our best chance," she shouted and ran out into the street.

They dashed over to the first house. At full speed, Lejla smashed the glass patio door and stormed inside. Lucas followed her, locking the wooden door and window shutters behind him. They were old and would withstand the assault for only a very short time, if at all. But every second they held off the undead increased their chances of survival.

Lejla ran deeper into the house, turned down the hallway, and spotted a narrow staircase to the upper floor. "This way," she yelled, taking three steps at a time. She kicked in a door, swung the muzzle from one corner to the other, shouted "Clear," and turned her attention to the room opposite, which she also found to be empty.

Downstairs, the zombies were pounding on the shutters. Lucas appeared on the upper landing.

"You take up position in that room there," she ordered, jerking her chin toward the door across the hall. "We'll take them in the cross fire from up here." She tossed her backpack to the floor. From it she dug out her spare ammunition. He did the same.

The wood in front of the patio door burst open.

"Are you ready?"

"In a second, just a second," he replied frantically.

The first footsteps were echoing through the lower rooms. He positioned himself in the doorway and pointed the gun toward the first floor.

"*Here they come!*" shouted Lejla and started firing.

The first figure made it up four steps before being thrown backward by a well-placed volley. The rear guard crashed into the tumbling body, climbing over it, preventing each other from advancing while being riddled with lead.

The muzzle flashes partially obscured Lejla's view of the rampaging mob, whose corpses were piling up at the foot of the stairs. But the corridor was so narrow that it was almost impossible for her and Lucas to miss their targets. Gradually, it filled with smoke that threatened to obscure her vision.

"I need to reload," she called over, changing magazines and firing at the windowpanes behind her. A breeze then began to carry away the smoke. The attack came to an abrupt halt. Lejla and Lucas looked at each other.

"That can't have been all of them," she whispered.

"They're cooking up something new. I can literally smell it," he replied, locking in a full magazine.

"Keep your eye on the stairs! I'm going to look out the window."

Carefully, she crept over and peered out over the razor-sharp spikes of glass. "*Fuck*," she yelled suddenly, throwing herself backward onto the double bed. At the same time, she fired into the air.

She caught a creature that had climbed onto the balcony midleap into the bedroom. Lejla got up, ran to the window, and shot down three more undead.

"Do you need backup?" shouted Lucas between two volleys.

"No, I've got them under control. How about you?"

"All safe."

"Okay. Hold the fort until I get back!"

"What are you going to do?"

But she had already jumped out through the window onto the messily poured concrete slab. Lejla's fear had long since given way to an anger that was a thousand times stronger than fear. When she was angry, she saw everything more clearly, acted quicker. She felt untouchable, invincible. Without pausing, she plunged off the balcony. Right kneecap first, she crashed into the face of a zombie. She landed on its chest, which cracked under her weight. Lejla rolled off, came up onto one knee, and fired. The facade of the house behind two of the wandering corpses was speckled with their gray bodily fluids. Another grotesque ran into the open, directly into her line of sight. Lejla fired. Then silence spread, disturbed only by the trickle of rain. Carefully, she circled the building. She peered into the adjacent barn with the collapsed roof and found nothing. Arriving back at the demolished patio door, she called into the house, "Frenchie, are you all right?"

"Yeah, but I can't get out of here. The stairs are jammed."

"Just jump off the balcony. I'll hold position here. But throw our stuff down first. "

Half a minute later, she heard his voice directly above her.

"Here, catch!"

She looked up as he was dropping a backpack. She caught it in one hand, then the second, and then Lucas's gun.

He sat down on the edge of the balcony and jumped. Down below, he wiped his palms on his pants. Then he began to load the emptied magazines with the cartridges from the pouch she had given him on the boat. She did the same. She pointed with the muzzle of the gun at the liberated undead.

"These ones are back to normal."

"That's quite a few for an area that's been cleared."

"I don't know what's going on, either," she said.

"So what now?" he asked.

"Well . . . I think it's time for Plan P."

"You mean Plan B?"

"No, I mean Plan P. As in Plješevica crossing."

"With all the . . . bears?"

"And lions and tigers, yes. Or do you want to risk getting caught in another zombie trap?"

"No, certainly not. But—are there really lions and tigers here?"

"What? Of course not. What makes you think that?"

"Because you just said so."

"You do realize that's just a quote from an ancient movie?"

"Um, I'm not big on films."

"Oh man. Whatever. You even hear the phrase in space operas. I'd be happy to lend the movie to you, if you'd like."

"Sure. As soon as I can speak Yugoslavian, that's the first thing I'll do."

"Don't worry, it's in English. Bought it at the market in Zadar two years ago."

"I'll make you a deal. If you get us to Bihać alive, I'll watch it. I promise."

"That's the spirit." She laughed, stowing two of the refilled magazines in the side pockets of her pants. She put on her backpack and threw on her olive-colored rain poncho. "How's your skull?"

"Buzzing quite a bit. But that could also be due to the noise in the stairwell."

"And you still have the recordings?"

He patted his breast pocket under his rain gear. "They're all there."

"Good, follow me!" She turned back and marched in an easterly direction past the house. One behind the other, they walked straight up to the slope and switched onto the first path that wound its way up the steep incline between spruces and beeches.

The forest smelled of rain and fresh earth. The higher they climbed into the low-hanging cloud, the worse the visibility became. They didn't talk much. Lejla had to force herself not to think about the zombie species that had first attacked. They stopped at every crackle in the undergrowth. She scanned their surroundings intensely, but they held no further danger. Nevertheless, the tension tugged incessantly at her nerves. She could not allow herself to be distracted. But whenever she let her eyes wander through the forest, she saw ice-cold eyes without irises watching her. She had to blink several times to dispel the illusion.

Hours later, they had not even reached the ridge. Constantly stopping to probe the area robbed them of nearly the entire afternoon. The rain had given way to one hundred percent humidity, which condensed on their capes. Drops of water flowed together there, leaving long trails.

The path became steeper and steeper. Lejla had to be careful not to slip on the wet ground. "Lucas," she said, "I think we'll soon have to make camp for tonight."

"I was hoping you'd say that. Trudging around in the dark in this forest is making me uneasy. Is there an old mountain cabin somewhere?"

"Yes, on the other side. But we won't make it there today."

"Then what should we do?"

"We'll spread our tarps out in the treetops and sleep underneath them in hammocks."

"Oh, okay," Lucas said simply.

Lejla led him up the path for another five minutes. "There," she said quietly, pointing to a cluster of oaks and beeches. "The rain will have washed away our tracks in a few minutes. If they haven't found us by then, we should be safe up there for the night. I'll climb the tree on the right. You take the one on the left. They're so close together that it shouldn't be a problem to throw the ropes between us at the top. We'll have to go all the way up, but the lower branches will hide us from unwelcome eyes."

She gave him time to get an idea of how high he would have to climb. Finally, he approached one of the gnarled oaks, grabbed the lower branches, and swung himself up. The bark was obviously wet, soaked through and slippery. The Frenchman was climbing carefully, Lejla could tell by his movements. She covered him until he switched over to the beech tree at four meters. After he'd climbed a bit higher, she signaled that he'd gone far enough. It took her less than five minutes to scramble up the tree opposite. She indicated to Lucas to secure his backpack to the trunk with a strap so he could have both hands free.

First, they spread out Lejla's tarp and secured it. Underneath, they slung and fixed a static rope between the trees to act as backup if the hammock came loose. Just two meters farther on, they constructed Lucas's sleeping place. They attached the two loose corners of the tarp to lower branches so the rain could not form puddles on them. The Newgoslavian looped a length of climbing rope with a loop around her upper body, hooking it onto the fixed rope with a carabiner. Then she swung herself into the hammock. She placed the strap of her weapon around her neck. Next, she holed up in her sleeping bag, hiking boots and all. It was unthinkable to undress while enemies might be lurking nearby. Her backpack hung from a hook close to her head, giving her quick access to it.

"Whoa, I'm not scared of heights, but I won't sleep a wink tonight," Lucas whispered, moving along the fixed rope over slippery branches toward his hammock. It took him a few tries before he was safely in the net. "At least it's dry," he said, as if to placate himself, spreading his sleeping bag over him.

Looking over at him, Lejla grinned. It was clear he wasn't having much fun on their excursion, so she tried to distract him. "Do you know what's beneath us?"

"Not a clue," he grumbled.

"Željava. Does that mean anything to you?"

He shook his head.

"One of the largest military bases from the Cold War era. Did your father also tell you about—"

"Yeah, I've heard of the Cold War, too," he interrupted before she could finish the sentence.

Swaying in her hammock nine meters above the forest floor, she nodded at him and went on. "At that time, Yugoslavia wasn't part of the western or the eastern alliances and was striving for its own sovereignty. To be able to assert itself as a serious opponent on the world stage, a lot of emphasis was given to military equipment, which was publicly displayed in annual parades. Defense facilities were also built—ultramodern fortresses. And one of those fortresses was built in the mountain beneath our feet. An underground battle station, so to speak."

"Like the Maginot Line?"

"Exactly. Smaller, to be sure, but equipped with its own jets and Russian MiGs. Completely self-sufficient and virtually indestructible from the outside. But even the strongest fortress isn't much use if you blow it up from the inside with fifty tons of TNT."

"Did they do that?"

"Yes, unfortunately. The Yugoslav army destroyed everything on its retreat after Slovenia and Croatia, then Bosnia and Herzegovina, declared their independence. Today you can only get one or two hundred meters down into the facility. And since you can't sleep, I'll tell you the story of how we hid in it and hibernated through the first winter of the pandemic."

"Okay," he said, by now almost mollified.

She cleared her throat and said, "All right, Frenchie. Now listen carefully.

"I was in the seventh or eighth grade at the time. The reports of an imminent epidemic led to panic throughout the city three weeks after it broke out. After years of feeling unimportant and excluded from world events, we couldn't even imagine being hit by a deadly disease. I mean, who would want to visit Bosnia? But the hair-raising information reached us in real time and firsthand via social media. France, Germany, and Austria had been infested for a long time without being able to get a handle on the situation.

"That spring, thousands of migrating people were living in the Balkans. Bihać was full of refugees from all sorts of countries to the east. In their desperation, they occupied empty houses and apartments of locals who were themselves seeking their fortunes elsewhere in the world. But the police drove them out, and they were forced to take shelter in the ruins of former Yugoslavian factories, which had been in operation for a short time at most after the civil war. The refugee camps reluctantly established by the governments did not improve the situation. The living conditions in them were so inhumane that from time to time the people living there burned them down to draw attention to the fatal conditions in them. In winter, they froze, and they starved for that entire first year. Western countries sent financial aid for temporary camps, but most of it disappeared into the pockets of corrupt politicians.

"Many locals found themselves barely able to survive week to week, let alone help others. That was my family's position, but we made friends with Shanti and Anand. Apart from them, only a few families made any connections. Most of the refugees hoped to move on soon anyway. But nothing like that happened. Frustrations increased on both sides. The tensions were exploited by nationalist movements for propaganda purposes as well as by the very same forces that had once been largely responsible for the civil war. I did not experience the war itself. About five or six years before I was born, a flimsy peace agreement had been reached, but the demon of separatism had not been exorcized. We had long since become accustomed to the fragile situation.

"I remember well the day when even the last bit of order in Bosnia and Herzegovina collapsed. My father was standing in front of the school, impatiently waiting for me. He had probably come straight from the field, a typical Bosnian seljak in his peasant clothes. I ran out to meet him, wearing conspicuous makeup and my jacket trimmed with fake fur, and I was ashamed to see him standing in front of everyone in the middle of the schoolyard in worn-out rubber boots covered in mud. He seemed to notice and made a face at the insult. It wasn't really his thing to pick me up anywhere, especially not after class. But that day, he wanted to be sure not to miss me, so he got out of the car. I went with him straight away to his rickety Golf 3. We drove out of town together to the Izačić border crossing, barely twenty minutes away. The booths where the Croatian border guards usually sat, allowing or denying entry into the European Union, were empty. The barriers were closed, but that did not stop the stream of people from marching past them into the promised land. They were cheering. *Sranje,* my father had scolded. *You see that? No border controls.* Unimpressed, I replied, *Yes, I can see. So what?*

"I had expected him to reprimand me for my disrespect. But he just snorted and jerked his head, indicating I should get back in the car. Just outside the city, he got a speeding ticket for going over sixty kilometers per hour. He didn't even swear. That was the moment I started to get seriously worried.

"His tone was serious. *You need to think now about what you can't do without over the next few months. And that's what you need to pack. That's all. One bag at the most. I want your mother to do the same.* His tone was serious. Not commanding, like the one I was familiar with— simply determined—as if in the foreseeable future I would be faced with a single decision whose outcome would depend on whether I trusted him or not.

"I responded in earnest. *And what will you be doing?*

"He clearly understood from my tone of voice that, contrary to his expectations, I had decided to follow his advice. *I'll go get the grandparents, and Shanti and Anand,* he replied calmly. *Make sure you and Mom are ready to leave in an hour, okay?*

"I told him that I could do that.

"He stopped in front of our house. Then he did something surprising. He bent down and gave me a kiss on the forehead. With a *Hajde, požuri,* he shooed me out of the car. *One hour,* he called after me.

"I nodded and hurried into the house. Part of me was confused, but the other, impelled by his words, was clear and focused on action. A few months, he had said. And only one bag.

"So I packed clothes, but I also thought about shower gel and laundry detergent, which—though I didn't know it yet—I would throw away soon afterward. Meanwhile, my mother was leaning against the doorframe, looking at me with amusement. *Tata told you to pack,* I said without looking at her. *Aha, are we going on vacation?* she asked sarcastically. We didn't have the money to go on vacation. But even if we had had, we couldn't have afforded more than a few days on the Adriatic. The prices had skyrocketed the previous season, and anything else was unthinkable. *We're going away, but certainly not on vacation,* I replied curtly, zipping up my bag deliberately loudly. *You need to pack now, too. For half a year,* he said. *He'll be back in forty-five minutes. We should be done by then.*

"Ignoring her disparaging look, I carried my travel bag to the door and called everyone in my contacts. They kept asking questions, to which I simply answered that I couldn't tell them anything more. I also mentioned that the border crossings seemed to have been abandoned, which was met with even more incomprehension.

"My friend Selma was the only one who drew the right conclusion. *E', jebi ga,* she cursed. *If this flu is in Zagreb already, it'll reach Bihać in a few days.* I replied, *I'm afraid it will, too. I'll get back to you as soon as I know what my old man's planning.* She said, *Okay, thanks. I'll go pack.* Before I could say any more, she had already hung up.

"My father was back an hour later, as agreed. Grandpa's hunting rifles lay between the seats. My grandparents looked at me questioningly, but I just shrugged, carried my belongings to the trunk, and took a seat next to my grandma in the back. Through the open door of the car, I heard my parents arguing in the house. Things weren't moving fast enough for my father, and my mother wasn't going to go along with anything based solely on his assumptions. Furious, he got into the car, turned around in the yard, and stopped by the front door with the engine rumbling. Mom appeared twenty minutes later. She had two suitcases with her. No one said a word. One ended up in the trunk and the other on my lap.

"We rushed westward through the villages on the outskirts of Bihać and then switched to dirt roads leading to the border with Croatia. I was about to call Selma when my father slowed down. Ahead of us, Sanel was sitting in the cab of his excavator, waiting and nibbling sunflower seeds. His family and Shanti and Anand sat next to him in their Opel Astra station wagon. *Stay here; I'll be right back*, my father said, getting out. He and Sanel talked for a while. We got more and more impatient. Then I heard a deep roar coming from behind us. Two, three trucks, seemingly fully loaded, were swaying after us. My father waved them on before getting back into the car.

"Sanel's digger clattered into life, and he set off sluggishly, escorted by us. Soon he left the gravel road and guided us across a meadow directly toward the runways on the old base. I expected Croatian rifles to rush at us from the surrounding bushes at any moment, but nothing moved. We passed the potholes created when the facility had been blown up and turned left two and a half kilometers later. Shortly after that, we arrived at the entrance to the underground hangar. Sanel dredged our way in, clearing away the mounds of gravel piled up in front of it. Then he disappeared inside.

"Father turned off the car. He told us to follow him. Two dozen other cars had now joined the trucks. We got out, and the others did the same. *This will be our home for the next few months*, he began, not mincing words. *I spoke to Dino in Zagreb on the phone this morning. Last night, the Croatian capital succumbed to the disease that has been spreading for weeks. And after only two days. Everything has fallen apart. As a result, there was no shift change at the border crossings. The morning crews simply didn't show up. Anyone under the command of the Croatian army or the police was summoned to Zagreb with immediate effect. It's like being at war, Dino says.*

"A crowd had formed a semicircle around him, and someone asked, *And what does that mean for us, exactly?*

"My father replied, *That we'll be dead or worse in less than a week if we don't manage to hide. I can't imagine any of you haven't seen a video on*

Messenger showing the infected, so I'll spare you any further explanation. From what's been reported over the last few days, we know they're specifically moving toward places where there are humans. It's conceivable they're following some kind of instinct that's guiding them to human settlements. They may be able to locate their victims by their sense of smell. Long story short—they could show up here tomorrow. So we don't have much time, and there's a lot to do. He pointed at the trucks and said, *Last week, a few of us secretly made arrangements to hole up here over the coming months. We have food, equipment, and even weapons to defend ourselves with if need be. We'll begin setting up the hangar immediately. It won't be comfortable, but it's our best chance. Please make way for the vehicles. I'll be right there, and I'll tell you what to do.* As soon we moved aside, the excavator drove past us.

"Over the next five hours, Sanel removed ton after ton of rubble from the depths of the cave. This created a lot more space and gave us enough material to build a gravel palisade nearly four meters high in front of the entrance once the trucks had disappeared into the crevasse in the mountain.

"The excavator carefully unloaded six huge concrete tubes big enough to walk through. We lined them up and buried them in gravel, careful not to cover their openings. Another truck was loaded to the brim with wooden pallets, planks, and beams. We used the planks to barricade the escape pipe and the entrance. Everyone lent a hand. Hardly anyone questioned what we were doing or my father's warnings. We parked the cars outside the barrier so that we could use them if we needed to escape—at least, that was the plan.

"In another truck, we found tents of all shapes and sizes. Two-person igloo tents, family tents with kitchenettes, army tents, and pavilion tents. Since the hangar floor was damp and had rivulets running across is, we first built platforms out of pallets. And that's what our new colony was built on. We connected the podiums with planks, creating the impression of dozens of small islands that had joined forces. I was given a two-person tent, an air mattress, and a sleeping bag, and I found a secluded platform deep in the cave and settled in.

"A little later, I went to see my father. He was sawing a board for the gate. *Stari,* I interrupted, *can I let people know where I am? And maybe invite a couple of them here?*

"He looked at me for a long time. His expression betrayed his inner struggle. *Yes, do that,* he said finally. *Don't let it get out of hand, though, please. We only have a few tents left.* I nodded eagerly. *They'll need clothing,* he continued. *Most importantly, they must bring nonperishable foods. Canned goods, pasta, rice, preserves.*

"I ran outside—there was no reception in the hangar—and called five of my closest friends. Three of them immediately approached their parents, who listened carefully to my father's instructions. The other two told me their families had also heard the news. They were about to leave for the south, to stay with family members. After finishing the calls, I returned to the cave.

"In the meantime, five solar panels had been installed directly above the entrance. The electricity they generated would drive several fans that would draw in fresh air during the day and expel stale air through the slots intended for the MiGs' aircraft rudders.

"The protective tarpaulin was slung over an area to the right of one of the trucks, which had now been emptied. On the trailer, a kind of makeshift field kitchen was set up. We had twelve bottles of gas to operate it. Someone had thought ahead and even placed an old wood stove on it, which we could use as soon as we'd exhausted our propane and butane supplies.

"The water supply, on the other hand, was the least of our problems. We had dozens of jerricans that we would fill up as needed at the Klokot spring two kilometers away.

"I asked my father, *You've been planning this a long time, haven't you?* I looked at the cargo from the fourth truck. Sacks of flour, rice, and pasta piled up next to cans of beans, corn, and chickpeas, and jars of jams and pickled vegetables. But I also discovered toilet paper and other cosmetics. *We started a week ago,* he confirmed. I asked, *But how did you pay for all this? The amount of food alone would cost a small fortune.* He grinned. *What do you mean, pay? Jasmin works as a store manager at the supermarket in Pritoka, as you can see from the logo on the trailer tarp.*

"Slowly I figured it out. *Ha, so he must have placed a big order, and before the cargo was unloaded, I guess Zdenko must have moved the truck off the company lot. That's his truck after all.*

"He confirmed my suspicions. *Absolutely right—the night before last, it was. If our fears had been wrong, the trailer would have been back at the warehouse in a couple of days. No one would have been any the wiser.* I said, *But what about the doormen? They work for an outside security company, don't they?* My father laughed. *Yeah, which one?*

"Suddenly I remembered that Sanel was the district manager of the security company that no doubt guarded the supermarket.

"In the evening, my classmates' families showed up. Their parents allowed Selma, Milijana, and Ela to set up their tents next to mine. That was one reason to be happy at least, and it made us forget our fears about the future. They looked fastidiously at the accommodation—unlike the people from Syria, Afghanistan, and Eritrea who had come here with us.

"They were now accustomed to living in difficult conditions and joked that this was the most civilized place they had stayed in a long time. At least there was enough to eat, and no one would freeze during the cold nights.

"We took turns preparing the food. To pass the time, we played cards and board games, taught each other songs, poems, and stories. It reminded me of prehistoric tribes who dwelt in caves, but I kept this to myself.

"Only a few days after we had settled in at the base, hordes of infected people poured into Bihać. As we later learned, they roamed the streets until many people were forced to leave their hiding places due to hunger and thirst. Their weakened state made them easy prey.

"No one had expected that in the coming weeks we were more likely to be fighting boredom than living in fear for our lives. Around the clock, a small squad scouted the immediate surroundings. At night, we retreated to the safety of our grotto. Behind the barricaded gate, several guards with loaded hunting rifles waited at the arrow slits for possible raids. The second half of the spring was almost uneventful due to our being so far from civilization. Just three times, small groups of infected strayed into the vicinity of the site; they were summarily beaten to death by our people at a safe distance from the hangar and buried in the forest.

"The remoteness of the base soon encouraged us to spend more time outdoors. This helped to reduce tensions that arose from living together in a confined space. We also reinforced the palisade with trunks of young birch trees, which sprouted everywhere. Life took a turn I never expected. I traded in my fancy clothes for camouflage pants and olive green T-shirts. There was no point putting on makeup, in any case. After the first six weeks, I didn't even know where I'd put my cell phone. The only thing I really missed was my former hobby of sitting outside a café and sipping a single espresso for hours on end due to lack of funds while giggling the day away with my girlfriends.

"There was hardly any privacy. Locked up in a cave with my parents, whose relationship was tanking, life became hell. I found their quarrels so unpleasant that the risk of being hunted by the infected seemed a desirable alternative to everyday life with them. As soon as the sun warmed the valley to thirty degrees, we stole out and ran down the runway to bathe in the ice-cold Klokot River. One of the oldest boys in our group had a Beretta, which his grandfather had supposedly given him as a gift. His presence made us believe we were safe.

"As soon as the weather changed and it started to rain, our refuge was flooded with torrents of water. But our pallet platforms meant we were able to keep our feet dry during these periods. Still, it wasn't pleasant. Everything was damp and clammy, and the fans ran slowly. There was nothing we could do but wait.

"In the middle of August, my father ventured into the city with a handful of daring comrades. They only found a few people; the undead had presumably moved on for lack of food. The city center, separated from the surrounding countryside to the north, to the east by the Una River, and to the southwest by a canal that supplied the city's hydroelectric plant, was a good place to make a fresh start. But it was a whole month before we left the safety of our cave.

"The population overcame its initial shock about six months after the pandemic broke out. We had long since realized that we wouldn't be able to return to the everyday lives we had known. We just wanted to survive from one day to the next. To this day, I don't know where we found the strength, but we picked ourselves up and laid the foundations for a new future despite the general misery and despair. We built a wall around the city center to protect us from attacks by the undead. We learned to cultivate the land without any technology and brought the harvest in by hand until someone had the idea of fitting agricultural machinery with electric motors and batteries, which made the work easier. Families and individuals came from the surrounding area to join our small community, which was increasingly guided by what my father had to say. His wealth of ideas and his bold foresightedness, which had brought us safely through the apocalypse, earned him an almost fanatical following. For us children and young people, however, the fall began with a shock, because he insisted that school lessons should begin again. We resented this because we thought the end of the world had exempted us from compulsory education. They rounded up teachers to run science and social sciences lessons. Agriculture and weapons training were added to the traditional subjects. Civil War veterans taught us how to use firearms and how to defend ourselves.

"My parents became increasingly estranged from each other. By the time my father left with his troops to search for survivors in the rest of the country and to put an end to the plague of the undead, they had both realized their marriage was at an end. Father's first trip lasted four weeks. He stayed away for longer each time. When he returned to Bihać, he told me about landscapes and people and battles and new places they had brought peace. Word of his success spread, and he became known everywhere by the name of Titwo. The troops became better armed as they came across smuggled weapons during their forays. As a result, in the third year of the apocalypse, they even were in a position to go beyond the borders of Bosnia and Herzegovina.

"I had barely turned sixteen when he decided it was time to take me with him. I hadn't seen much of the world yet, but I knew how to handle a variety of weapons. I also had some combat experience in the field. So we went to the farthest reaches of the Balkans, crossing rivers and mountain passes, wandering for days through valleys and gorges without seeing a single soul. In a few villages that had been self-sufficient for centuries and were difficult to reach, the apocalypse seemed as if it had never happened. We stayed there happily, recharging our batteries. I soon discovered that I liked sleeping out in the open or in a tent, taking out zombies, and being permanently on the move. My father, on the other hand, was constantly dealing with administrative matters, which is probably inevitable when you're building a new society. This forced him to retire almost completely from active duty. I guess my performance in the field was good enough for me to be given free rein to put together a team to continue his work. He, on the other hand, took care of the people's concerns. The borders of the country were fixed, and the danger of the undead had been banished from within them. There was not much left for my team and me to do.

"Securing access to the sea was an obvious goal. Zadar seemed ideal for this. It had a harbor and wasn't far away. Six or seven years had passed since the start of the outbreak. Some countries and regions had largely recovered. Entrepreneurs were slowly daring to seek out partnerships in remote ports again. We organized ships to patrol the coast. Restricting or even stopping trade was the last thing on our minds, but we had to make sure the disease was not reintroduced into liberated cities like Zadar.

"And then, one day, we heard about a three-master flying the French ensign that had ventured into the Adriatic.

"The strange thing," Lejla continued, "was that it was a war galley anchored off Albania. We sailed there immediately, more curious than concerned. There we introduced ourselves and sailed landward with part of the crew. You know the rest of the story, Frenchie. Frenchie? Are you asleep?"

"No, not at all. But I'm close," Lucas murmured.

"Then go ahead and close your eyes. I'm still with it; I can keep watch."

"Okay. Thanks," he replied.

Barely five seconds later, she heard him start to snore.

At dawn, she had to admit, contrary to her assertion, she had also fallen asleep. So she hadn't noticed when exactly the rain had stopped. Thanks to the tarps, they had stayed reasonably dry. However, it was still foggy. They waited until the visibility was better before dismantling their bunks.

They stowed the equipment in their backpacks before swinging down the trees. They quickly found the path they had been on the day before. In the mist, which had thinned, they marched up to the ridge. The temperature was gradually rising.

Lejla hoped the sun would make an appearance soon. But an exclamation from Lucas put her on the alert. Her gaze followed his finger, which was pointing to a small patch of higher ground ten meters to their right. A skeleton, gnawed to the bone, was protruding from the earth. The empty eye sockets of a human skull glared at her. Lucas looked around frantically, his gun at the ready.

"Calm down; it's been there a while," she remarked tersely.

"Who were they?" he asked.

"Presumably a poor soul who wanted to get to Europe. Probably tried to get there at night, in the middle of winter. Froze to death or was killed by wild animals. Beaten, robbed, and abandoned naked in the wilderness by Croatian border guards as a result of illegal pushbacks. Take your pick—it could have been any of them. The infamous Balkan route ended right here back then." She pointed to the ground at her feet and gave a bitter laugh. "That's the irony of fate, Lucas," she called over her shoulder as she walked on. "You scrape together all your money, put your life in the hands of unscrupulous gangs, flee halfway around the world, and survive storms in a shabby rubber boat on the high seas if you can. All because you want to escape poverty and inhumane living conditions, only to fail in fucking Bosnia on the brink of achieving your goal." Lejla shook her head. "No asshole can think up sadder stories than the ones written by life, Frenchie."

Wordlessly, they walked on for another half hour until the clouds parted, sending rays of sunshine to the broad green valley at their feet. "There," she called out, pointing southeast at a dirty white oval splotch. "That's Bihać. We're as good as there."

"About time," Lucas replied.

They drank from their bottles and ate half a flatbread each before setting off on the last leg of their journey.

CHAPTER 4

BIHAĆ

They completed the walk into town in three hours. Careful to make as little noise as possible, they communicated only by hand signals. They stayed vigilant. They weren't sure what awaited them in Bihać and along the way. Lejla wore a closed expression. *She's worried about the zombie attack yesterday*, Lucas thought. She'd believed the area was safe—and now this. In her place, he'd have felt just the same.

Meanwhile, the clouds dispersed, giving way to a bright blue sky and a brilliant midday sun. The warming earth released moisture, making it difficult for them to breathe. They were surrounded by the rich smell of decaying leaves. Flower buds were about to open. But he and Lejla had no time to enjoy the beauty of nature. All their senses were focused on a possible ambush.

In the valley, they followed the Klokot River. The houses along the road to the town looked deserted. Any that had not been ravaged were gradually falling apart. They saw broken windows and soot-blackened walls. Courtyard driveways with rusted car bodies. Overgrown front yards surrounded by fences covered in creepers.

This impression changed as they got closer to the city center. They saw more and more clean windows, some with white curtains. They went past simple buildings, mostly unrendered multistory brick and concrete blocks, their balconies without railings. In the distance they heard a dog barking. But they did not meet any people.

"This is strange," Lejla said nervously. "Where is everyone?"

"Maybe they've barricaded themselves in? Or got themselves to safety?" said Lucas without taking his eyes off the surroundings.

"Hmm, I hope so. Come on, it's not far now," she replied.

At the end of the path, they stopped by the remains of a bridge. A ditch holding crystal clear water separated them from the six-meter perimeter fence on the other side, a mosaic of boards, corrugated metal, and even glass that had evidently been foraged from various car models. Lucas and Lejla looked around. Far and wide, there was no one to be seen.

She curled her tongue as if to whistle in the direction of the palisade—and paused midmotion. Lucas's gaze followed hers. The heads of two people had appeared above the parapet. They eyed the arrivals with hostility. But then they seemed to recognize Lejla and looked more friendly. She was smiling now, too. They shouted something down from the fortification, and she answered with a cheeky undertone. The guards laughed. Moments later, a well-oiled drawbridge was lowered, clearing the way into the city's interior. With a motion of her head, Lejla indicated for him to follow her.

They enjoyed a warm welcome. She introduced him to the reception committee. Like Zadar, the city had a heterogeneous population. People from the Arab world, the Far East, Africa, and southern Europe surrounded her. They greeted each other in English, their rough Balkan accents sounding like dull handsaws in his ears. A woman addressed him in French. She had left Congo a long time ago, she explained, and like the other migrants here had been stopped at the European Union border.

He learned how happy she was about that now. Lucas saw that people were wearing clean, wrinkle-free army clothes, as if they had recently taken them out of the linen closet. And everyone was armed. Despite the reunion, everyone spoke in hushed voices. Lucas knew all too well why. He didn't want to attract the attention of any zombies that might be roaming around, either.

Without him noticing, the drawbridge had been closed behind them. They were finally safe. He relaxed and let his shoulders drop. His boots suddenly felt several times their actual weight. He could do with a hot bath now, or a bed at least.

"Hey, Lucas, let's go," Lejla said loudly, interrupting his thoughts.

"Where to?" he inquired.

"First to pay our respects to my father. Then to my house. Are you hungry?"

He nodded.

"Very good," she said. Her eyes were shining.

She led him past the bridge along the defensive wall to the right. Every twenty meters, he saw a guard crouched behind the parapet, peering out through one of the car windows.

"Something happened. Something serious. Earlier today, everyone was advised to retreat behind the walls. We haven't had that in four years," Lejla said, glancing at the many people they were seeing with travel bags.

They were moving in an orderly and disciplined manner, as if they had already practiced evacuating from the danger zone many times.

"Everyone's been wondering where we are. My father is out of his mind with worry."

"Couldn't the guards tell you any more?"

"They had strict orders to send me to Tiz immediately." Lejla turned left between two apartment blocks. They crossed a courtyard and stepped onto a wide promenade that was also full of people. "These are the first volunteers to hear about the upcoming mission to Shkodër," she murmured, leading him up a stone staircase to the entrance of an official-looking building. Guards saluted, and one let the two of them in. On the second floor, she selected a corridor that branched off to the right, walking purposefully toward a door. Lucas had to hurry to keep up with her. He saw her raise a fist, heard her knock at the same time as pushing down the handle. Without waiting for an answer, she entered. He squeezed through behind her before the heavy door slammed shut. They were in a conference room, the center of which was occupied by a long table with chairs for at least fifty people. Sparse light filtered through thick curtains, illuminating only half the room, where a gaunt figure stood hunched over a stack of papers.

Lejla called out, "Ćao, stari," and the man looked up.

"Hey," he said.

Lucas wondered at the annoyed undertone. The father should have been pleased and relieved that his daughter had returned unharmed. He was waiting stiffly, his hands clasped behind his back, for her to approach him. She embraced him. Tiz was wiry with cropped hair and a pronounced aquiline nose. Dark circles under his eyes and stubble told Lucas that Lejla's father had had little opportunity for personal hygiene lately. He kissed her forehead almost involuntarily. A tension seemed to drop from him. *Unimaginable, how worried he must have been about her*, Lucas reflected. *I just wonder why he's reacting so coolly.*

The two of them talked in Yugoslavian for a three whole minutes without paying any attention to him. He heard a few Albanian terms but understood nothing else. Lejla pointed to her stomach, where she had been stabbed, then in Lucas's direction. She gestured wildly, even slamming her fist into her palm once. Later she mimicked a rolling motion, so he suspected she was telling him about the accident with the pedal quad.

Again, she turned around and drew Tiz's attention to him, earning Lucas an appraising look from the Newgoslavian. He seemed to continue listening to his daughter, but never took his eyes off Lucas.

As soon as she had finished her report, Lejla's father crossed his arms over his chest. "So, Frenchie, what's up?" he said.

Lucas tried not to let his uncertainty about Tiz's dismissive behavior show and blurted out the first thing that came to his mind. "I came from afar just to say bonsoir." He immediately realized that he had succeeded in doing the opposite, because both father and daughter looked at him in amazement.

Lejla said, "Are you a poet now, or what?"

"Um, no . . . I just . . ." he stammered, trying not to make the situation even more embarrassing. Three agonizing seconds passed with no one saying a word. Lucas's face flamed up. Embarrassed, he looked away.

"Okay, you seem all right," Tiz said, holding out a hand to Lucas. "Thank you for saving my daughter."

"I . . . that was . . . nothing special . . ."

Tiz laughed again. "Oh, it undoubtedly was!" he said. "And welcome to Newgoslavia. It must be a huge culture shock."

"No, not really," Lucas claimed with a grin. "It's just that the zombies are a little weirder than they are at home."

"Yes, manners are rough here," said the older man.

Lucas seized the opportunity to ask the question that was on his mind. "I haven't understood much since we arrived. Can someone update me about what's going on?"

Tiz motioned to them to sit down. Once all three were seated, he continued, "A week ago, you radioed in about what was going on in Albania. As a result, I put out a call for volunteers." He propped his elbows on the edge of the table and held his hands over his mouth, yawning. "Within a few days, dozens came forward. Most have arrived here now. But we won't be able to send them all out."

"Why's that?" asked Lucas. Out of the corner of his eye, he saw Lejla stiffen. The tension in the room seemed to increase. Puzzled, he looked back and forth between the two.

Tiz looked at him. "What do you know about the political turmoil in Newgoslavia?"

Lucas shrugged. "Not much. Only what Lejla told me on our way here. That is, I only know her version—that religious groups want to stir up nationalism and divide the population."

"His father is a political scientist," Lejla explained, pretending to be impressed, her voice dripping with sarcasm. "I guess he needs more facts before he can come to his own conclusions."

The men ignored her.

"You're welcome to study the history of Yugoslavia, Frenchie. We have plenty of books about our past, even some in French. But I hope you don't become a witness"—he gestured with his head toward his daughter— "to the truth of her statement, because history repeats itself so many times until mankind has learned from its mistakes."

"What do you mean?"

Tiz took a deep breath. "The religious camps you mentioned are gaining strength again. As always, they initially seem to be united and are presenting a common enemy to fight."

"And who's that supposed to be?" asked Lucas skeptically. "You?"

Tiz snorted. "Me? No way! It's the zombies. And they want to use the planned liberation of Shkodër to get back into power. What will happen after that, I can only guess. But I can't think of a scenario where any of it ends well."

He looked out the window, ruminating.

Lucas had another burning question. "But what would the people gain from it? The locals know how the game is played, don't they? So what are you worried about?"

Tiz returned from his thoughts. "I can answer all your questions with one sentence. Not everyone in Yugoslavia had access to education, even before the pandemic, and that's also in the interest of these sects."

"Hmm, yes, I see," Lucas murmured thoughtfully. "The lower the level of education, the easier it is to manipulate the population's religious zeal or nationalism."

Tiz nodded and drummed his fingertips on the table. "And now they're trying to strengthen their position by setting me in a bad light."

Lucas looked at him, surprised. "But what does it have to do with you?"

"For one thing, I'm assuming they want to instigate a rash act on my part to turn people against me."

"Which, with your temperament, is not such an outlandish thought," Lejla interjected, looking serious.

"Maybe that's why they attacked you in Zadar," Lucas mused aloud. "To draw Tiz out?"

"We have no proof of that, but it's quite possible," Tiz replied. "And secondly," he continued, "there's another thing I need to tell you."

Lucas raised his eyebrows questioningly.

"There was an incident about six months ago at the Kresnice border crossing, a small bridge east of Ljubljana," Tiz continued. "The guards have been missing ever since. At first we didn't know what to make of it. But this morning, we got a visitor. And he knew more about it."

Lucas waited eagerly for Tiz to reveal more information. Lejla was also looking at him attentively. But her father remained silent, watching the two of them as if waiting for a reaction. Then he looked over to the darkest corner in the conference room and gave a nod. Slowly, Lejla and Lucas turned around. Only then did he see a black-clad figure enthroned on a cushioned armchair, his hood pulled deep over his face. Gloved hands were clasping the armrests.

"Oh," Lejla said, "the ranger's here, too."

"Please," Tiz hissed. Lucas recognized in his tone the same displeasure at one of her remarks as he had heard from Sanel on the boat. "For once in your life, hold your tongue!"

She rolled her eyes, apparently without a trace of guilt.

"Okay, stari," she said, winking at Lucas. Apparently, she was having a hard time staying serious.

The figure rose, smoothed its black robe, and came toward them. Its movements were so fluid that Lucas had the impression it was floating on air. Suddenly, as if aware of imminent danger, the hairs on his arms stood on end. He jumped up, his hand fumbling for his weapon. With difficulty, he kept himself calm, warning sirens blaring inside him. Next to him, Lejla clenched her fists and took a combat stance.

Tiz stepped between them and held him and Lejla by the wrists. "It's all right. This person is on our side."

But the feeling of alarm did not decrease. The closer the figure came, the faster Lucas wanted to run away. And then it was standing barely two meters away from him. He felt his heart pounding in his carotid artery. *What the fuck is this?* This thing, looking at him out of the shadows of the hood, slowly raised its hands and uncovered its face. A muffled sound of horror escaped Lejla's throat. The figure's right cheek was marked by three deep scars running diagonally from forehead to chin, splitting both lips at the corner of its mouth. On its neck, Lucas saw healed wounds that could only have been made by a rope.

The nose looked as if it had been broken a long time ago and inexpertly set. The person looked from him to Tiz's daughter and back again. "Good afternoon," it said in a rasping voice. "I bring news from the north."

Lucas hoped he wasn't showing how much the figure's hoarse voice was bothering him. "And the people who ambushed you are most likely the same as the people who invaded Kresnice," the figure croaked.

"This kind of activity requires a tactical military response. Who's behind this? Who's importing undead into liberated areas?" it asked.

"Maybe someone who wants to accuse Tiz of being incompetent at fighting zombies?" Lucas hoped his ideas didn't sound too much like a conspiracy theory.

"That's our guess, too," the figure replied.

Lucas breathed a sigh of relief. He wasn't the only one who thought so.

"But the rest of the insurgents need to be located urgently, and before they expand their numbers. How many attacked you?"

"Lucas and I took out three of the special breed. There were fifteen, sixteen normal ones," Lejla said.

"These special ones—were they unclothed? With no sexual characteristics?"

"Yes, exactly. They lay in wait for us and launched a coordinated attack. Shortly after that, the others appeared." Lejla briefly explained what had happened the day before.

"The main thing is to eliminate the hunters. There may still be two or three of them wandering around. But you should be able to deal with them," said the entity.

"Hunter? Do you mean those special zombies?" interjected Lucas.

His interlocutor nodded. "Yes, they were bred in Germany, specifically to hunt humans. I've spent the past few years trying to eradicate them. Hopefully, these three were the last."

"What?" exclaimed Lejla, "Who on earth would breed such monsters of their own free will?"

"It would take too long to explain in detail. And while some of them are still out there, we don't have the time."

"Well, at least we took care of the superzombies," Lejla added.

The robe nodded. "Thank you for taking the work off my hands."

"And you were going after them all by yourself?"

"Yes."

"Tough," the Newgoslavian remarked appreciatively. "But how's it looking in Germany now? Communication broke down years ago. Is anyone still living there now?"

"Very few people, and only in three cities: Berlin, Cologne, and Würzburg. There are also a few villages and farmsteads where communities have been established. That's all that's left."

"Well, that's a lot less than we have. What the hell happened there?"

"As I said, it's a long story that has to do with the people who, among other things, created the hunter species."

"You'll have to tell us about them at a better time," Lejla said. "Is it all right if Lucas and I go now? We're hungry, and we need to have showers."

"Go ahead. Our visitor and I have a lot to talk about, anyway," Tiz said.

"Okay, roger that," she replied, holding her fist out to them before leaving the hall with Lucas in tow.

"So," she turned to Lucas, "I hope lunch is ready."

"What's on the menu?"

"Krompiruša, hopefully. I love it!" She rubbed her belly.

"And what would that be?"

"Potato pieces baked with onions in thinly rolled dough. Do you know Turkish börek?"

He nodded.

"It's basically the same thing, only without the meat filling. We call it pita. There are lots of different kinds: zeljanica with spinach, sirnica with cream cheese. You can also have it with pumpkin filling. But krompiruša is my favorite. On the other hand, I don't really care what there is. I'd stuff just about anything in my mouth right now, I'm so famished!"

In front of the town hall, they turned right. They'd walked scarcely a hundred meters, then Lejla said, "There, in that tower block; that's where we live." She pointed at a multistory building that might once have been blue but now looked grayish. In many places, the plaster had crumbled away, revealing red bricks. Laundry was drying on the balconies. Lucas guessed the plants in the countless flower boxes were herbs, tomatoes, and bell pepper seedlings.

The closer they got to the skyscraper, the denser the commotion around them became. Lucas ran after her, shielding his rifle with both hands. Suddenly, he gave a surprised "Oh."

She stopped abruptly and looked at him. "What's wrong?"

"That woman over there," he said, pointing over several heads to a woman dragging a crying child behind her. "She just slapped that boy in the face. I could hear it all the way over here."

"So?" she asked, unimpressed.

"What d'you mean? She hit a child in the face!"

"Maybe he's hers."

"So what? Are you allowed to beat up children on the street just like that?"

She shrugged. "It's a normal part of our upbringing around here. It never did anyone any harm. You clearly don't come here often."

With that, she turned around and walked on. Lucas was seething inside but was too tired to get into a discussion.

Two minutes later, Lejla led him into a dark, musty stairwell. "Watch your step," she warned on the way up. He took care to avoid the worn-out sections. The walls were covered with names and slogans. At some point, they must have run out of pens and markers and had switched to scratching.

On the second floor, Lejla stopped in front of a door and took off her boots. He followed her lead. Then she knocked.

When the door opened, Lucas's senses exploded under the onslaught of perceptions that hit him. The scent of cooking rose to his nostrils. An older woman with a colorful headscarf and an even more colorful kitchen apron peeked through the crack in the door. She gave a cry of joyful surprise when she recognized Lejla. As she pulled the young woman into an embrace, she called out behind her. A gray-haired man in an oversize sweater appeared in the hallway of the apartment, clapping his hands and raising his skinny arms in jubilation. "Hajde, hajde," he insisted, opening the door. Joyfully, Lejla said something that sounded like "Evo, hoćemo," before gesturing to Lucas to step inside. Unsure how to behave, he smiled sheepishly and entered.

The apartment smelled even more intensely of a freshly prepared meal. His stomach growled loudly. Following Lejla, he hung his gun on the coatrack. He put down his backpack beneath it.

"This is my grandma, Dragica, and my grandpa, Milutin," she explained. "They don't speak French, and they have hardly any English, but I'll translate everything." He was introduced to the grandparents, who welcomed him with visible enthusiasm.

Lejla led him to a small bathroom with a toilet, where they washed their hands. "I'm starving." She moaned, handing him the towel.

Lucas nodded eagerly. "It smells fantastic!" he replied. Before he could even hang the cloth back up, she tugged him into the kitchen and over to the laden table. Various pots were steaming over a wood-burning stove. In the half-open oven, he caught a glimpse of a circular baking tin containing snail-shaped rolls of dough, the surfaces of which were baked to a golden brown. Milutin offered him a seat. Dragica set the table while Lejla talked incessantly, pointing at Lucas from time to time. Her grandparents responded with oohs and aahs. Without asking if he wanted anything to eat, Lejla's grandmother filled his bowl to the brim with tomato soup in which pea-size lumps of dough were floating.

"Trahana," Lejla explained and began to spoon the dough balls in. Milutin patted him paternally on the back of the head, while Dragica encouraged him to eat with a "Jedi, jedi." The soup was hot and tasted sour and invigorating. He hadn't quite finished when he was given another ladleful without being asked. Lejla lifted her dish to her lips to slurp the last of her second helping.

Her grandfather grabbed a tea towel from the back of the chair, used it to fish the tepsiya out of the oven, and placed it on the wooden board that was used to place hot objects on.

"Yes!" Lejla exclaimed happily, "Just as I hoped!" Using a spatula, she cut off large triangular pieces of the dumpling, which she handed around.

Imitating his hosts, Lucas reached out with his bare fingers.

Milutin plonked a good portion of mixed salad next to his krompiruša, giving him a toothless smile. Lucas thanked him and immediately focused on the pita in front of him.

The crispy baked surface contrasted with its juicy interior, which, along with the hearty taste, made it difficult for him to recognize when he was full. The grandparents watched his expression constantly, apparently wanting to be sure he liked it. When he thought he had finished and was about to sit back, they served him a second piece. He tried in vain to refuse.

"Don't be like that," Lejla said with her mouth full. "They'll keep bugging you until you eat it all."

"But I can't take any more." Lucas groaned. Nevertheless, he forced himself to eat the second portion.

He spent the afternoon in what he happily called a food coma. His stomach hurt. Besides, Lucas's entire system seemed to be fully occupied with digestion, which took up almost all his energy. He got heartburn from the high fat content, which Milutin cured with a glass of rakija. The heat from his insides then made him sleepy. Dragica probably saw it in his face and maneuvered him into the living room, telling him to stretch out on the couch. He heard Lejla speaking to him as if through a veil, but in retrospect he couldn't remember what about or whether he'd said anything in reply.

In the early evening, he came to again. The apartment was quiet and cozy. Lejla was asleep in the armchair across from him. Her legs were crossed over each other on a stool. An open book lay across her stomach. Without waking her, Lucas got up. From the kitchen, he heard voices and fire crackling in the oven. He tried to remember the way to the bathroom. He went into the hallway and turned left into the bathroom. There he relieved himself and washed his hands and face before going into the kitchen.

Dragica called him over to the table as soon as she caught sight of him in the doorway.

Tiz sat opposite her with an empty plate in front of him.

"Oh, Lucas," he said as Milutin raised a small glass to him and downed it. "Would you like something to eat?"

"No, thanks, I've eaten enough to last me all next week. But I would like a glass of water."

Tiz translated, and Lejla's grandmother poured him one. It was ice cold. He suddenly realized how thirsty he was. He drank it down in one gulp.

"What's your plan for the next few days?" asked Tiz.

"Tomorrow we want to go through the footage to create a presentation from it," Lucas replied. "Lejla thinks a good presentation would help attract more fighters."

"Well, I don't know about that," Tiz said noncommittally. "When you're done, come see me so I can get an impression of it in advance."

"Sure." After a brief pause, Lucas went on, "And what happened with your visitor?"

"Headed off again to scout the area for undead."

Nodding, Lucas took note. "Um, would it be all right if I took a quick shower?"

"Of course. You know where the bathroom is? There's a full bucket of water in there. And take this big pot of hot water with you."

"Okay, thank you very much."

First, he carried the pot to the bathroom before retrieving the backpack with his clothes. After washing, he changed. Freshly washed and in clean gear, he immediately felt more comfortable.

Back in the kitchen, he found Lejla finishing off the salad.

"Where's your father?" asked Lucas.

"He's gone back to greet the incoming troops and allocate them somewhere to stay. D'you feel like a walk through the city with me?"

"I need to radio my sister to report in. But after that, I'd love to."

"Sure, we can head out whenever you're ready."

"As far as I'm concerned, we can make a start right away."

Lejla turned to her grandparents, who accompanied them to the door. In the stairway, which was now dark, they used headlamps. Outside, it had turned colder. Lucas pulled the zipper of his jacket all the way up.

Lejla asked, "Will she be around at this time?"

"One of our frequencies is constantly monitored. Someone will then call her to the device. I just hope the signal's strong enough."

"It always reaches Corfu okay."

She took him to a building with walls that tapered upward, built long ago out of stone. It looked like a black pyramid stretching upward. Across the street, he saw the remains of an ancient church. Only the bell tower remained, with various dishes and antennas attached to it. The two structures were connected with cables as thick as his arm. Lejla led him around the stone building.

"Centuries ago, when the Balkans were part of the Ottoman Empire, this was a prison. After the Second World War, it was converted into a museum. Today it serves as a radio station." Inside, she was greeted joyfully. Lejla returned the greetings and introduced Lucas. After chatting for a minute, they were assigned a station. "Give my love to your sister, you hear?" she said.

"Sure," he replied, selecting the frequency with the rotary controls. Lucas thought through what he wanted to discuss with Lena.

He imagined her subsequently radioing Maman from her cabin to relay the conversation with him. He heard their voices in his imagination.

"Marseille, this is the Jacques Cousteau. *Marseille, are you receiving me? Over."*

"Bonjour, Jacques Cousteau, *this is Marseille. Receiving you loud and clear. What's the news? Over."*

"Oh, Maman. It's Lena. There's a lot to tell you. I've no idea where to start. Is everything okay with you? How are Grandma and Dad?"

"I'm doing wonderfully, thank you. Especially now I know you two are doing well. Grandma is getting fitter by the day. She misses the farm and ultimately wants to go back. But we're still waiting for it to get warmer up there. The mild Mediterranean winter has definitely done her good. Dad is alive and well—out fixing things or at least tweaking them, as usual. Have you heard from your brother?"

"Yes, we just spoke. That's why I'm calling you."

"And is he okay?"

"Yes. We met some people from Newgoslavia a week ago. He's currently traveling with them."

"Newgoslavia? You must mean Yugoslavia."

"No, they've actually given it a new name now. And they've offered to help us. Anyway, Lucas and his team managed to get to the bottom of the rumor we came here to investigate."

"So, is there any truth to it?"

"Absolutely. They even took photos and videos in Shkodër. It looks bad in there."

"Hmm . . . What are you going to do next?"

"Well, we have to get the people out of there. Or at least try to. But we need even more support. We managed to round up a few volunteers from Corfu. But that's not enough."

"Hmm . . . I could ask around to see if there are people here who could support you. But I can't give you much hope. You know how hard it was to get your little fact-finding mission going.

"And convincing someone to go back into combat after all these years of peace; that's not going to be easy."

"Yes, you're absolutely right. Do you have any other ideas of people we could contact?"

"Well, no one who lives in your area."

"And do you know anyone who might want to help but doesn't live in the area? Please don't make me drag it out of you. You know how I hate that."

"There are some survivors in Sweden I've been in contact with for two years. As far as I know, they were part of a resistance group that liberated Scandinavia."

"You mean they'd go to the trouble of crossing the entire continent for someone they've never seen in their life? I find that hard to imagine."

"They certainly wouldn't. If they did, they would sail. And they might know other people who'd be willing to help."

"I wish I'd inherited your optimism and not Papa's restraint. Well, it's worth a shot. Can you radio them right away?"

"I'll do that. Because of your coordinates . . . You're in Corfu? And you can stay there a while longer?"

"Yes, we're just by Kassiopi. And I can stay here as long as it takes. Will you let me know if you reach anyone?"

"Of course. And, Lena . . . ?"

"Yes?"

"I didn't even ask how you were doing before. So . . ."

"I'm fine, Maman. It's a little boring right now. I'm trying to read and write. But the weather's great, so I'm sunning myself on deck most of the time."

"Ha, that's lovely. Stick with it, enjoy it. You never know what tomorrow will bring."

"Stick with your optimism. It suits you better, Maman. See you soon. Say hello to everyone. Over and out."

"Will do. Take good care of yourselves and say hello to Lucas. See you soon. Over and out."

After speaking with his sister for ten minutes, Lucas followed Lejla out into the street. They walked past the basketball court, where a game was underway in front of quite a few spectators in the glow of the floodlights—probably the only performance you could attend inside the Bihać palisades. They bought salted popcorn on a street corner before stopping at the railing over the moat.

Lejla said, "This canal gets its water from the Una River. At its end is an electric plant that generates electricity for the city. Just a fraction of its capacity supplies all our households. So it's not under too much pressure. We hope it'll continue to serve us well for many years."

"And you grew up here in town?" inquired Lucas.

"Yes. My birthplace is barely half a kilometer from the spot we're standing on right now. In the years after the outbreak, the whole family barricaded themselves in the center, and we settled in well. But my grandparents will be going back there soon. All that stair climbing doesn't suit them at their age." She looked at him. "If you want, we can go and see it tomorrow."

"Yeah, sure," he replied. "I'd like that."

Lucas wondered when he'd last spent time alone with a woman. He couldn't say for sure. But now, strolling beside Lejla through her city, listening to her voice as she told stories from her life—he felt emotional. He liked her, and he liked how he felt when he was with her.

Whenever their elbows touched, as if by chance, an electric shock shot through him. He would have liked to hold her hand. Embarrassingly, he found himself trying to make the funniest or smartest remarks he could when he was around her, to get her to like him, too. When she suggested going back home to watch a movie together, his pulse quickened.

In her grandparents' apartment, she told him to sit down on the couch. A flat-screen TV hung on the opposite wall. Next to it he saw a shelf full of Blu-Ray discs.

"What do you like?" she asked, rummaging in her backpack. He saw her pull out the discs she had bought in Zadar.

"What do you have there?"

"A musical, an action movie, and the third one's supposed to be a drama."

"Whatever you feel like. I've no strong preferences." *As long as I can sit next to you, I don't care what we watch*, he almost let slip.

She inserted the disc and started the movie. Then she poured the rest of the popcorn into a glass bowl and sat down next to him.

He couldn't follow the film. Every few minutes he moved millimeter by millimeter closer to Lejla. He also refused the popcorn. As soon as she had emptied the bowl, she drew her legs up and leaned back. Her fingers lay between them, just five inches from his. *Is that deliberate?* he wondered. He could hear his own heart beating loudly. Was it an invitation to take her hand?

But what if he had misunderstood the signs? How would she react if he simply touched her? The situation might become uncomfortable for him, that was clear, but if she looked at him askance, he could pretend it had been unintentional. He decided to try his luck.

"Hey, Frenchie," she said just as he was about to put his hand on hers. She had her eyes on the TV and probably hadn't noticed. "Your sister, what was her name . . . ?"

In his agitation, he had frozen into a marble statue. He managed with difficulty not to choke as he answered. "Lena?"

"Yeah, right. Tell me, does she have a boyfriend?"

"Who, Lena? Um, no . . . That is, not that I know of."

"Are you guys close? I mean, if she had one, she'd be bound to tell you, right?"

"Um . . . yes, I think so," he stammered. "But Lena doesn't care much for men." *What's she driving at?*

"Well, well," Lejla said, looking at him. Her grin stretched from ear to ear. "D'you think she'd go out with me sometime?"

"Go out?" He quickly swallowed his disappointment, hoping Lejla hadn't noticed. "I'll see what I can do," he replied.

His shoulders eased at the thought that the situation hadn't ended in complete disaster.

She held her fist out to him. "I'd appreciate that."

Lucas returned the gesture. "I'll put in a good word."

Lejla laughed out loud. Then she rested her head on his shoulder, her eyes back on the screen. He snuggled up to her and managed not to move until the movie was over.

Being enmeshed almost around the clock in the concerns of his newly acquired family robbed Lucas of all sense of time. When he and Lejla weren't playing basketball during the day, they were fine-tuning their presentation or helping prepare shelters for the volunteers who were arriving. Time flew by. They visited her family home. They went on several walks to the nearby hill to look out over the city and into the valley below.

"This is where the picture of you and your parents that I saw at Sweet Chili was taken," he exclaimed joyfully the first time.

"Hey, good noticing," she replied, punching his shoulder.

Once she led him for two hours through the forest past the hill to an Ottoman ruin that had towered over the village of Sokolac for centuries.

Their friendship grew stronger and stronger. At midday, Lucas would help Dragica in the kitchen or carry logs up from the cellar for Milutin. They saw Tiz when he looked at the pictures after dinner and commented on their report.

The night before the meeting with the newly arrived troops, Lucas tried to count the days he had spent in Bihać so far, but he was not sure if it was seven or eight. Then he went over his lecture twice in his mind before finally falling asleep, exhausted.

Lejla woke him at dawn for breakfast, and then they went to the town hall, where they were taken into the main chamber. The day before, they had helped to remove the tables from the room, replacing them with long rows of chairs.

They quickly found their seats in the front row beneath the window. Standing and talking in front of a school map that hung on the wall were Sanel, Tiz, and the hooded figure they hadn't seen since their arrival in Bihać. Sanel nodded in greeting, but the other two took no notice of them. They waited and watched as the hall filled.

"Are you nervous?" she asked.

"And how," he replied. "I've never given a talk in front of so many people, let alone in a foreign language."

"Oh, you could do it standing on your head. Let the pictures speak for themselves, and then you'll have them in the palm of your hand."

"Yes. I'll just do what my father does when he's talking to big gatherings. True, he's usually talking about distributing supplies for the winter, but it's the same thing in practice. His strategy was always to imagine that everyone in the audience was his friend, and that he was going for a pastis with them afterward. That always made his nerves go away. At least that's what he claims."

Lejla laughed, which in turn made him feel lighter.

Lucas looked at the colorful mixture of people around him. Women, men, and some people he couldn't assign a gender to, even when he looked closely. Ethnically, almost all continents were represented—from India to central Asia, from central and North Africa to Scandinavia—but the majority had Balkan features. There were different age groups and all sorts of body sizes. All had gathered here today for a single reason. Lucas's mouth went dry. He was about to speak in front of all these people. The best-case scenario was that he'd succeed in persuading even the most skeptical among them to participate in the military operation. He knew that some of them had already decided in favor of it. These had come to the lecture to get a feel for the enemy. Hopefully, he'd be able to deal with all the questions he was about to be asked.

The conference room had now filled up completely. The hooded figure sat down next to Sanel at the other end of their row and folded his gloved hands beneath the wide sleeves of his robe.

When Tiz looked up from his notes and cleared his throat loudly, the murmuring gradually died down. Smiling, he waited a few seconds until he had everyone's full attention. The acoustics carried his voice all the way to the back rows. "How many years has it been since we last sat here together? Three, four?" he said.

"Three," came the answer from several places, followed by murmurs of agreement from the crowd.

"So for three years, our country has been free of the undead. Three good years in which we've had peace. In which we've been able to rebuild villages and towns. A time in which we have found a new order that allows us to move forward together." He glanced around the room. Like a wave, a nod went through the ranks of those present. "But while we are working toward a joyful future, not far from us entire communities are still suffering under the yoke of the zombies."

"Then the rumors are true?" asked a deep, feminine voice.

"Yes, they are. And before anyone starts to question that, I'd like to ask Lucas to come forward. He returned from there a few weeks ago and brought some material that confirms all of our suspicions." He raised his hand and beckoned Lucas over before sitting down in a chair at the edge of the podium.

"Have fun," Lejla teased him.

Taking a deep breath, Lucas stood up. He felt his heart drumming in anticipation, as it had in many of the battles he'd fought. Arriving at the podium, he flipped open the computer and asked for the curtains to be drawn and the lights switched off. For a moment, the room went dark, then the ceiling-mounted projector came on. Someone lowered the screen. Meanwhile, he clicked around on the laptop. An older aerial view of Lake Scutari appeared on the white screen behind him. Controlling his nerves, he straightened up, stepped away from the picture, and cleared his throat.

He said, "For those of you who don't know me, my name is Lucas Morel, and I'm from France. Like most of you, I've spent the last few years rendering zombies harmless—though you might not necessarily be able to tell by looking at me, because of my age."

Some of the audience laughed amiably.

"In our hunt for the undead, we've learned a lot about them. For example, we found out how they get food. Although we still don't know how they can survive winter temperatures. But a few weeks ago, we discovered something we're particularly worried about. I'd like to share that information with you today."

Lucas paused so that the audience could take in what he was saying. When he was sure everyone was following him, he continued, "Last year, we heard reports of a zombie nest in the south of the Balkans that was apparently mind-bogglingly large." He showed a picture of the entire Adriatic coast, "Here, right in the middle of Shkodër." He tapped an area in the lower quarter with the wooden stick. "At first, we didn't believe the rumors, but they intensified. So we sent a reconnaissance team to find out what was going on."

Another pause. "I took charge of the operation myself. We also had a good three dozen people from western Europe on board. The expedition left from Marseilles. Our first stop two months later was Corfu, where we encountered a small enclave of Albanian, Greek, and Macedonian survivors. According to them, the rumors were all true. They speculated that the relatively mild climate in Shkodër was why the location had been chosen; the proximity to the Adriatic Sea guarantees comfortable temperatures even in winter."

The next slide was a zoomed-in aerial shot of Shkodër with the lake to the north. To the west, the foothills of the Enchanted Mountains were clearly visible. "East of the lake and north of the city is fertile land that was used for agriculture before the outbreak. It still is today. The produce that was resold then is today being used to feed the three thousand who are imprisoned in Shkodër." Silence followed his words. Lucas took a deep breath and exhaled. "That's more people than there are in most major European cities."

Someone interrupted him. "Where did that exact number come from?"

"We have different sources. Albanian scouting parties we met have been monitoring the area for some time. But they are far outnumbered by the undead and cannot intervene themselves. We also have information from escapees. They've provided firsthand reports. I met an escapee myself in Corfu."

He clicked on the next picture. The screen showed a portrait of Nesha, which he had taken with the compact camera on the day she left for Prokletije. Her cheeks were sunken, her hair dull. She wasn't smiling—yet she radiated a power whose origin Lucas could only understand in retrospect. He swallowed. "This is Nesha. She gave us the knowledge to assemble and send out a small scouting party, of which I was also a member. To get the information I'm about to share with you, we went deep behind enemy lines. From there, my team scouted the south of the district, while Nesha snuck in to Shkodër from the east, to provide us with the following footage."

Tapping the keyboard, he projected an aerial view of a city district onto the screen, including an area bordered with a white diamond. Within it, four interconnected factory buildings could be seen, each marked with a different color. "Each of these buildings serves a different purpose. The pictures you are being shown now were smuggled by Nesha. There are many more of them, but in order not to exceed the time frame of this meeting, we're showing you only some of them."

With the tip of his stick, he pointed at the red area. "These are house women, who live there with their babies and small children."

The next slide showed a fish-eye shot of a warehouse. The beds in it stood close together. Silhouettes of pregnant women were visible along with small children running around in the aisles. "Girls and women from fourteen to thirty years old are held captive there. Their primary purpose is to produce offspring. Otherwise, they work in the fields." Two other slides showed similar images at other times of day, as was evident from the longer shadows. On the fourth, a massive male figure loomed over the beds. "Here we see a collaborator, known in Shkodër simply as a collab. These people are not infected, but they work for the undead."

Low laughter rang out, as if his audience didn't believe him.

Lucas did not elaborate. He continued, "In addition to guard duty, the collabs ensure these women are in a state of permanent pregnancy."

Someone inhaled sharply and expelled their breath in a hiss. In the next photograph, all the beds were occupied. It was one of the shots taken early in the morning.

"We don't know exactly how many women total are living there, but we assume it's between twelve and eighteen hundred. The children stay with their mothers until they are three or four years old. After that, they are separated from them."

He switched back to the picture with the differently colored buildings. "The offspring are then brought here." Lucas pointed to the blue building and displayed a new slide—a different perspective, this time from slightly higher up than the picture of the women's camp. Here, too, countless beds and sleeping places on the bare ground. Just little figures scurrying about. As far as he could in the twilight, Lucas looked into the faces of his audience, who were following the slideshow as if spellbound. He waited five seconds. In the next shot, a concentric circle of tots had formed around a cot. Their fists raised and their mouths wide open, they seemed to be chanting at the top of their voices. "The children who live here work up to twelve hours a day during the sowing and harvesting periods, without any breaks to speak of. In the periods in between, they are left to their own devices. Often there are fights, which are frequently fatal for the younger ones. The collabs, who instigate brawls for their own entertainment, like to intervene to de-escalate things toward the end," he added sarcastically. The next picture showed a grown man dispersing the pack of children with hefty punches and smacks. A small body lay motionless on the ground.

Lucas switched slides but waited a moment to allow people to process what they were seeing. "In the third building," he finally continued, "shown here in green, food is being prepared for the imprisoned people." Figures standing at several long tables appeared on the screen, engaged in some task that could not be precisely identified. These images were also taken from an elevated perspective. "All the fruit and vegetables harvested are consumed here. They've even thought of the winter season. They dry herbs. Eggplants, zucchini, peppers, and tomatoes are boiled down, as you have done here in the Balkans for centuries. The staple food, along with corn, is wheat."

The slide changed. "Here you can see the cooking stations where porridge is prepared daily. This is then distributed to the camps." The next image showed long rows of people with buckets in their hands, presumably waiting for them to be filled. Next to them, others were stirring waist-high cauldrons.

"Finally, you'll see the facility that was created exclusively to ensure the continued existence of the zombies, shown here in purple. This is divided into two areas. The first is for recruitment, as the imprisoned call it. All male youths over the age of thirteen or fourteen who are reasonably strong are infected in order to maintain the undead population. They're probably selected because they could become a threat if they were allowed to develop normally."

This series of photos now showed two men fishing out individual youths from a kind of cage. One was being taken over to a third supervisor sitting at a table. "The collabs have contaminated tools, which they use to slightly injure their victims. On the hand, leg, or arm." The boy, who appeared to be infected, was pushed through a door into the open.

After that, a completely different picture appeared. Unlike the previous ones, it was deprived of all color. The floor shone darkly. Unidentifiable objects lay all around. Although Lucas had seen the footage several times already, his voice failed him for a moment at the sight of it. Striving to retain a matter-of-fact tone, he reported, "This is the hall where the wandering corpses are fed. This photo was taken around an hour after forty zombies devoured fifteen people. Women who can't have children, people who are unfit for fieldwork for health reasons, live out their last moments here. Older boys and young people of both sexes who are of no use to the system due to exhaustion, injury, or some other disability, are given to the zombies as food. We all know how this plays out, so I won't show you any more images." With that, Lucas ended his presentation.

For a long time, no one dared say a word.

"I have a question." A voice came from the back rows. Some looked toward it. "Is it a good idea to free these people? I mean, many of them have lived there for years. Would they be able to adjust to life outside the camp? If they even want to, I'm not even sure they could survive outside. What I am saying is, where will these people be housed? Who's going to take care of them, provide for them? I assume you're not planning to leave them down there, are you?"

A murmur went through the crowd. People whispered among themselves. Lucas couldn't tell whether they were agreeing or disagreeing with the questioner. The latter had apparently quickly decided that the audience was in favor his concerns and continued, "Do we even have enough food to tide them over until the next harvest?"

"What is this crap? How can you think for one second that those people *want* to stay in there?" Lejla hissed at the questioner. "Would you like to be zombie food? Yeah, I'm sure *you'd* be happy about that. I can't believe you're talking so much shit!"

Tiz, who had been watching in silence until then, exhaled, clapped his hands on his thighs, and got to his feet. Gently he placed a hand on Lucas's shoulder; the young man was glad to be taken out of the line of fire. He sat down next to Lejla.

"No one will *have* to rescue, take in, or feed anyone if they don't feel morally obligated to do so," Tiz explained. "However, the rest of us will use our resources not only during the expedition, but also afterward, to give these people a new, more dignified life. Ships have been ordered to take the survivors to a safe place in the event of a rescue mission, which is currently very likely. It has not yet been determined where this will be, and that's of secondary importance at this stage."

This time, there were numerous nods in the audience—confirmed agreement.

But the questioner was not to be dismissed. "But there are just too many of them. How will they survive in the outside world? We don't have enough food for *all* of them! They'll starve to death. Besides, you know how fragile our newly built societies are. When people who have been cooped up in Shkodër for a decade arrive, we can say good-bye to our achievements. They'll simply overrun us. They won't abide by our rules. They know only one law—survival. And they only think about them-selves. Community values and norms are alien to them."

It irritated Lucas that Tiz, in contrast with his usual irritable manner, answered calmly. "You have to decide. Either they'll all starve to death, or they'll destroy our society. They can't do both at the same time."

"Yeah, well, what I'm saying is . . ." the questioner stammered. Appar-ently, Tiz had thrown him off his game.

"What about the anomaly you talked about?" interrupted another participant. "Does it exist?"

"We weren't able to confirm that. None of our footage shows anyone who might be a candidate for that. It remains unclear whether such a person ever existed."

"Can someone explain to me how the zombies got this far? It just boggles my mind," said a woman in the front row.

At that, everyone fell silent.

When it became clear no one was going to speak, Tiz said into the silence, "I'd like to try my hand at an answer. As you know, I, along with many of you, have had years of experience in the zombie war. And our visitor from the north has also brought a great deal of new information."

Tiz inclined his head toward the hooded figure, who nodded in acknowledgement. Then he continued, "As we all know, the disease takes possession of the body of an infected person, overwriting the exist-ing metabolism where necessary. In addition, it is able to access the information that the host body has—and pass it on with each subsequent infection. Whether this has always been the case or whether it is due to the evolution of the plague, I cannot say. The fact is that the undead act on instinct as a result."

"I don't understand," someone else said.

Tiz massaged his neck and looked up at the ceiling. "Let me give you an example. Once a species learns what food is, it looks for the easiest way to get it. Zombies access the embedded knowledge of their pre-species, which explains their appetite for human flesh."

"But people weren't cannibals before the apocalypse," someone objected.

"Right," Tiz said. "But the plague doesn't know that. To it, human flesh is the most readily available food source."

"And then the undead get the idea to set up this kind of facility? How did they find out how to do that?"

"Ha," someone remarked disparagingly, "you do know what parts of our agricultural economy looked like before the outbreak, don't you?"

"Yes, I do, but . . . Still, it all sounds a bit far-fetched to me. And these collabs, or whatever they're called. Why hasn't anyone challenged them? The whole discussion leaves more gaps than it can fill."

Lucas looked at Tiz as he struggled to find a plausible answer. But before he could reply, the black-cloaked figure stood up. Goosebumps came over Lucas, as they always did when the figure moved. With its strange floating gait, it came to Tiz's side.

The voice under the hood grated on his ears. "This is indeed something that would require the existence of the anomaly I mentioned earlier. A being capable of communicating with humans as well as the undead. Someone who can act instinctively and yet in such a planned and structured way as to be able to create environments like those in Shkodër."

"No, we've never seen anything like this before," said another member of the crowd. "These kinds of apparitions only exist in fairy tales. You can say what you want, but I'd have to see it to believe it."

"What is it exactly that you want to see?" the voice under the hood asked, almost threateningly.

"Well, an anomaly like that, for example."

In the silence that followed, Lucas heard his heart hammering wildly. The figure calmly removed its robe, folded it once in the middle, and placed it gently on the table. At the sight of its face, many of those present stiffened. It looked at Lucas and asked him to turn on the light. He obeyed. Meanwhile, it took off its gloves. People in the front rows, who had the best view, flinched. Chairs squeaked. The figure bared its left arm, which was gray up to its muscular biceps.

The chaos that ensued lasted almost a full minute and only came to an end when Tiz, after yelling in vain for calm, fired a shot at the ceiling.

Meanwhile, the figure remained unimpressed, motionless, watching the confusion. Many had drawn pistols and were waving them toward it. Lucas looked at Lejla, whose mouth was open in amazement. Only then did he hear Tiz's voice. The man was screaming his head off. His face was flushed. He stood like a wall between the angry crowd and the figure with the rolled-up sleeve.

"*Silence now!* Shut your damn mouths!" He received venomous looks in return, which he ignored. "What kind of pathetic bigots are you? Is that any way to treat our guest? Calling them names and threatening them with guns? Put your guns away, right now. All of you!"

He met every gaze until the others looked away and holstered their firearms. "If any of you feel uncomfortable, there's the exit. And anyone who gets abusive again can come outside with me. Then we'll settle this in private. Did that get through?"

Hard-faced women and men looked at Tiz as if they wanted to jump down his throat, but they sat down again once their anger had faded.

"Good. Now listen to what our visitor has to say." The Newgoslavian turned to the figure with the zombie arm. "Please forgive the confusion. Our culture has never been known for civilized behavior, I'm afraid. But please"—Tiz cleared the stage—"proceed now, Backup."

CHAPTER 5

REYKJAVÍK

For the seventh day in a row, Cassiopeia sought comfort in the place that was familiar to her. She sat in the tall grass, her legs crossed. The view of the seemingly endless sea never altered, except for the changes brought by the seasons. The wind rustled through the tough stalks at the foot of the Holmsberg lighthouse. That, too, was as it always was.

A gust of wind tangled Cas's long black hair. She brushed the strands off her face. She liked it when the world around her held no surprises. But now her mama had sailed away, and nothing was the same. Cassiopeia felt an emptiness inside that she, at eight years old, didn't know what to do about. This was the first time Mama had gone away for a long time. Cas couldn't remember a day when they hadn't spent at least a few hours together. But suddenly that had all changed, and she hadn't had time to prepare for it. Cas didn't like it at all. But she liked it even less that her mom was gone.

She had found out through an overheard conversation between her mother and her grandfather. Where she was traveling to, Cas didn't know. The names of the countries, seas, and cities were unknown to her. She didn't understand why the people there needed Mom's help. Cas had heard countless eerie stories about the calamity that had befallen the rest of the world. But she'd spent her whole life in Iceland, where there was no pandemic, and she had no concept of the threat. She would have loved to have sailed with her mom. She'd have accepted the change just to be with her mom, even if the trip was going to be dangerous. After all, she could have stayed safely on the ship while the adults went ashore.

Given the tales of the barbarian people who were supposed to live on the Faroe Islands to the southeast, it might even have been better for Eva to take her along. In Cas's imagination, the people of those islands were more vicious than the flesh-eating undead. While she had never set eyes on either, the rumors about the barbarians were no less horrific. They were even believed to eat children's flesh. Moreover, they were accused of kidnapping children since they had few of their own. Whether the stories were true, no one knew.

It was supposedly safe in Iceland. Cas was now living with her grandparents. One day, Eva, her mother, had simply said good-bye to her.

The security she had always known was gone in one fell swoop. Sadness dominated her every waking minute. She hardly ate, couldn't sleep at night, and was tired during the day. She found school tedious. She'd ride past it on her bicycle in the morning to stare out at the lighthouse for hours and listen to the whistling of the wind. By now, someone should have noticed she was skipping class. Tomorrow at the latest, probably, her class teacher would come knocking on her grandparents' door, asking about her. But she didn't care. She didn't want to learn anything or see anyone. She longed for her mother.

The blue sky and the sunshine gave her a little comfort. Absentmindedly, she held in her lap the spear Eva had given her. Rays of sunlight flashed on the blade at one end of the staff. The lighthouse behind her would be in the same spot a hundred years from now. The wind and the rolling sea in front of her would be there for all eternity. Nothing changed very fast here. Soon she felt herself becoming calmer.

Cas reached for her satchel to take out her water bottle. She noticed a movement out of the corner of her eye. A dry twig cracked. She lifted her head but saw only the sky above the grass behind the orange-painted lighthouse. Had someone come to service it? Many lives depended on this one working perfectly. Perhaps Magnús, the caretaker, had gone inside without Cas noticing? But he had no need to hide from Cas. He would have said hello and almost certainly asked why she wasn't at school.

Might it be that an elf from the Huldufólk was speaking to her? Grandmother knew countless stories about the mystical people who lived in hiding. Here and there, they would show themselves and even play with human children. Would Cas finally get to set eyes on one of the álfar? Because the Huldufólk didn't talk to humans, and because it was bad luck to address an elf by its true name, they communicated through noises. Grandma never tired of saying that if you stayed very still, you could hear soft clacking and popping sounds. So maybe it wasn't a twig that had cracked at all, but an elf trying to tell her something? She shook her head. No, Cas was eight years old and no longer believed in such fairy tales, no matter how much she wished them to be true.

It was probably just the wind blowing in the grass. It had snapped a dry stalk. She was alone.

Cas remembered why she was holding the backpack. With her free hand, she laid the spear down in the grass, took out her bottle, and drank.

A shadow appeared behind her. She wheeled around, panting. An unknown person was standing where no one had been five seconds ago, staring at her. A whole group of people seemed to have grown out of the ground.

The arrivals' clothing was unlike anything Cas had ever seen in Iceland. Some were only wearing pants and stood motionless with their torsos exposed. Some had scarred skin painted over with sooty black paint and strange shapes drawn on their skin.

Scary tales about barbarians kidnapping children shot through Cas's mind. She began to tremble. The arrivals were silent.

A lone figure stood apart from the group that surrounded her. She eyed Cas. The area around her eyes, all the way around to her clean-shaven temples, was painted with a shiny black band. On her torso, she wore a dark, threadbare tank top. As if obeying an inaudible command, the crowd between them parted. The figure came closer and bent down over the spear. Her cold eyes looked down at the weapon. She tested the tip of the blade with her thumb. Her nod gave the impression she was satisfied with it. Unhurriedly, she pointed the blade at Cassiopeia, whose breath caught. Was she going to die now? Or would they kidnap her to turn her into a savage? Suddenly, she understood that all the horror stories were real.

The figure approached her. Cas's eyes filled with tears. The water bottle slipped from her fingers and landed on the grass. Shaking all over, she began to cry.

CHAPTER 6

ATLANTIC

As I write this entry, I leave Iceland with mixed feelings. I find it difficult to admit precisely what I'm feeling, even to myself. So, it's easier to start with this hollow phrase.

In fact, though, I feel like I've been relieved of a burden. I'm finally on the road again after all these years spent in Reykjavík—so uncharacteristic for me as someone always on the move and never staying in the same place for long. But because I had to leave my daughter, Cassiopeia, alone, my guilty conscience is hard on my heels, even here in the middle of the Atlantic Ocean at the latitude of Ireland, the north wind driving us southward. At the Strait of Gibraltar, we hope to catch up with the Scandinavian crew, who are two weeks ahead of us and have traversed the Baltic Sea and the English Channel. From there, we're supposed to sail together across the Mediterranean all the way to the Adriatic Sea. At the moment, I can't think about what lies ahead for us. My thoughts keep returning to my daughter.

Cas is eight years old. A glance at my wristwatch tells me she should be at school right now. It's been over forty-eight hours since we said good-bye, and it wasn't easy. She barely made a face, which made it even harder to leave. If she had cried bitterly, I could have comforted her. But she was silent. And I keep asking myself, whether I'm a bad mother.

Unsuccessfully, I try to convince myself that the answer to this question doesn't matter. After eight years of permanent parenthood, I'm just glad to escape Iceland. Cas is old enough by now to spend a few weeks without me in the care of her grandparents, even though there hasn't been a single day since she was born when she wasn't with me. Have I spoiled her? Probably. But I thought it was appropriate to make life as comfortable as possible for a fatherless child who was born barely a year after the end of the world. On the other hand, I didn't treat her like a tender plant; I prepared her for difficult times. In the remote areas of Iceland, we went on survival trips for days, living only on what we could find in the wilderness, sleeping in caves and camping out in the open, even when the temperature was below freezing. To warm ourselves up, we occasionally sought out one of the many hot springs. All this in a setting that would have gotten me into trouble with the Youth Welfare Office before the pandemic.

For her, these trips were nothing special—as long as she could be by my side. She accepted harsh weather conditions stoically and was even willing to suffer hunger. I was proud of her. The depth of our bond flattered my maternal ego. For her self-protection, I fashioned her a spear like Backup had. Her toy weapon is only half as long, but proportionally speaking, it's big enough. The edge of the blade was blunted. When Cas practiced at home, I put a cork on it so she wouldn't hurt herself. In my view, she's too young for that. But at the martial arts school in Reykjavík she's attended from the age of six, they teach her and other children self-defense—even with stabbing weapons and blunt instruments.

Every day, I told her about her father.

In the first few years after his death, I struggled through countless outbursts of tears, and the sting in my heart caused by Patrick's absence now hurts less. Or have I just become so used to mourning him that it has become a part of me?

I often struggle to remember the time we spent together. I wish I hadn't lost my diaries from the time before the outbreak. Without them, I could only tell Cas the stories of the past as I remembered them. How we met while studying in Copenhagen, and how, after our third date, I had to admit to myself that I was in love. I told Cas about our escape through France and how we braved the elements to get to Mallorca. About the people we met there. About the friendships that had developed out of adversity. I told my daughter everything I could remember, even our last hours together and how Patrick sacrificed himself to save us both.

The older she got, the more she resembled him. Even though her dark hair is more like mine, she has inherited his gray-blue eyes. But above all, the stubbornness and the tendency to sarcasm, which are already evident at her young age, are the biggest clues to who her father was.

My girl is growing up in safety and, at the same time, is aware of the dangers lurking outside her little world—as far as her eight-year-old brain can comprehend and process. She knows about the zombies, but she also knows about the presumed threat to us from the Faroe Islands.

It is a very strange story.

Norwegian sailors, who now call at Reykjavík two or three times a year, bring not only merchandise but also sailor's yarns and rumors. They seem to have spread the word about my story. It is rumored that the handful of survivors of Vágur, who managed to escape from the undead horde in the arena, might arm themselves for a retaliatory strike, directed at me. I see this as a remarkable case of cognitive dissonance, because, ultimately, I am the one who was wronged. But so be it.

After escaping to other islands nine years ago, the survivors have been desperately trying to make ends meet ever since. Their population, which was nearly wiped out, produces hardly any offspring. The available manpower is just enough to cultivate or trade essential foodstuffs. They hardly have any modern technology, and their culture has taken a huge step backward. I don't believe they present a threat to us, especially because they should have more important things to do than to pursue me after so many years.

Leaving Iceland was unexpectedly difficult even though I was able to leave Cassiopeia with my parents. It was obvious that we'd have to cut the cord sooner or later. Nevertheless, it caused me pain. However, my joy over my new freedom increased the farther we sailed from Reykjavík. Being stuck on an island since the beginning of the pandemic and seeing nothing of the world, experiencing little that was new except being a parent, and being trapped in the same routine every day did me no good. Besides, the trip is too important for me not to be on it.

A stiff north wind is driving us south at an average speed of around twenty knots. To cover the three thousand and four hundred nautical miles to the Adriatic, we need at least three weeks. We must not waste time; we have a job to do. The crew I joined on the way to the Balkans has now become a reasonably well-drilled team. Since post apocalypse weather forecasts aren't always to be trusted, the crew of forty aboard the luxury yacht works in shifts to make the most of the night breeze. It could always change direction the next day, forcing a slower pace on us.

As soon as we'd established a certain routine on board after three days on the open sea, I decided to continue working on my memoirs between shifts. I'm itching to put the events of the past weeks down on paper. I need to get them off my chest. Usually, I would have read my last entry beforehand to get into the flow of writing.

The day before I left, I put it and three pens with the pile of clothes I stowed in the duffel bag that evening. But now I can't find it. Even the pens are missing. Losing diaries has become my hobby, I guess. It was futile to rack my brain about where they'd gone—if they weren't in the bag, I hadn't packed them. My fellow travelers provided me with writing materials.

Now I have two pens and three pencils. I found enough paper in a small storeroom where a stack of halfway usable printer paper was lying next to an antique fax machine.

Sitting at my desk in front of the huge window, through which I can make out the horizon in the far distance, I watch the isolated blue smudges in the overcast sky. Rays of sunlight turn the gray sea azure wherever they hit it. I turn around and, for the first time, I don't see the yacht as a workplace.

The sailing ship used to belong to a Russian billionaire and must have cost a fortune. The interior was equipped with every imaginable bell and whistle that you could get at that time. Unfortunately, the oligarch was on a sailing trip in the middle of the Atlantic when stock prices plummeted due to the outbreak of the zombie infection, so he feared for his riches. He loaded his family into the helicopter parked on the hull of the yacht before unceremoniously heading east, probably hoping to salvage some of his possessions.

The crew he left behind, on the other hand, was forced to settle in Iceland. None of them felt able to pay the enormous daily berth prices the ship was accruing. As long as these costs were not paid, the port administration wouldn't allow them to leave the port. However, when it became clear that no one was coming to retrieve the luxury vessel, it became the property of the Icelanders.

In the years that followed, it was used for transporting passengers and goods around the island. The cabins were rebuilt to give it greater capacity. All unnecessary features were removed. For a while, the ship even served as a mobile hospital, but this changed when most of the people in need of care were relocated to Reykjavík. The yacht was unsuitable for fishing, as it would have been enormously expensive to equip her with containers and net winches. So for the last two years, it lay jacked up in the harbor—until three weeks ago, when I received a message to go to the office of the Crisis Response Unit.

Curious, I answered the call. The official, who had presumably drawn up the invitation himself—a muscular man in his early fifties with gray hair and a small belly bulge under his dark blue uniform—introduced himself as Arnar Dagursbur.

After the usual greetings, he slipped me a handwritten transcript of a radio conversation. He seemed to be in a hurry. My brows furrowed; I read line after line. The content announced the discovery of a population in danger and appealed to the Icelandic government to assemble a relief force and send it immediately to the Mediterranean.

Once I had taken in the first half, Arnar, who was sitting across from me with his arms folded, casually interjected, "We immediately told the applicants it was unlikely we'd be able to grant their request. Our rapid response unit is only responsible for Iceland, especially since everything was eventually sorted out through international solidarity as the epidemic progressed."

"There were times when the unit was even stationed in Afghanistan as part of a peace mission," I said without lifting my eyes from the page.

"Before the pandemic, yes. But things were slightly different than they are today," he replied, piqued.

"Why?"

"Surely you've noticed that the world has changed drastically since then."

"Technically, yes, but that doesn't absolve Iceland's government of its moral duty to help people in need. It's not as if we're suffering from over-population. And the unit has been active in Kosovo. If I'm reading this correctly, the new trouble spot is right around the corner from there. Don't you have a veteran who knows the area?"

He smiled. "Yes, we do—me. I was stationed in Kosovo at the time."

"And why aren't you going yourself?"

Arnar pushed his chair back from the table and placed his left leg on the countertop. With both hands, he pulled back his trouser leg, revealing, a prosthetic leg underneath. "Kabul, 2004. A Taliban suicide bombing that was supposed to be for my superior."

"Oh shit, I'm sorry," I said, genuinely affected. "I didn't know."

He waved my apology away. "You couldn't have; it was a long time ago. But you'll understand that I wouldn't be much use to anyone with this."

I nodded diplomatically. "But I'm still unclear why you called me in."

Again, he smiled mischievously. "Come with me."

With these words, he led me out of the office. On the way to the harbor, we exchanged some harmless small talk. Turning past a three-master, we stepped onto a wide pier where a crowd of people were standing in rows. Despite the semidisciplined lineup, they didn't seem like an army.

People were wearing everyday clothes, and their hairstyles were all kinds of lengths. Most of them were in their early twenties, but there were some older ones, too.

Five people in uniform and holding clipboards were walking between the rows, looking overwhelmed. They were entering data while sending the people in civilian clothes back and forth across the port area.

"What's that supposed to be?" I asked, probably sounding more condescending than I meant to.

Arnar pursed his lips. "A small group of teenagers also intercepted the message. Before we could react, they sent an urgent request to charter the ship you see here for a supply run.

The office, which had not received any communication about the message, saw no reason to deny it to them."

It took me a few seconds to process what I had heard. "Wait a minute. You're giving this sailing ship to kids who want to use it to go to Albania? To challenge hundreds, if not thousands, of zombies?"

"Mm-hmm, yeah, that pretty much sums it up—except for the part about the kids. Everyone who has volunteered is of legal age."

Stunned, I looked at him. "Oh, that makes it much better, of course. Can't they be stopped? It's pure suicide."

He shook his head. "Legally, our hands are tied. The ship doesn't belong to the government; it belongs to the people. Anyone can use it, as long as they specify a meaningful purpose."

"And it was declared as a supply run. So they saw no reason to deny the request. And if they tried to stop the trip now, they'd have no reasonable justification."

"But what if the ship is lost en route? Can't you make that argument?"

"They've even thought of that. They'll leave enough crew on board to sail it back if the mission fails."

"These are children. Hardly any of them are older than twenty. I'm guessing most of them have never held a gun before."

"I'd disagree there. Here in Iceland, it's not uncommon for parents to teach their children to shoot polar bears."

"You're out of your minds." I was enraged. "How can you be so ignorant? Might it be because hardly anyone in Iceland has ever seen an infected? A horde of undead is not the same thing as a polar bear. A bear might run away when it hears loud noises. Zombies don't. A long-range gunshot is completely different from hand-to-hand combat, which they'll undoubtedly have to engage in."

With each of my sentences, he stiffened more and more. "I didn't invite you here to tell me what I already know."

But I couldn't stop myself. "And I have a feeling that neither the government nor the rest of the adult population are getting enough information about the zombies. Not to mention these infants. They don't even know what they'll be facing out there. You have to educate them about the dangers first, long before you can even think about basic training in how to conduct a war.

"Only then would it be possible—maybe—to send them out there with some sort of a minimal chance. Led by someone who knows exactly what it fighting zombies is all about. Someone who has experience and could coordinate the whole operation. Someone who . . ."

I froze. I turned to Arnar and looked him in the eye. He held my gaze. "Forget it. No way!" I held out the communiqué to him.

He made no effort to take it back. His hands clasped behind his back, he said matter-of-factly, "Finish reading, please!"

He jutted his chin toward the paper.

Astonished, I lifted the paper up to my eyes. Between the lines, I could see other, more indistinct letters. Only then did I realize that the message continued on the back.

I read. At the point where it was explicitly suggested I be personally informed about the events, my breath caught in my throat. But when I came to the name of the person who had provided the information, I let out a muffled cry, releasing all the longing of the last few years.

"But that's . . . it can't be . . ." I stammered awkwardly.

Arnar grinned broadly. "Aah, so you two really know each other?"

Tears welled up in my eyes. "Sure, I know her. I mean, that can only be her. She's the only person with that name who knows me. And she's alive. My God, she's alive," I whispered. "Where did you say she was?"

"Sweden."

"Sweden," I repeated as if in a trance. "How did she find out about me?"

"I assume that the sailors . . ." Arnar continued.

"Yeah, I get it," I interrupted him, still engrossed in my memories. The initial joyful shock soon ebbed, and the desire to do something helpful awoke in me. My palms became damp with sweat. My heart began to race. In my mind, I saw myself shooting across the ocean. I felt the wind in my hair and the rise and fall of the swells. Images of zombies passed through my mind's eye. Disgust and a destructive rage flared up in me.

Those feelings faded instantly when I remembered what I was—a mother with a child who needed special attention.

"Just to be clear, I will not be leading an expedition." I shook my head. "This mission has to happen without me." He looked at me questioningly. "I have a child," I continued, though he probably knew anyway. "And I'm a single parent. I don't want to risk Cas growing up an orphan. This apocalypse has already robbed her of her father. If it were just me, none of this would be a problem. But under these circumstances . . . I just can't."

He looked at the tips of his shoes and was silent for a while. "Hmm, that's understandable," he said. "Repeatedly venturing into the infested areas would be just as unappealing to me. And that's after all the sacrifices you had to make to escape them."

Thinking of my last days with Patrick, I nodded. Then I pulled myself together and waved the message. "How do you know this person really is who they say they are?"

"What do you mean?"

"What if this is a trap?"

"Who'd be interested in that?" said Arnar seriously, but he snorted right afterward. "Oh, you mean the savages from the Faroe Islands? They certainly wouldn't have ordered a whole squadron of armed men," he placated. "Come back the day after tomorrow. We'll contact Sweden at eighteen hundred hours. Then you can see for yourself whether they're trying to pull the wool over our eyes or not." His voice became more serious. "There must be a reason why they're explicitly asking for you. For me, at least, it's obvious. If such an expedition were a success . . ." Arnar paused meaningfully. Finally, he went on, "Like most people in Iceland, I know your story. For many, you're a kind of legend. And to be honest, I, myself, am . . . a fan."

I frowned suspiciously. "Just don't expect me to give you an autograph."

Laughing, he replied, "No, that won't be necessary. But if I may say so, you are one of the few people in Iceland I would call a zombie veteran. In fact, most likely the only one. No one else has as much experience dealing with the undead as you."

He raised an arm and pointed to the east. "You, on the other hand, experienced the pandemic from the beginning—and were forced to fight the undead. Your expertise is essential to the success of this expedition. And, as for your daughter—she will be in good hands with her grandparents. Of course, we will provide you with any assistance you may need."

Slowly, I shook my head. "My child needs her mother. At least until she's old enough to get along without me. And that's going to take some time."

I put all the conviction I could muster into my voice.

Arnar frowned his already wrinkled face, looked at me closely, and then nodded.

"Would you at least help us with the preparations? Train the team so they don't plunge headlong into disaster completely unprepared?"

"I'm not in favor of supporting this suicide mission." I sighed. "But they probably won't let me talk them out of it. Maybe I can at least do something to increase their chances of survival." Then I nodded. "All right. Let me know when you're done recruiting, and I'll come and teach these babies as much as I can."

This compromise was obviously not what Arnar had hoped for. But he agreed. "As I said, it'll take a few more days. I know where to find you."

"I'll see you the day after tomorrow anyway."

He looked amused. "Of course. That's certainly what the petitioner wants—although she won't be edified to learn that you rejected her proposal."

"Are you trying to change my mind by making me feel guilty?"

"Mm-hmm, I'd be lying if I denied it."

"See you soon, Arnar. I have to go now. Cassiopeia will be home from school soon, and I haven't cooked anything yet."

Smiling, he nodded. "Good-bye, Eva. I'll be in touch once the troop is finalized. That is, if we don't see each other tomorrow evening. You're welcome to drop by just before six."

I shook hands with him and made my way home.

On the day of the planned contact, I was so excited that I can't remember what I did before the appointment at six. But certainly, I didn't disturb the routine I had been following for years—getting Cas ready for school in the morning, working with my parents in the greenhouses in the garden, and cooking dinner for us all around four o'clock. My eyes wandered to the clock every other minute. I also squinted at the sky, which was reluctantly letting through rays of sunlight to charge our small car. Its battery was aging but still performing at just over half its initial capacity. Given the short distances we had to cover, this was enough. So far, we'd had to have minor damage to the electric motors repaired four times, which had only cost us a few kilos of freshly harvested vegetables. After that, the vehicle was almost as good as new again.

An hour before the scheduled appointment, I stole out of the house, unplugged the car, and drove into town. Thirty minutes later, I parked in front of Arnar's office building. I was waved through at the front desk. I climbed the stairs to the second floor, where I knocked on his door. Entering, I saw him putting a file back onto one of the shelves.

He looked at me and smiled, "Ah, Eva. I knew you would come."

"Wasn't that hard to guess, was it?"

"Hmm, you're probably right. Would you like some tea? Or some lupin coffee? We still have time."

"A tea would be great," I replied.

He reached for his phone and ordered our drinks. "So, how was your day?" he asked.

"Apart from the fact that I'm very excited—normal, I'd say."

"Actually, I wanted to check in advance whether you'd like to talk to Sweden alone or whether it's okay for me to be there. But we can . . ."

"Yes, we'll see about that when the time comes," I interrupted him. My obvious nervousness seemed to amuse him.

The tea arrived. We talked and drank until Arnar glanced at the clock. Clapping both hands on the table, he said, "It's time." He led me down the poorly lit corridor to the radio room. A young female technician wearing large headphones was sitting at one of the tables. She looked up briefly when we arrived but was immediately engrossed in her work again.

Arnar headed for a free radio station, where he took a seat. He handed me my own headset. It beeped loudly, forcing me to turn down the volume. Meanwhile, my companion fiddled with a few buttons and dials. The numbers on the digital display rushed upward until they reached a certain frequency. The clock showed two minutes to six. I looked over at Arnar, who gave me a thumbs-up. He spoke into his headset, gave his name, and inquired in English whether anyone could hear him.

He did that seven times in a row.

And then we received an answer.

"Hello, Reykjavík; Umeå here. Over." The sound of her voice almost took my breath away.

"Hej, Umeå. I have been assigned to handle communications regarding your request."

"Ah, wonderful. And in the meantime, do you have anything to report?"

"Yes, mainly good news. We've already had volunteers come forward. As soon as we get enough food together and the team trained, we'll send them out."

"That's really great news, Arnar. On the Swedish side, we've already completed the preparations. Our team is leaving in four days. My suggestion would be that we meet at the Strait of Gibraltar."

Arnar thought. "Hmm, that might work. We'll probably be ready to go in two weeks. With a good wind, we'll need another two to get there."

"And the trip will take us almost a month anyway. Whoever gets there first waits." She laughed and he joined in.

"That's the way it's supposed to be. By the way, I have someone here who wants to talk to you."

"Um"—she paused, audibly struggling to compose herself—"Is she really there?"

He nodded, giving me the floor.

My chin trembled as I spoke, "Hi, Waltraud. It's Eva."

She whooped.

First we laughed, and then we cried. Once our tears had dried, we talked for three hours about what we had been through. Arnar's presence didn't bother me in the least.

He drew back a little and brought me tea from time to time, and even a late dinner. My mouth full, I listened to Waltraud's stories, howled, giggled, and heard equal outbursts of emotion from her. She knew as little as I did, however, about the whereabouts of Backup and Franca and the youngsters she had once rescued with Patrick. Over all the years, their names had slipped our minds, but we pieced them together after a few attempts.

My throat was scratchy from hours of talking. At some point, there was nothing left to speak about. With heavy hearts, we said good-bye, promising to meet as soon as she returned from the Balkans. I asked her to say hello to Jens for me before we ended the conversation. I then needed a few minutes to collect myself. Our bond probably went deeper than I had suspected.

Arnar took me to the parking lot. Before I got into my car, he asked me to come back in three days. I smiled wanly, nodded, and drove away.

As agreed, I appeared three days later in the harbor, where again a huge crowd had gathered. Arnar was watching the action from the ship's rail. As soon as he saw me, he waved me up.

"That was quicker than I thought," I greeted, nodding in the direction of the pack.

"I guess word has gotten out. We now have more adventurous people than we can accommodate. So we have to screen them. On the one hand, that's good, but on the other hand, it throws off our schedule."

"What criteria do you use to decide who can come and who can't?"

He shrugged, his eyes roaming over the crowd. "We can't be too picky. But it boils down to the fact that they don't make it to the second round if they're too young or too old. After that, we pick the fittest ones. In the final pass, we test how they work in a team, how well they follow orders and the like. Fourteen people have also turned up who belong or used to belong to the army or the police. We'll probably put them in charge."

"Not bad. To get all that organized in such a short time . . ."

"Well, we don't have much else to do. Everyone involved in the project was delighted to see some action."

I snorted. "If only they knew what they were in for. Absolute greenhorns."

Arnar nodded. "The ones we've chosen are being trained to use weapons. Many of the senior applicants have let us have their hunting rifles."

"Smaller handguns would be better than bulky rifles. But I have an idea how we can optimize that."

"That's exactly why you're here, Eva. In addition to the shotguns, we've got a dozen or so carbines, which are better for long distances. In the fourth round, it'll be a matter of dividing up the weapons according to the volunteers' skills."

"We have the people to take care of it. We'll get some rapid-fire weapons from the state, unofficially, of course. No one wants anyone to see our relief effort as a waste of resources."

"Very good. How much time have you allocated for instruction?"

"Two weeks, during which we will work close to twelve hours each day. I am sure that another handful of them won't be able to cope with the pressure and will be eliminated. During the trip, there'll be time to discuss everything we don't have time for now. Food for the journey is just waiting to be loaded. Our sea farms produced enough algae last year to ensure the emergency stores are full of algae protein. As for carbohydrates, we have packets of instant cereal-potato powder ready to go. We've also produced far more of that than we needed. We planned our quantities for crises, such as crop failures, which fortunately didn't occur. We produced new ones anyway, and that's gradually forcing us to get rid of the older rations. Depending on how big your team gets, you'll have supplies for several weeks. If not months or a whole year."

"But we'll need a lot more food. Probably all you can spare."

"I don't quite understand . . ."

"Assuming the mission is successful, the question of how the rescued people are going to feed themselves remains. They can't stay there. We'll have to move them to safer territory. And once the resources from the surrounding area are used up, what happens then? If they starve to death after a few weeks, the whole operation will have been for nothing."

"Hmm, that's true. I'll come up with something. Don't worry," Arnar said, hastily scribbling notes. "For my part, there are a few more things to say about the ship. It was built in line with the owner's instructions, to sail quickly and safely over the seas. Everything can be controlled automatically. But if the electronics fail, the crew must know what to do. We'll need to teach you that and a thousand other little things in workshops. But that needn't concern you."

The planned two weeks ultimately turned into three. Physical and psychological tests had produced far more rejects than initially expected, which made another wave of recruitment necessary. But then the team of forty was in place, and after the initial basic training, it no longer seemed quite as pathetic as I had feared.

Some of the rejected soldiers who were able to step out of their comfort zones and not leave the field in contrition agreed to help repair the ship. They did their part for the expedition, loading ration packs and water on board, clearing the hull of shells, and coating it with antifouling paint.

With the ones we'd selected, we drove kilometers into the wilderness for outdoor survival training. My expertise was mainly in the behavioral patterns of the undead and how to avoid them. The recruits were relatively familiar with their vulnerabilities. However, many did not realize the fatal effects that small things such as body odors could have. So I explained why it was sensible to answer the call of nature far away from the campsite and bury it as deep as possible. To wash with sand and herbs. To eat largely unseasoned food, which surprisingly did not bother anyone.

The officers let me take the lead and seemed to etch each of my sentences irrevocably in their minds.

I usually only saw Arnar shortly after sunrise when the shift started. However, late in the morning of the twelfth day, he joined me as I watched from a safe distance while the ship was launched.

"They leave the day after tomorrow," I said in a voice that sounded more wistful than I was comfortable with.

"And the crew is eager to finally set sail," he replied. "They seem to have enough discipline to ensure the venture won't be a disaster."

I nodded and took a deep breath. What I was about to say was something I had been thinking carefully about over the previous few days. "What if I were willing to review my position?"

He looked at me unsurprised. "Are you saying you would—might—go with them after all?"

I nodded.

"And that's the reason I saved one of the officers' cabins for you," Arnar said with a grin.

"I haven't completely changed my mind yet, though!"

"Hmm, that's up to you. But what made you . . . start to change your mind?"

I shrugged. "Most likely it's simply wanderlust. Besides, I find it hard to bear the thought that my friends will be exposed to those stinkers again without having me by their side."

"As I said, your bunk is waiting for you."

"Don't rejoice too soon, Arnar. First, I have to inform my family. And they won't approve. Cas certainly won't. My mother will get up in the middle of the conversation and leave the room without a word. And my father . . . well, I don't know how he'll react at all."

"Then sort that out first. The ship leaves the day after tomorrow at sunrise. I can arrange for you to be picked up two hours before that."

If someone was picking me up, I wouldn't have to worry about getting the car back to my parents, I argued to myself spuriously. I put that item on the pros side of my list. "Yes, that would be really good," I replied. "But please don't be disappointed if I can't bring myself to do it in the end."

He shook his head slowly. "No, don't worry about it. But if you do, we'll give your family all the support we can." He looked me urgently in the eyes. "Because, for this mission, we need you, Eva, to have a clear mind and a clear head. The same is true for you as for all the other participants. If you're not a hundred percent focused, you're of no help to anyone."

We said good-bye. Inwardly, I'd long since made the decision to join the trip. I wanted to support the recruits, I wanted to help Jens and Waltraud, and I wanted kick the stinking zombies' asses again. No matter how hard I tried to maintain a facade of normality, Cas seemed to sense my tension. She wouldn't leave my side and watched me with her saucer eyes. My heart threatened to burst at the thought of having to confront her with my decision.

We ate lunch, did homework, and rode our bikes to Holmsberg Lighthouse. Mariners appreciated its reliability when they sailed back into Reykjavík waters on stormy nights. The same was true for those who went out fishing. Since the seas had restocked, they didn't need to go far out to get a bountiful haul. On winter days, the fishing boats returned long after sunset, guided safely into the harbor by the beacon.

Back at home, I got the impression my parents had long since seen through me, but they didn't want to talk about it. My mother was silent and monosyllabic, as she always was when she disagreed with something. Her stiff posture spoke of undisguised disapproval. At dinner, my father was also taciturn. Plagued by my guilty conscience, I barely touched my food. I put Cas to bed as usual around eight o'clock. I lay beside her and read to her while she clung to me. But when she finally fell asleep, it was another hour before I dared break away from her embrace. I listened to her steady breathing, smelled her hair, and sang softly to myself even though she had long since drifted off. When the clock reached ten o'clock, I plodded downstairs. By now, I had gathered enough courage to tell my parents about my decision.

At this hour, they were sitting in the living room. By the light of the floor lamp, Father was browsing one of the books he had already read several times. Mother was connecting with her simple roots and was either knitting new clothes or mending worn-out ones—I couldn't tell which. I sat in the armchair in front of them, and I revealed that I was once again heading out into the wide world.

"Mom, Dad. Can you please take a break from reading and knitting? I need to talk to you. Mom, you don't have to throw your stuff down like that. You can't just leave now, can you? Mom! Please stay and talk to me, even if it you don't want to. *Mom!* I don't believe it . . ."

"Eva, let it go . . ."

"But, Dad! It's driving me crazy. She pulls this stunt every time. I can't talk to her like a normal adult when something doesn't suit her. And you just shrug. That's a great help. Thanks a lot!"

"Eva! What's wrong with you?"

"What do you think's wrong with me? It drives me nuts when she treats me so condescendingly. How have you stood it all these decades?"

"It's not about me right now. You've been acting strangely for weeks."

"Oh, Dad! You know I was asked to help with the preparations for the expedition to the Balkans. Because an enclave of three thousand people has been discovered in Albania."

"Yes. You haven't talked about anything else since. Have there been complications?"

"No, everything's gone more or less to plan. Today, the ship was launched. Tomorrow, it will finish loading, and it'll sail the following day."

"So?"

"I don't know whether . . . I told you I refused to go with them. But the longer I've been involved, the more personally invested I've become . . ."

"I still don't understand what you're getting at."

"Oh, you know very well—please don't take me for a fool. I've been on this island eight years now. Before Cas was born, I barely stayed in one place for six months, for years. It's not that I feel trapped. But then somehow . . . I do. Besides, Jens and Waltraud are there. Oh, I don't know, it was probably a stupid idea to even think about going away again. I probably just wanted to talk to you guys about it so you'd give me a piece of your mind and I'd be able to see things clearly and reasonably again."

"Hmm, but ultimately it's not that simple, is it?"

"I don't know, Dad. I just don't know."

"Frankly, I'm surprised we're only having this conversation now. I was expecting it much sooner. Don't look at me like that. I know what makes you tick. I know how hard it is for you to stay in one place for long periods of time. But there hasn't been any other way for the last few years."

"I already know that . . ."

"Please let me finish! That's just the way you are, always on the road. True, if circumstances demand it, you can turn it off—you have for eight whole years. But no one can run away from themselves without it destroying them."

"What are you trying to tell me, Dad?"

"Please don't put me in the position of having to make your decisions for you. I'm sure you understand what I just said."

"I'm not even sure I want to, though! After all, this is not a vacation; it's a war deployment . . . Cas could . . . Oh crap, I don't know what to do!"

"Oh, I think you do. I suspect you're too afraid of your own courage to say what has long been obvious to your mother and me."

"How . . . is it so obvious?"

"Obviously."

"But what about Cassiopeia?"

"What do you think will happen to her? Just because you're away for a few weeks? She's old enough to wean herself off you now. Mom and I will take care of her while you're gone."

"The question is more whether *I'm* ready for it."

"Well, that's an idea you'll have to come to terms with quickly."

"Hmm. Arnar did say you'd have whatever support you need."

"So, you see—everything's been thought of, and you can take part in the mission with a clear conscience."

"But aren't you afraid something might happen to me?"

"Well, after all you've been through and survived, I'm convinced there's not much that could bring you to your knees. It takes people like you to fight. Besides, your service saves lives—and makes Cas's world a little safer. Otherwise, there'll never be an end to it."

"Oh, Dad . . ."

"Don't cry, Eva . . . Just come back safe and healthy!"

"I can't stop right now. It's like a rock falling off my chest. What's Mom going to say about it?"

"Don't you worry about her. She guessed from day one that your involvement wouldn't be limited to the preparations."

"What a load of crap. Somehow, I imagined this conversation differently. And it turned out a thousand times better than I thought it would. Thank you, Dad."

"It's obvious. Just please take very good care of yourself out there—but that's what you're going to do anyway, so I'll spare you . . ."

"Cas? *Cas!* What are you doing up there? Why aren't you in your bed asleep?"

"What?" my dad asked.

"Dammit. Cas was on the stairs and overheard us. And I wanted to tell her in person."

"Oh, she'll be fine with it. As I said, it's long past time for her to spend a few days without you. It'll do her good. Go up and calm her down. I'll beard the lioness in her den and break the news to her."

"Dad?"

"Hmm?"

"Am I . . . a bad mother?"

"Oh God, what on earth do you mean, child? You've taken better and more intense care of your daughter over the last eight years than most people I've had the privilege of knowing in my life. Cas has turned out to be a wonderful girl. The only thing you need to do for her right now is give her some space to grow out from behind your shadow."

"Well, I just don't want her to hate me for it."

"There's no way around that. At some point, every child hates their parents. At least for a while. It's part of the weaning process. The sooner that starts, the sooner you'll get through it."

"But I . . ."

"That's enough, Eva. Stop feeling sorry for yourself. And get up there with your daughter."

"Okay. Thanks, Dad. Good night."

"Good night, dear. Give Cas a kiss for me, will you?"

"I will. Sleep tight."

Cas was lying in bed and turned her back on me as soon as she saw I was there. The room was softly lit by a string of lights. I lay down next to her and hugged her. "Mama will be back soon," I whispered in a desperate attempt to soothe her.

There was no need to beat around the bush, even though I didn't know how much of the discussion with my father she had overheard. Cas stayed silent and snuggled up to me. That was her way of giving me her approval.

"Grandma and Grandpa will take good care of you. And I'll be back before you know it."

Her hand sought mine. A firm pressure exhorted me to be quiet. I didn't need to say any more.

We spent the following day together, ignoring the fact that I would be gone for several weeks starting the next day. My mother must have worked things through with my father because she was more talkative than the night before.

For his part, my father didn't let anything show, but I was familiar with the dynamic between them. Once again, he had stepped into the breach for my sake and neutralized her displeasure.

A sea of anticipation and guilty conscience roiled within me. Almost in panic, I clung to the role of mother. At the same time, my adventurous heart, which had had short shrift in recent years, was rejoicing.

As best I could, I ignored my conflicting feelings. I forced myself to devote all my attention to Cas, as if it were possible to store it up for the time she would spend without me.

But she remained silent. I knew she wasn't showing her feelings and was closing herself off to the pain. I spent the last night by her side, crying for quite a while long after she had moved on to the land of dreams.

Two hours before the alarm on my wristwatch went off, I finally fell asleep. The short sleep was anything but restful, but my excitement drove me on. Without waking Cassiopeia, I slipped out, showered, and grabbed the duffel bag I had packed the day before. Avoiding the stairs that creaked, I descended to the first floor.

A light was on in the kitchen. Wearing a bathrobe over her nightgown, my mother was leaning against the countertop. In her hands, she held a coffee cup. A second one stood steaming on the table. The smell alone made me more alert.

"This one's for you," she said gently, as if to put an end to the tension between us.

"Thanks, I could really use that. Barely slept." I grabbed the cup and took a sip of the hot drink.

We were silent. It was not an uncomfortable silence. More of an unspoken mutual peace offering.

"Don't worry about Cas," she said at one point.

"Hmm," I muttered.

"Just make sure nothing happens to you while you're away."

"As I said, my job is only to coordinate the troops." I shrugged. "I don't need to get involved at all."

"Very good." She sipped at her cup. "It would be lovely if we could go sailing together again sometime. After you get back."

I had to grin. "Yeah, like we did in Grandpa's dinghy."

She nodded. "Those were the days." Her gaze went past me into the distance.

"How would you like it if we actually did it? We could sail around Iceland. Maybe over to Greenland," I suggested.

"I would love that."

"Well, now you have an extra task—find a suitable boat by the time I get back."

I saw her blink away her tears. "That's a good idea, Eva. Dad would be beside himself if he could sail close to the wind again. And I'm sure Cassilein will love it, too."

"Yes, but only if you stop calling her that."

We both laughed.

Through the kitchen window, I saw lights approaching. A vehicle stopped in the driveway.

"Thanks for the coffee, Mom. I have to go now." A lump in my throat, I went over to her and hugged her as she wrapped her thin arms around me. Then I left the house.

"Good morning," Arnar said as I got into the car. "Have you had any coffee yet?" There was a thermos in the center console.

"Yeah, but some more wouldn't do any harm today."

"Help yourself while it's hot."

I sipped it cautiously. "Have you been to the port yet?"

He nodded, running his hand over his tired face. "All night. It took us a little longer to finish loading the last of the supplies. But by the time we get to the port, everything will be shipshape."

"Any news from Sweden?"

"Just that the *Vasa* is on schedule."

"And Waltraud and Jens?"

"Still in Umeå. But they should be ready to go in the next few days. Are you looking forward to seeing them again?"

"And how! Even if I would have preferred the circumstances to be different." I took another drink of coffee. "But you can't have everything in life."

"How was it saying good-bye to your family?"

"Better than I hoped. But I still feel terrible."

"Why?"

I shrugged.

"Mainly because I'm leaving Cas behind. I don't usually care what people say about me. But if people called me a bad mother, that would bother me."

He snorted cheerfully. "What if you were the father?"

"What . . . then?" I replied, nonplussed.

"Well, would you be worrying about it as much?"

I shrugged again. "As a father, certainly, but people would probably be less likely to criticize me for my actions. It's more acceptable for a man to go out into the world to seek adventure."

"Well, you see. Why should it be any different in your case?"

"That's what a good friend would have said." I felt a little comforted.

We were approaching the brightly lit harbor. We unfastened our seat belts and got out after the car stopped.

We shook hands and said good-bye. Arnar wished us all luck, looked up at me, and waved. Standing at the railing, I returned his gesture. Then I went to the main mast. A young sailor I had met on the field excursions saluted awkwardly. I looked at her. My brain cast around for her name. She blushed when I didn't immediately return her greeting.

"You're Lífa, aren't you?" I asked.

"Yes, ma'am," she replied shyly and saluted again.

"There's no need for you to salute all the time. This isn't the U.S. Navy," I tried to joke.

She blushed even more.

To help her out of the awkward situation, I asked, "Do you know how I get to my cabin?"

I knew exactly where it was, but I felt it was my duty to give Lífa some small sense of achievement. She was twenty-four years old and would have far worse to deal with on this mission once we arrived at our destination.

She nodded but made no effort to move.

"Would you show me the way?" I asked very slowly.

Only then did she turn around and lead me through the ship. I followed.

I settled into the spacious cabin, lay down in the bunk, and waited for the journey to finally begin.

With the first rays of sunshine, we set sail. Farewell calls came up from the harbor. Once they had faded away, I went on deck. Under full sail, we were rushing south. The crew, although not yet completely familiar with the yacht, seemed confident. Unswervingly, they held their course. The length of the hull meant I could hardly feel the swells.

The driving wind caught my shoulder-length hair and forced me to tie it into a chignon.

The farther we got away from Iceland, the more excited I became. But I told myself that my sweaty palms were just a sign of my growing need for adventure. Or the anticipation of rekindling an old friendship. But in truth, my demons, tired of hibernation, were awakening.

Sometimes they whispered loudly, sometimes softly, fueling my hatred for the undead.

They didn't seem to care that I was putting myself in such danger that could cost me my life. They saw their chance had come to quench their thirst for revenge.

Once again, we were going into battle.

CHAPTER 7

UMEÅ

"Pass me the seventeen," Waltraud requests, lying on the roller board under the fuselage of a light aircraft. She pushes off with her heels and rolls out a bit. "I'm not getting anywhere with this right now." With her left hand, she holds out the socket wrench to Jens. The scarred tissue of her latissimus tenses whenever she stretches.

He takes the ratchet from her. Shortly afterward, she hears him rummaging in the toolbox before passing her the rotator wrench she wants. She thanks him and disappears under the plane again. Although the Gedore tubular won't fit, she gets the narrow seventeen in without any problems.

Rolling back into the daylight, she says, "Right, now you can give me the sheet."

He nods and grabs the curved aluminum sheet from the storage cart standing next to the plane. He also picks up a box of screws and a cordless screwdriver. Waltraud rolls back under and gets ready to close the opening to the propshaft. When she's done, she rolls out. She wipes the oil residue from her fingers with a cloth.

"Do you want to check the electrics again?" asks Jens.

Waltraud looks at the bulging skin on his face, which makes it difficult for him to move his lips when he speaks. She strokes his cheek with her fingertips. "No need," she replies, kissing him. "I'm sure it's working."

His unusual hyperflexibility had decreased greatly after their accident, but Waltraud has long since gotten used to that. Now he's merely about as flexible as most people.

Waltraud struggles free of her smudged coveralls, which may have been dove blue at some point. She's unlikely to need them again for the foreseeable future, so she tosses them carelessly over the back of the chair. She pulls a patched lumberjack shirt and gray sweatpants over her long thermal underwear. In the hangar's kitchenette, she fills the kettle, retrieves two mugs from the closet, and pours a concoction of dried stevia and mint leaves into them. She returns with the steaming mugs and hands one to Jens, who's getting out of his workshop clothes as well.

"Are you really sure you want to fly to southern Europe on only two thirds of the batteries?" he asks. His gaze wanders over to the forty-five-meter wing of the four-seater, its surface covered in gleaming solar cells.

"Yep," she replies confidently, sipping her tea. "Thorbjörn used forty percent at most on his night flights. Only that one time," she adds, "when the airstream pushed him off in the wrong direction—almost sixty. But he was sticking strictly to his route back then. We, on the other hand, can drift until the sun comes up again and then return to our route if necessary."

She can tell from the unbroken corner of his mouth that he is smiling. "Okay," she continues placatingly. "The batteries aren't the newest, but we checked them and weeded out the ones with the lowest power." She points to the corner of the hangar, where gray cuboid packs are piled up. "Even the test flight to Riga and back went well."

"We were flying during the day. We could have just switched over if circumstances . . ."

"Oh man, Jens, when did you become such a square?" she interrupts him. "Where's your sense of adventure?"

"You're acting like our lives have been boring as hell and devoid of adventure for the last ten years," he comments with amusement. "But so be it. You're right—the crate's half the weight now without all the batteries." He takes a big gulp and sets the cup down. "How about it? Feel like an adventurous trip?"

"That's the spirit," she replies perkily, finishing her tea.

The aircraft, stripped of its faulty batteries, can be pushed out of the hangar with ease. Since the small airport and its single runway were not intended to provide shelter for aircraft with the wingspan of an Airbus, this one had to be specially built. The unused area to the northeast of the main building was ideal for the purpose. In record time, almost overnight, they had built the hangar out of which they have just taxied the aircraft into the Scandinavian sun.

Waltraud has positioned herself—in a mirror image of Jens—next to the fuselage. The delicate structure under her hands looks fragile and, in fact, is. The surface of the flying wing is equipped with almost twenty-five thousand tiny solar cells, and the underside is covered with a thin plastic film. The aileron is made of gossamer mesh. The rest is an intricate latticework of cables, wires, microchips, and carbon and fiberglass components. All the components have been measured and cut to the last millimeter to save every superfluous gram of weight.

The five electric motors mounted at the rear of the plane, and which drive the propellers, have been custom-made for engineer Thorbjörn Eklöv's ambitious project. The retiree and amateur pilot, who wanted to break the Piccard-Borschberg world record of 2016, invested all his knowledge and most of his fortune into the prototype. His test vehicle had four seats and could carry up to fifty kilograms of luggage per passenger. After initial flights across the Baltic Sea and to Spitzbergen, he was on the lookout for interested parties to sponsor his little adventure. Just as donors became aware of the project, the pandemic broke out, making its way across Finland to Sweden in the fall of the same year. Thorbjörn Eklöv did not meet the fate of ninety percent of the Scandinavian population—he survived. Waltraud met him five years ago, after she and Jens had liberated Umeå with the Norwegian troops.

The following summer, when the north had been cleansed of the undead, she learned of Thorbjörn's project. He, physically depleted after many winters of deprivation, was unable to take matters in hand himself. However, he was pleased by Waltraud's enthusiasm. Nevertheless, it was to be two years before Waltraud returned to Umeå from her trip to the Mediterranean and resumed the aircraft project with Thorbjörn. They are now pushing along the result of this collaboration.

Squinting past the cabin, she spots Thorbjörn in the tower. Sometimes he volunteers to take on a shift or two on the radio. She waves quickly; he returns the greeting. "Thor's up there again," she says to Jens.

"Yeah, I see him, too. Did he spend the night there?"

She knows the question was meant as a joke. "A little distance from his project wouldn't hurt him," she confirms.

But she thinks she understands why he's so committed. *Apart from his marriage, it's all he has.*

At the start of the runway, they turn the plane. The old man waves again from behind the glass panes of the tower. The wind sock on the roof shows only a moderate north wind. Waltraud takes a deep breath and climbs into the cockpit. Jens is fastening his seat belt and putting on a headset. She looks around and locates hers on the shoulder rest. She then presses the main switch. With a barely audible hum, the aircraft comes to life. Lights flicker on.

Thorbjörn's voice sounds close to her ear. "Hello, you two, can you hear me? Over."

"Loud and clear," Waltraud answers. Once the lights in the cockpit show the machine is ready, she adds, "We're good to go. Over."

The conversation makes no sense since there's no air traffic anywhere. For Thorbjörn's sake, they still play the game every time. He sends them down the runway. Waltraud pushes the lever at her knee forward. The rotors turn faster and faster until the plane rolls forward with a gentle jerk. They reach the maximum speed of one hundred and twenty kilometers per hour with the lever halfway down.

Two hundred meters farther on, they are in the air. They rise in a long spiral until they are at the same height as the scattered clouds. The city diminishes below them, but the sea to the east and the forests to the west become larger and larger.

Because the cabin has neither pressure equalization nor heating, they stop climbing at one kilometer. If this were a real trip, they might have to fly twice as high and dress warmly beforehand since their leisure clothes wouldn't do them much good, despite their thermal underwear.

"Everything all right up there?" Thorbjörn's voice says in her headphones.

"Yes, all values are stable. The plane works perfectly. Once again, I must say that your bird is wonderful, Thorbjörn. And today, the view is fantastic. If you like, we'll come down and take you for a spin."

"That would be great, Waltraud. But I'm reporting in to give you a message."

"What's going on? Has Dennis been in touch?"

"Not since yesterday. But there's no reason to believe his Black Masks aren't doing well or that they won't stay on schedule."

"Then what's it about?"

"You've just been sent a message from France. I guess there's been a little change of plan."

"Uh-huh, and did they say what it was about?"

"Your final rendezvous point at Shkodër remains the same, but you're to make a stopover about four hundred kilometers north of there."

"Why's that?"

"A new team has agreed to participate in the rescue mission. They'll probably be joined by fighters from the former Yugoslavia who are gathering in Bihać.

"You're to coordinate the troop merger with them, the Black Masks, and Eva's team."

"Hmm, can't they do it themselves?"

"Well, from what I've been able to glean, it's not exactly straightforward."

Waltraud moans. "Oh man, always this Balkan—"

"It is not just that. Someone's smuggled zombies into the area."

"What do you mean, smuggled zombies?"

"I can't answer that question, I'm afraid, except to say that I assume some aerial reconnaissance would be handy for the troop movements. That's all I know. That's why you need to come down and talk to Miriam in person."

"Okay, Thor. We'll start to descend now. See you in a few minutes. Over and out."

He replies, "I'll hold the runway for you. Over and out." Waltraud can't help smiling at his words.

She switches frequencies and says, "What do you reckon?"

Jens shrugs. "It's not much different from the original plan. The only change for us is that we'll have to leave a little earlier. Our rations are packed, our weapons are ready. Other than that, there's nothing wrong with meeting some new people. What do you think?"

"Well," she says, "having more gunmen with us is no bad thing, to be sure. But here's hoping they keep their act together and don't shoot each other in the face."

"From what I've heard, they're getting pretty good at it now," he counters.

"Where did you hear that again?" she wants to know.

"Some merchant was telling stories from southern Europe the other day. Supposedly, he sailed to Zadar to sell his wares."

Lost in thought, she says, "Hmm." Then she leans into the angle of the wing, which is spiraling downward.

* * *

Two days later, they arrive on the airfield shortly before sunrise. Jens feels confident. The sky is partly overcast, but the cloud cover is low. It will be no problem to fly above it and make use of the plentiful solar power. They keep warm clothing handy in case turbulence or adverse winds force them to climb higher. They have often practiced putting these on in the confines of the cabin. But now, the plane needs to be pushed to its takeoff position. Jens looks ahead, spotting a figure on the runway. Thorbjörn is already waiting for them. Jens is not surprised. Even though the old man is smiling, he can see the melancholy in his face.

Yesterday they took him for a long spin. A three-hour trip, venturing across the Gulf of Bothnia, passing over Vaasa in Finland on the return flight, as well as some of Sweden's fir and birch forests, which explode with green in spring and have countless lakes. Thorbjörn, who seemed to have regained some of his vitality in the process, expressed his thanks through tears. "I didn't think I would ever get up in the air in it again. You have given me great joy. There is no one I would rather bequeath this treasure than you."

After landing, he patted the fuselage of the plane like the neck of a beloved horse. "May it bring you happiness wherever you may go." Another tear ran down his cheek. "But now I'll go home and leave you to pack. My Åsa has been complaining for weeks how little she sees me. She thinks I should set up a bed in the tower, I'm here so much. That will change now. But tomorrow I'll definitely come and see you off." He patted Waltraud on the shoulder, pinched Jens's good cheek, turned, and walked away.

As promised, Thorbjörn had appeared the next morning. As soon as he had disappeared inside the main building, they pushed the plane back into the hangar. They quickly stowed their carefully packed belongings and weapons in the rear. The length of the fuselage allowed one of them to take a nap during the flight if necessary. They placed the provisions and the water directly behind their seats.

Once they'd completed these tasks, they sat down at the table in the hanger, ate, and studied their route for the umpteenth time. They had marked the route they hoped to take on the map, including a single stopover in Visby on Gotland, which was reckless in Jens's opinion, not least in view of the lack of weather reports. Since they didn't have much knowledge of the situation in mainland Europe, they were less happy about further landings. If they wanted to fly over the entire continent in one go, they would have to rely on their battery power for a night in the air. In an emergency, there was always the option of landing in Brno, Graz, Vienna, or Zagreb and waiting for sunrise. They would need a sunrise like today's so they could take off without any problems.

Jens returns his thoughts to the present. *Thirst for adventure*, he thinks and shakes his head.

"What are you thinking about?" asks Waltraud.

"Nothing special. I'm really looking forward to our next Robinsonade," he replies sarcastically.

She ignores his tone, feigning surprise and whispering close to his lips, "Do you really mean that?"

After all these years, she can still make him breathless. The skin of his scarred hand is no different in color or texture from the skin on her neck, which he caresses tenderly. The few nerve endings that have fought their way back to the surface are enough to allow him to feel the warmth of her body. "Yes," he breathily replies, surprising himself by actually meaning it. But she has already turned her attention to Thorbjörn.

"Don't let me stop you," he calls out to them. "I just want to say a quick good-bye—and then hurry back before Åsa notices I've sneaked out."

"What about the control tower?" inquires Waltraud. "How are we supposed to take off without you?"

"We all know very well that that's unnecessary. You only went along with the game for my sake, so that I wouldn't feel completely superfluous. Now let's say good-bye, and off you fly."

"Thank you for everything, Thorbjörn. We'll take good care of your bird," says Waltraud, hugging the old man.

Then it's Jens's turn to say good-bye. "I hope we'll see each other again soon."

"Highly unlikely." The old man smiles. "You young people deserve a different life. Not here, where it's cold, and nights can last for weeks. The world is big—there are better places to grow old. Now, off with you before I change my mind and take the plane back."

Laughing, they move away.

Jens's heart is racing with excitement. He is actually looking forward to the task ahead. They get on board. With a hand signal, Thorbjörn sends them down the runway. They do a farewell lap for him before pointing the nose southward.

Jens breathes in and out deeply. His hand searches for Waltraud's. She takes it and looks into his eyes. He sees the same anticipation in them that he's feeling.

Once again, they're embarking on a journey into the unknown.

CHAPTER 8

DEPARTURE

Lejla had never flown before. Her hands were shaking with excitement. In the cramped cockpit, she poked Lucas unintentionally in the ribs with her elbow while trying to fasten her seat belt in the row behind Jens and Waltraud.

Since it was a prototype, the interior of the solar aircraft was spartan. Wiring harnesses ran along the open unclad skeleton, disappearing into the control console at the front and the fuselage at the rear. None of this instilled her with confidence in the machine's capabilities. She tried to convince herself otherwise. *Waltraud and Jens flew here from Sweden in one hop—everything will be fine. Just don't make a fuss.*

"Are you guys ready?" asked Jens.

"Just a minute," Lejla called out. She heard Lucas's buckle click, a second before her belt clicked into place, too. "Okay, we're ready to go."

Waltraud gave a thumbs-up. With four flicks of her wrist, she activated the electric motors. The vehicle trembled as the rotors began to turn.

On the Golubić sports airfield, built long before the apocalypse on the southeastern outskirts of Bihać, the aircraft gradually picked up speed.

Lejla took a deep breath. She thought about the morning the day before yesterday, when Waltraud and Jens had landed in the very place they were about to take off from. That morning, she had been sitting at breakfast with her grandparents, Lucas, and Tiz. She was sipping her first tea of the day when her father's radio trilled.

"Yes, what is it?" her father said.

"Just received word from the people you're waiting for. ETA is ten o'clock," a voice replied over the static.

"Good. Did you send them the coordinates of the airstrip in Golubić?"

The person on the other end answered in the affirmative.

"Okay." Tiz ended the call. Turning to Lejla and Lucas, he said, "So now we just have to let Backup know."

She and the Frenchman nodded.

Half an hour later, they were on their way to the hotel by the city park, which was located close to the center. In the parking lot in front of it, they found almost a dozen pedal quads and eight electric tandems that could be operated by several people at once. In addition, there were countless bicycles with and without electric motors. In the middle of everything stood three battered e-cars, their partially cracked windows gleaming in the morning sun behind welded grills. Across the street, in a make-shift shelter, horses were being groomed. The transportation belonged to the armed forces that had recently arrived. Everything was ready for departure.

Hardly anyone had expected such a huge response to Tiz's request for help. So it had taken longer to procure and distribute appropriate quantities of ammunition, weapons, food, water, and clothing. Now all they were waiting for was confirmation from Zadar that there were enough ships to take them to Shkodër by the fastest route.

Backup's report that no more undead had been detected in the area allowed life to return to normal outside the walls around the city center.

For the new arrivals, this meant a little more comfort, as they could move out of their crowded quarters into some of the empty apartments in other parts of the city. Important guests like Backup, on the other hand, were accommodated at the hotel. Lejla, Tiz, and Lucas climbed the three steps into the lobby.

To the man at the reception, her father said, "We'd like—" He faltered, as if he were not sure how to make the request.

"To see the person in the black robe?" the receptionist finished for him.

Tiz nodded.

"Do you want me to phone ahead, or do you just need the room number?" the hotel clerk asked.

"Both," Tiz said harshly. The receptionist merely smiled back. Lejla blushed with embarrassment. *Will I ever stop being ashamed of my father?*

She should have been used to his embarrassing behavior by now. But she still wanted to sink into the ground every time he acted up.

Once the receptionist had told them the room number, they climbed the stairs to the third floor. Lejla knocked. Shortly afterward, the door opened. Backup was standing in the doorway—dressed in black, of course.

"Oh, it's you. Good morning. Please come in."

The three of them accepted the invitation.

"How far along are your preparations?"

"We're as good as done," Tiz explained. "Today and tomorrow, we'll distribute the rest of the equipment, and everyone will leave for Zadar the day after tomorrow."

Backup nodded, as if signing off on the schedule.

"We're here for a different reason, though."

Backup looked him at him expectantly.

"The two people we're expecting from Scandinavia should be landing in an hour."

"Where?" Backup's voice was hoarse.

"Four kilometers outside town," Tiz replied.

"Then we've no time to waste," Backup said, grabbing the cloak and leading them hastily out to the parking lot. Tiz talked to the watch commander, who assigned them two pedal quads. They got on in twos.

"D'you know why Backup got so nervous in the hotel room?" asked Lucas, when Lejla had maneuvered her vehicle out of the parking space, and they were out of earshot.

"Backup seemed more excited than nervous to me," she countered. "I suspect Backup knows the people who are headed this way. He implied as much when we first got word of their arrival. If there's a backstory, I think we're about to hear it."

Lucas nodded. Following her father, Lejla turned left.

Tiz, Backup, Lejla, and Lucas arrived half an hour before the flight was scheduled to land. They parked their vehicles at the end of the runway access road. They walked between crumbling hangars onto it, inspecting every square meter. Armed men secured a wide cordon around the area.

"Can I ask you a question, Backup?" said Lucas, scanning the sky for the plane.

"Sure," came the confused-sounding reply.

"These people we're waiting for now . . . have you met them before?"

Backup gave a loud, raucous, throaty laugh.

The eyes of the figure in black shone. "You bet. If you want, I can tell you a few tales until they arrive. I've been through a lot with those two," he croaked melancholically. "Meanwhile, we can double-check the runway. Not that a single pothole has been overlooked."

Over the next half hour, Lejla, Tiz, and Lucas learned how the story of Backup and the guests they were expecting had played out.

"So, it's safe to say that I've met them before. Or at least, I once knew who they used to be," Backup concluded the narrative.

In the meantime, they had reached the end of the runway. The people who had been charged with repairing it the previous day had done a good job.

The strip of field, which had not been used for almost a decade, was free of bushes and creepers. The pastures around it had been mowed, the molehills leveled. It resembled a golf course, like the ones there had been pre-apocalypse. An improvised wind sock indicated a weak breeze from the south.

Tiz glanced at his wristwatch. "You should be able to see them in a moment, if their calculations were correct."

"There's no doubt about that. They'll be here on the dot," Backup replied. Lejla saw her father nod, although his expression was skeptical.

"Come on." She led Lucas to the nearby river. "This will make the wait seem shorter." The bank was sandy and fell away gently. They took off their shoes. Barefoot, they waded into the crystal clear water.

"It's a pity we didn't take bathing suits. I feel like swimming," said Lejla.

"It's pretty icy, though," Lucas remarked.

"At first. But after a few minutes, everything goes numb, so you won't mind a bit of cold."

"Ha, ha! Are you actually always this funny?"

Before she could give a sarcastic answer, she heard a whistle. She looked over at her father, who was beckoning with one hand and pointing at the sky to the north with the other. She looked where he was pointing. Five seconds later, she spotted a short black line silhouetted against the blue. It grew longer and longer until, half a minute later, Lejla could make out the outline of the plane.

"They're here," she said—redundantly, because Lucas must have spotted it as well. The hum of the propellers was clearly audible now.

They slipped on their shoes and joined Tiz, who was sitting in the grass next to the runway. Backup was walking up and down right next to him, his hood pulled low over his face. Lejla wondered what the hood was all about. But before she got around to asking, the plane touched down.

Waltraud looked at the console again. All values normal, the headwind was no obstacle to their landing. During the night, they had flown over Croatia, which had used up eighty-seven percent of their battery capacity. But since the sun was shining overhead, they had been able to regain sixty percent.

She had spent the final hours before sunrise dreaming in the sleeping bag. They were the kind of dreams you immediately forgot when you woke up. Only an unpleasant afterimage remained. With the first rays of sunshine, she relieved Jens at the helm, who then crawled into the pre-warmed sleeping bag. Three hours later, it was time to wake him up. In the cold, two thousand meters above sea level, her breath came in white clouds.

"Jens?" she called back.

"Hmm?" he replied.

"You can start waking up. We'll be there soon."

"Just five more minutes," he mumbled sleepily.

"All right," she allowed with a grin.

Ten minutes later, he was sitting next to her, brushing his teeth with one hand. In the other, he held a water bottle. He took a sip, gargled, and spit out the contents through the small side window. They were flying over long mountain ranges separated by broad, forested valleys. An emerald river meandered from the south.

"Can you see the runway yet?" he inquired.

"Yes. If you follow the course of the river, around the last quarter. Three fingers south of town."

Jens nodded. "Now I can see it, too."

"I'm making the approach," she warned. The sound of propeller blades in the air died away. Waltraud knew they were still working and continuing to provide lift, but the frequency of their rotations was so diminished that they were almost sailing toward the ground. At the edge of the runway, she spotted people looking up at them.

"That'll be our welcoming committee," she said to Jens as soon as they were within a hundred meters. Receiving no reply, she looked over at him. He was staring intently straight ahead and didn't seem to hear her. "Jens, are you okay?"

He pointed ahead. "There . . . The figure in black."

"Yeah, the one with the cowl and the hood?" She shrugged, smirking. "Did they bring in Jedis for backup?"

"The way that person's moving . . . Their posture . . . looks . . . familiar."

"We'll soon find out," she said skeptically. "Hold on! Landing in ten, nine . . ." At the end of the countdown, the plane touched the ground, bounced briefly, and taxied straight ahead. Waltraud gently applied the brakes. As soon as they came to a stop, she exhaled, undoing her seat belt. Before she could say anything, Jens had jumped out. She followed him out into the open. He didn't wait for her but walked straight over to the people waiting a hundred meters away. The hooded figure didn't move. Behind her, three more people were waiting. Jens stopped five meters in front of them. Waltraud hurried after him and took his hand in hers. Then he introduced her.

The young woman and the man of about the same age, who were in the background, smiled kindly when Jens called his and Waltraud's names. The hood bowed. The gloved hands moved upward, revealing the weather-beaten face. Sudden joy flashed through Waltraud. Tears welled up in her eyes. Jens uttered a sound of surprise.

Backup just grinned and said, "Hello, you two. It's been ages."

"Let's give them some privacy," Tiz whispered, walking toward the pedal quads. Lucas and Lejla followed him, while the trio behind them hugged each other and let out delighted cries.

"They'll have a lot to talk about," Lejla said.

Around twenty minutes later, they were ready to head into town. The plane was emptied before being maneuvered to the southern end of the runway. Jens and Waltraud took their belongings, including their weapons, with them.

"If it's all right with you, we'll take a step back today," Backup said to Tiz. "We've been out of touch for years, and we need some time to ourselves. I know it's not great timing—just before we're due to head out tomorrow. With regard to that, I can tell Waltraud and Jens our plan later today."

Lejla's father nodded. "Do what you think is right. But let's go back now. I still have a lot to do."

Lucas wondered why Tiz had wanted to come along at all if he was so busy elsewhere. He behaved very differently from his own father, who was in a similar position of leadership. Outside the hotel, Tiz said a quick good-bye before hurrying away. Lucas and Lejla exchanged small talk with the arrivals before Backup whisked them into the hotel for the rest of the day.

Since Lucas and Lejla found themselves without a task, they decided to help the Newgoslavian troops with the final preparations. They met Tiz again in the old movie theater, which served as a weapons and ammunition store. Although everything was going according to plan, Lucas noticed an inner tension in him, worse than usual. Every hour, he called the marina in Zadar, which repeatedly assured him the ships would arrive the next day as agreed, loaded with supplies for the crossing. In two days, they would definitely be ready to set sail. But that did not seem to be enough for Tiz. He instructed the guards to double- and triple-check all volunteers, and he checked them himself. He kept harassing individuals if they were going too slow or too fast for him and could not immediately tell him which order they were following.

By the evening, Lucas had exhausted his patience. He screwed up his courage and asked Tiz outright, "I don't understand why you're panicking. We've completed all the tasks, so there is nothing in the way of our departure. But you're communicating stress as if everything's going wrong. Can you tell me what the problem is?"

The look on Tiz's face told him that he was suppressing one of his choleric outbursts. When he was sure he could halfway control himself, the Newgoslavian said, "You know, fighting the undead out there is extremely dangerous. But it's kind of calculable. You weigh whether you have enough people and enough resources to take out the next zombie mob. If the risk is too great, you don't do it. Otherwise, you attack them. Simple math. But this time, it's different. We're also dealing with people who are targeting my daughter. Maybe me, too, but that's less important. I can't tell you if any of those hundreds of people"—he indicated the troops with an outstretched hand—"some of whom I've never seen before, are out to kill her. And she'll be among them from the day after tomorrow. I have to try to eliminate any risk to her. Do you understand now?"

Lucas nodded slowly. "If it makes you feel any better," he said, looking Tiz in the eye, "I won't leave her side. No matter what happens.

Zombies or regulars, I don't give a shit—I'll flatten anyone who gets too close to her."

Tiz sniffed. He looked at Lucas for a long time, as if he could tell from his eyes whether he was speaking the truth. Despite the discomfort he felt, Lucas maintained eye contact. The Newgoslavian put a hand on his shoulder, nodded approvingly, and walked away. Lucas was left somewhat perplexed.

The next day, after he and Lejla had assured each other several times that there was nothing more to do, they met Waltraud, Jens, and Backup, who had just finished breakfast in the hotel restaurant. As they had with Backup, they hit it off right away. Lucas regretted that they could only eat unseasoned food before the mission to improve their chances of escaping the zombies' sensitive sense of smell. After all, the culinary delights he had previously discovered in Bihać were worth sharing with his new friends.

They spent part of their time together poring over a map. When they took off tomorrow, an hour after sunrise, the volunteers would head toward Zadar in a convoy. Waltraud and Jens, on the other hand, would monitor them from the air. At their destination, ships would be waiting after the mission—if it was successful—to take the escapees far away from the place of their ordeal. To the north, Biograd was standing by, to the south, Corfu. However, they would not confront the survivors with these options until the operation was completed.

It would have been just as pointless to decide all the tactical details without consulting the troops from Iceland and Scandinavia. They would have to wait until they were all together in the waters off Albania.

The next morning, the time had finally come. Lucas had only had a little sleep, in the last few hours before sunrise. Nevertheless, he felt alert. He knew this was due to the adrenaline coursing through his body. Before Lejla had even crawled out of bed, Lucas dressed and headed for the hotel. He knocked on Backup's door, which promptly opened. Jens stood in front of him. In the room behind, Waltraud was just pulling on a T-shirt. He saw burn scars on almost every uncovered part of her body.

"Hello, Lucas," Jens greeted. "What brings you to us so early?"

"Hi. I thought of something I wanted to ask you. Can I come in?"

"Go ahead," the Dutchman replied.

"Where's Backup?" asked Lucas in surprise once the door had slammed shut behind him.

"Backup set out long ago to identify potential traps along your route. If there's anything fishy going on anywhere, we'll know about it right away."

"But that wasn't the deal," Lucas said skeptically.

Jens took a handy radio set from behind his back. "We thought it'd be safer to keep that part of the plan quiet. These days, you never know—do you?"

"You mean the attack on Lejla and me?"

Jens confirmed, "Yes. But tell me, what brings you to us?"

"Then I assume you've also heard about the attack in Zadar?"

Again, the Dutchman nodded. Lucas continued, "Lejla's father may be strange and, yes, a difficult person. But he's so worried about her. He fears it might happen again. Possibly on the way to Zadar. That's why I wanted to ask if it would be possible for her to fly with you?"

Jens's gaze drifted over to his companion. "What do you think?"

She shrugged. "Sure, why not. Three people and some luggage for five hours in the air won't be a problem. Besides, we're expecting a sunny day." Waltraud looked at Lucas. "Would you like to come, too?"

Caught off guard, he replied, "Um, I'd love to."

"Then get your things and fetch Lejla. We'll leave in half an hour."

"All right," he confirmed and hurried out of their room.

He found Lejla at her grandparents' apartment, already dressed and chewing on a roll. "Um, I don't think that's a good idea," he said, glancing at her breakfast.

"What? Where have you been?" she replied with her mouth full.

"I've arranged alternative transportation for us. We're flying with Waltraud and Jens."

"Why would you do that? And couldn't you have asked me first if I even wanted to?"

"Sorry, there wasn't time. I only thought of it fifteen minutes ago. I was just with them. Waltraud said it would be all right."

"You want me to fly in that thing? With you?"

"Yeah, why not?"

"You're braver than I thought."

But Lucas had already recognized the adventurous twinkle in her eyes. Ten minutes later, they met Waltraud and Jens in the parking lot. Lejla dismissed a driver who was supposed to take them to the plane on the pedal quad and asked her to inform her father about the short-notice change of plan. Then she got behind the wheel herself.

"Just so you know," she explained as everyone pedaled along, "I've never flown before."

"Then I hope your stomach is made of steel—or at least that you didn't eat breakfast," Jens said.

"I ate a jam roll. And drank a cup of tea."

"Let's see if you can keep that down, then." The Norwegian grinned at her from the passenger seat.

Half an hour later, they were sitting in the loaded plane. Once everyone was strapped in, Waltraud started the engines.

The vehicle rose doggedly into the air, climbing ever farther northward.

"Is it true that you once pushed Backup off the roof of a nine-story hotel?" asked Lejla. They were nine hundred feet above the ground by now, she could tell from the cockpit display.

"Hey, I saved our lives that time," the pilot defended herself. "Besides, he volunteered."

Jens laughed. Then he switched on the radio. "I'll ask what's going on down there."

Leaving the smell of human perspiration behind once again brought enormous relief. After all the years of resistance, I was practiced at suppressing the call—the mixture of gluttony and wild reproductive instinct that incessantly tried to overcome my reason. To turn this body into a lethal zombie machine and open the floodgates of the disease to the world of the healthy.

But I won't cave in.

The human part of myself has developed a daring way of dealing with all the conflicting emotions that constantly rise in me. This has been the only way of allowing me to relax, at least briefly. In order to be able to work off the frustration that is "not mine," the hatred of all living things within a given area that is "not mine," I eliminated the undead whenever I came across them. But that only silences the voices like them inside me for a short time.

Oh, how depressing it was to stand at dawn over the cadavers that had been executed in the deserted house by the young couple. To discover the dead bodies without being able to single-handedly jab a spearhead through their eye sockets. Without being able to crush their skulls with a single punch of my infected arm. I felt cheated. Deprived of the opportunity to destroy their last scraps of life. To liberate them and give myself the morbid satisfaction of getting rid of unwanted siblings. So I was left only to look at their rotting corpses, which even the wild animals were giving a wide berth.

The radio on my hip buzzed. Silently, I thanked it for the distraction. "Backup here," I said croakily, hoping my tone didn't betray my inner struggle. But I had become adept at masking it.

"Jens here," my old friend said. "What's the situation down there?"

When I heard his voice, I couldn't help grinning. The gray sky of my thoughts gave way to a Mallorcan blue. "The first quarter of the route is safe. Have you already left?"

"We just took off. If you spot us just above you, let me know."

I agreed.

We signed off.

A modified e-bike, which had been my faithful companion for two years, stood on the road. Depending on the incline and surface conditions, it could go up to forty-five kilometers per hour. The three batteries, two of which were mounted on the frame and one on the luggage rack, covered an average range of a hundred and twenty kilometers. Only the charging times left much to be desired; it could take up to six hours depending on the voltage of the power supply. However, a built-in generator ensured they charged when I rode downhill. I climbed on and headed south.

Five minutes later, I cycled past the trap of felled spruce that Sanel's troop must have pushed into the ditch on their way back.

I passed the spot cautiously. But nothing moved. It smelled like a living forest, where spring was coming. Minutes later, I heard a humming noise above the treetops, coming closer and closer. I looked through the canopy and spotted the delta-shaped glider in the sky, probably carrying my friends.

Two hundred meters farther on, the forest gave way to meadows on both sides of the path. My black clothing was undoubtedly easy to spot on a road bleached by the elements. "You're right over me," I radioed up. The plane descended and flew a tight loop at thirty meters. I waved. The wingtips waggled in response. Then the plane glided away. For half an hour, I followed its flight across a sky dotted with clouds.

The smells that drifted over to me during the ride continued to testify that the area was deserted. There was no change either on the main road or on the freeway before the Velebit mountains. At the entrance to the tunnel, I took my spear out of the holder on my back. I was hoping at least for an ambush at this point, but I was disappointed.

The fact that the battery indicator had dropped to two percent by the middle of the tunnel bothered me far less. Its capacity increased minutes later with every downhill bend I negotiated.

I reached Zadar three hours ahead of the convoy. It was early afternoon when I rolled in to the marina, which was easy to find from the old road signs. A lively hullabaloo prevailed there. Hawkers were obviously waiting impatiently for the arrival of the troops to get rid of at least some of their goods. Dozens of ships were moored at the quay, ready to leave with the first rays of sunlight the next morning. Jens, Waltraud, Lejla, and Lucas were standing on a jetty, watching for me.

They pressed a water bottle into my hand as soon as I dismounted in front of them. Only then did I notice how thirsty I was.

"And you're sure you won't be exposed to any danger aboard your ship?" Jens asked the Newgoslavian.

"Yes, definitely. I can rely on the crew a hundred percent, at least," returned Lejla.

Jens nodded. "In that case, we'll move on with Backup. The troops from Northern Europe arrived in Corfu the day before yesterday," he said. "We'll use the five days until your arrival to discuss possible courses of action with them."

Everyone agreed. We said good-bye. Lucas and Lejla went toward their blue-painted ship. Before following Jens and Waltraud, I drank the bottle dry. The pedal quad got us to the lonely airport of Zadar in barely half an hour. Minutes later, we were rising into the sky. Here above the clouds everything seemed so calm, so harmless, so far from death and destruction. It awakened in me a feeling of security I had not felt for a long time.

CHAPTER 9

REDEMPTION

On the last night before the long-planned deployment, the stars twinkled above us. Waves splashed against the ship's hull. In the company of Jens, Waltraud, and Backup, I sat aboard the Icelandic ship, wrapped in a blanket against the night chill. Someone from the crew had provided us with a small fire pit that radiated additional warmth. Long conversations were followed by minutes of silence, when we stared into the flames, lost in thought. Lejla, Tiz, Lucas, and Lena had gone to their teams earlier in the evening, to brief them for the upcoming mission. I thought about the past week, since Waltraud, Jens, and Backup's early morning landing on a dirt road near Hamallaj. I had brought them to my ship by rowboat, and they had settled into two of the vacant cabins. The couple had not filled in Backup or me before they arrived, so we weren't prepared for a reunion. Their surprise had succeeded, and the spark of friendship quickly blazed again. My joy was just as great, even if the cynic in me was immediately on the lookout for the next stroke of fate that would ruin my mood again.

We used the remaining days until the arrival of the Newgoslavian troops to bring each other up to date. In the first evening after our work was done, we met up again, and I got the impression I wasn't the only one feeling a touch melancholy. Backup, Waltraud, and Jens let me speak first, and I wondered why. They certainly would have had more to tell than I did. Did they want to hear about Patrick's last days and hours so that at least his spirit could keep us company? This idea comforted me in my sense of loss, which had become more intense around the old crew.

Backup's relationship with Patrick had been the strongest after mine. His grief over the fate of a good friend was almost physically palpable. After such a long time, however, Backup had become much more withdrawn, more easily irritable, and more weighed down by thought. After hearing my story, though, the metamorphosis was more than understandable to me.

But Patrick's absence was not the only cause for gloom. Franca was also missing from our circle. Backup reported that she hadn't been seen since her abduction in Berlin. There weren't even any rumors about her whereabouts, so we could only speculate about whether she was still alive.

The fact that I had a child gave all three of them huge delight. They bombarded me ceaselessly with questions about Cassiopeia and obviously wanted to meet her. "Whenever you come to Iceland," I affirmed.

Soon, members of our allied troops had heard about our storytelling sessions and gathered on the deck of our ship to listen to them. But nothing in the world could have prepared me for what I experienced on the fourth evening. We had just been talking about our time together in Mallorca. During Waltraud's description of her experiences in a hotel on S'Arenal, I noticed a young Frenchwoman watching me. I wondered why she was staring at me like that and whether we knew each other from somewhere.

Before I could talk to her, she got up and left the ship, disappearing for almost half an hour. I had already forgotten her when she was right there in front of me, holding something wrapped in an old plastic bag.

Out of breath, she held out the package to me and said, "I believe this is yours."

I looked at it in amazement, flipping back the faded newsprint cover that seemed to contain a book. At the beginning, the lines were neatly written in ballpoint pen, but the last pages were hastily scribbled in pencil. Even before my brain took in what she had handed me, my knees buckled. I recognized my own handwriting. I was vaguely aware that it was now Lena's turn to tell her story to the large group, so I took the opportunity to leaf through my old diary in amazement.

"You are the Eva who wrote this, though, aren't you?" asked the young woman.

My voice failed me. All I could do was nod.

"I thought so," she continued. "And when you talked about a Patrick, I was sure of it."

"What's that?" exclaimed Jens curiously.

"It's my old diary from the early days of the pandemic," I croaked as soon as I was able. "Where did you get it?"

"My father found it nearly ten years ago. In an abandoned car. I thought you might want it back."

"Oh. You dear thing," was all I was able to say. Silently I held it out to her.

But she refused. "No, it's yours. I know it by heart anyway. As a teenager, I admired you for what you experienced and how you fought the zombies. You were almost like superheroes to me. It motivated me to become active myself and to take up the fight against these creatures. That's why I always had it with me," she added, smiling sheepishly.

I hugged her with gratitude before she sat back down in her chair.

"Is there anything in there about Patrick?" Backup chimed in.

I nodded.

"Read it to us, please. I'm curious to know what mischief the guy got up to before he got on my nerves."

Despite the distressing events described in the book, which I didn't really want to be reminded of, I pulled myself together. I read to them until late in the night.

Over the next few days, we worked out a plan to combine our different troops in the most effective way. Twenty kilometers south of the intended deployment point, we brought my greenhorns together with the small team from western Europe and the Scandinavian Black Masks, where they underwent further training. True to their name, the Scandinavians hid their faces behind balaclavas during combat. Otherwise, they wore a combination of rugged civilian and military clothing that showed evidence of their many previous engagements. Besides a few firearms, most of them had swords and long-handled hammers, which they wielded with frightening strength and precision.

Unfortunately, the western European unit that had been waiting for our arrival off Corfu had only a small number of fighters. On the other hand, some of them had detailed knowledge of the terrain, which was a huge advantage.

The extra drills yielded positive results after only three days. The self-confidence of the Icelandic volunteers increased, as became clear in the practice fights. They struck more accurately and had more discipline in stressful situations. Their ability to respond to and follow orders improved, which would be a matter of life and death on the field.

My confidence in the success of the proposed rescue mission grew every day. And when the convoy of seven ships with Newgoslavian troops appeared, I had scarcely any more doubts. The convoy was led by a three-master with a huge spinnaker, in whose hull were stored enough weapons to fight a war, as they let us know.

From the very beginning, I remained true to my resolution to be only an observer. I stayed in the background while the leading members of the various parties on board the *Sinji Galeb* sat down together at a table to plan for the landing and further action.

Waltraud and Jens spoke for the Black Masks, who had now adopted my charges. The Newgoslavian leader, Tiz, brought his daughter and a young Frenchman on board, representing the western European troops. For two days, hunched over maps, they went over possible scenarios until, on the second afternoon, they brought the discussions to an end and went off to brief their forces.

They had decided on a very simple tactic. Each of our sailing ships had at least five lifeboats capable of carrying between eight and twenty-two people. Under cover of night, we would row them up the Buna River, landing at dawn on the southwestern outskirts of Shkodër. Dividing into three teams, we would approach the zombies' area from the south, east, and north before the sun even rose. The southern and eastern units were given the task of luring out the undead, thus paving the way for the northern team to enter the factories. The rest of the plan was relatively simple—kill as many zombies as possible with the least possible casualties and rescue the maximum number of people.

Provided the mission was successful, we would be able to quickly remove the wounded and those most in need of help in boats. The fittest would have to make the thirty-kilometer walk, escorted by armed men, to Velipojë, where our ships would be waiting to take them to a safe place.

Jens and Waltraud offered to observe the troop movements from the air, and this was unanimously agreed upon. I was given the honor of accompanying them. Backup had other goals to pursue, which were not discussed.

"Did you speak to your sister in the end?" Lejla's voice whispered through Lucas's headphones. He had to suppress a laugh because of the feigned casual tone in her voice. He now knew the Newgoslavian well enough to interpret this behavior as an attempt to mask her nervousness. She was riding in one of the boats ahead of him and impossible to pick out in the gloom of the cloud-darkened twilight. In contrast to the open sea, the sky above them here on the river was overcast. The cloud cover absorbed the starlight that would otherwise have betrayed them. But it was enough to enable helmsmen with night vision devices to find their way.

Lucas wanted to conserve his batteries though, so he left his switched off. Sitting in their respective dinghies, they advanced deeper inland. By his reckoning, they were only half an hour from landing.

The night was almost silent. Since it was cool, no insects were chirping, but scattered wolf howls, a common sound in the southern Balkans, were carried to them over the cold air. Occasionally, Lucas heard oars being carefully dipped into the water.

"No, I haven't talked to Lena yet," he whispered back. "Have you?"

"When was I supposed to do that? I barely got to see her. Besides, you promised."

"I'll do it as soon as we're through here. Now shut up, or do you want the stinkers to hear us?"

"Don't deflect, Frenchie. You agreed to set me up on a date with your sister. And I insist on it."

"Stop bugging me," Lucas replied cheerfully. He guessed more than saw the puzzlement on the faces of his team, which turned toward him at those words. "Take good care of yourself when we're out there, okay?" he added.

Her tone was serious. "You, too, Frenchie." Then she went quiet again.

He concentrated on the impending landing. Soon he would leave the boat and make an arc around the city center to reach the former industrial area. His destination was the east end of Shkodër, while Lejla would lead her unit to the city from the south. These were the areas least controlled by the undead, as he knew from Nesha. Backup, on the other hand, planned to work alone, trying to locate the phenomenon known as the anomaly. About anything else that might follow, Backup had refused to comment. The Black Masks were given the task of providing passage to and across the bridges for the escapees, as well as securing the landing site until the escapees arrived. Then they would form the rear guard, protecting their escape from the undead—provided any of the latter survived the invasion.

The closer they got to the landing point, the more Lucas's inner calm gave way to the tension that gripped him before every mission. He felt his heartbeat pounding in his jugular. His palms began to sweat. He checked the drop lever of his weapon with his thumb and released the safety. Seconds later, the boat slid over sandy ground. Immediately, he activated his night vision, swung his feet into the ankle-deep water, and ran. On dry land, he paused until his small main team had gathered around him. Ramona, Angela, Argiris, and Matteo were there this time, too. Their faces glowed green behind their night vision goggles, looking strangely familiar, as if he had just experienced déjà vu. They nodded, indicating they were ready. He would be leading the entire unit, which consisted of dozens of similar teams. Lucas set off at a run.

They crossed an abandoned freeway construction site. The next moment, they were standing by the backyards of the first of the city's houses. Lucas bent over to create a smaller target and aimed his gun. His steps set a brisk rhythm, but at the same time, he scanned everything ahead of him. They were to advance to the industrial area without much ado, avoiding violence so as not to raise the alarm prematurely. Once they had freed the prisoners, however, there would be no reason to spare the zombies. But first, he had to find his way there.

Since the street names at intersections and house addresses were indecipherable in the darkness, Lucas would have to trust his compass until he could follow the position of the sun. But although it wouldn't rise for another hour, the eastern sky was already growing lighter.

Lucas peered around the corner. The picture he saw was like every other city he had seen in the past four years. The achievements of human civilization were rotting away. Nothing was stirring, living or undead. With a wave of his hand, he ordered the rear guard to advance. Angela and Matteo did as instructed, securing the next intersection before beckoning to him, Ramona, and Argiris. The rest followed at a distance of twenty meters. In this manner, they worked their way forward block by block.

After three hundred meters, Lucas wondered when the first undead would cross their path. When they still hadn't met any resistance fifteen minutes later, he began to suspect that something was very wrong.

The day before, Lejla had flown over the mission area with Lucas, Waltraud, and Jens. Without attracting attention, they had glided through the air without engine power at a great height, reconnoitering the city. She recognized many of the factories from Nesha's recordings and the videos and photographs the young Albanian had smuggled out. Lejla sketched out the major streets on a notepad, marking prominent buildings, intersections, and parks that would serve as landmarks.

She now led her hundred soldiers across one of the intersections. They moved forward with discipline, taking street after street. They were now only two kilometers from their destination, which Lejla hoped to reach in half an hour. *We're making good progress*, she mused. *Much too good for my taste.* She distrusted the unexpected quiet. At the latest, she'd firmly expected to encounter the undead by the time they were halfway there. But they had passed this point without incident. Five hundred meters farther on, and still nothing had happened.

But all at once, the mood changed. Muffled gunshots sent her spinning around. Around fifty meters behind, someone was firing. She could clearly make out the muzzle flashes in the twilight. Lejla activated her radio. "What's going on back there?" she said into her throat mic.

"Enemy contact. We've found a nest," was the reply. The fire continued. "A big one, it looks like."

"Are you okay?"

"Yes, actually. But there are really a lot of them."

"What do you mean by a lot?" She had assumed that, first of all, she'd encounter a smaller number, and that fighting them would attract more zombies, which was what had happened on most of her previous missions. They'd almost never been surprised by a larger group. Suddenly, a chill ran down Lejla's spine. *Can it be an ambush?* Shots were still being fired. Frantically, she turned around and looked ahead. Around ten meters away, shadowy figures were running toward her. *Damn it,* she cursed silently and fired. If the undead trapped them on this street with its high walls around the courtyards, things wouldn't look good. Emphatically and precisely, she ordered, "We're not far from the target. Follow me!" Lejla switched her weapon from serial fire to single shot. Which team was closest to theirs; who could get to them the fastest? Her father was leading the unit to the north. He was too far away. Lejla selected Lucas's frequency. "Frenchie, can you hear me?"

His answer came through promptly. "Yes. Are you okay?" he whispered.

"No, the undead are suddenly flitting all over the place here." She darted into a side alley and took out two stinkers.

"It's much too quiet for that where we are. I don't like it. How far are you from the deployment site?"

"Maybe another kilometer. Fuck, there are more and more of them."

After a short pause, he said, "Listen, according to my map, in two hundred meters you'll come out at a traffic circle where we can meet up with you. You just have to hang on for ten minutes."

"But that's not the plan that was agreed."

"Screw the plan; we have to improvise now."

"Okay, see you in a minute." Lejla glanced back. The discipline of her unit had not diminished. They were following her closely.

She took off at a run. Three minutes and two empty magazines later, she stepped onto the multilane traffic circle with the planted central island that Lucas had talked about. Countless cars were parked close together, forming a barrier of metal around the island. It was now light enough for her to do without her night vision device. Lejla tore it from her head and threw it away. The number of approaching zombies had increased. Running at full tilt, she jumped over the hood of one of the cars. Then she rushed to the green area in the middle of the traffic circle. "Follow me," she yelled unnecessarily. Her team followed hard on her heels, though in a somewhat less orderly formation than before their encounter with the undead. With a minimal lead over the latter, who were prevented from breaking through by the surrounding vehicles, the unit gathered around their leader. Lejla noticed that some of them were missing. Now they were surrounded by the zombies.

The onslaught came in one fell swoop from all sides. Lejla realized they'd never be able to stop so many of them. *Damn it, where is Lucas?* She fired her next magazine until it was empty.

Over the years, the spear had become an integral part of my life. Since the start of the pandemic, I had it modified several times by experts. It was already on its fourth blade, after the previous ones had become blunt, chipped, or even broken off. As I walked through the streets of the Albanian ghost town, I tried to remember the early days when I had constructed the first version myself. But the images in my mind had faded. Far too much had happened since then, and it was only the very best of it I wanted in my memory.

The current opportunity to rekindle old friendships had also reopened wounds I would have preferred to keep closed. The loss of numerous loved ones was getting to me. The gray twilight in the sky reflected my mental state with frightening accuracy. But that gave me no further help on today's mission. I tried to shake off the depressing thoughts and focus on my task.

Like an undead, I lifted my nose and sniffed. The silence of the ghost town could not hide the fact that they were lurking everywhere. Those who had caught my scent followed me into the shadows. I sensed their astonishment at the presence of an individual unknown to them, who at the same time seemed familiar. In their pheromone language, they referred to me as a half-half—I was probably not the first anomaly they had come across. But in their eyes, I was thoroughly unlike anything they knew. Besides astonishment, I noticed respect in their messages, maybe even submissiveness.

Learning to communicate with the undead had taken years. The complex exchange of odor molecules created an effect on those who received them, calling to mind images that were supposed to signal a specific fact or idea, like words do in the world of the living. But there the similarities ended. Whenever zombies spoke of food—and they were permanently hungry—I saw humans in my mind's eye. They had degraded humans into objects whose sole purpose was to ensure the continuation of the zombie population. Every time I smelled a pheromone cloud, I had to sort through these impressions, declare them as nonhuman, and internally distance myself from them. This made it easier to put hunger and my sex drive and the resulting need to reproduce in check. This process had now become second nature to me, but it had not always been the case.

I had also learned to use the sweat glands on my left wrist for the same purpose. I signaled to the most curious and most aggressive zombies who were pursuing me through Shkodër that I was not a threat. They far outnumbered me, so I wanted to avoid any confrontation for the time being. Once again, I breathed in the pheromone-filled air and filtered out the information I needed. Then I went on.

Immediately after landing, I had separated from the rescue forces. I took a path away from their planned routes and walked northward through Shkodër, while the number of gray figures following me in wonder grew. News spread that another half-half was in town. They came from everywhere. I hadn't counted on being an attraction that would distract the zombies from the rescue units by its mere presence. But our luck was not to last long.

When I was around two-thirds of the way across the city, the undead suddenly sent out a warning signal. Some of the human troops had been sighted. Abruptly, the wandering corpses rushed away. If my hunch was right, it was Lejla's team that had been spotted. It took me all of five seconds to understand that this was an unfortunate development.

Our units were numerous and well armed, but our planning had considered it unlikely that most of the undead would form a single group. Encountering and fighting isolated zombies and smaller groups was something we were used to. There was no reason to believe things would be any different in Shkodër. And without me, it would probably have remained that way. But my presence had brought them together. Just like that, they were rushing toward an intruder whom they could overrun by sheer force of numbers. I smelled their emotions, their unbridled hunger, and their nymphomaniacal reproductive rage. I also felt this desire—it rolled through me like a murderous tsunami—and I had to resist it with all my might until I was more human than zombie again. Then I ran after them.

Lucas approached the masses holding Lejla's unit at bay. As soon as he reached the outer edge of the traffic circle, he dropped to one knee, took aim, and began firing selectively. The first line of his team took up position to his left and right and starting firing. Behind them, the second line came to a halt and fired at the zombies over the heads of those kneeling. The third provided backup.

"We're east of you," Lucas informed the Newgoslavian. "How's it looking?"

"Better not ask." There were short pauses between her sentences, interspersed with bursts of rifle fire. "Half my people are dead. And the zombies keep on coming. We can barely keep them from entering the traffic circle."

"There are loads of them," Lucas confirmed. "Did you reach Tiz?"

"Yes. It'll take him a good ten minutes to get here, though. He's already almost at the north entrance of the factory."

"Oh," was all Lucas could think of to say.

And then the zombies abruptly stopped their efforts to break through. They turned their heads back and forth as if looking for a signal they didn't agree with. Lucas ordered a cease fire, mesmerized by the action. He gestured to his team to close ranks. Through the resulting gap, undead poured toward the center of the square, mingling with their kind. No one dared breathe. At the southern edge, Lucas sensed more movement. He stood on tiptoe to see what was going on there. The undead shrank back, forming a cordon through which walked a dark figure armed only with a spear.

"Fucking Backup!" Lejla's voice in his headphones sounded stunned. Lucas had never heard anything more fitting. The admiration he heard matched his own.

Backup ran toward the traffic circle, climbed over a car hood, and approached Lejla. Through her radio, Lucas heard the fascinating person say, "Take the path behind me to get out. Surround the traffic circle and wait for my order." Lucas saw Lejla nodding, apparently incapable of saying a word. He was surprised she couldn't think of a sarcastic response. Then he fiddled with his radio to tell Tiz to proceed to the deployment site as originally planned.

"What's going on?" Tiz's mood had reached its limit.

"I . . . have no idea. I'll tell you later," he replied.

"What about Lejla?"

"She's fine. We'll be at our deployment site in a few minutes." Then he signed off.

Lejla led the remnants of her team from the traffic circle. Some of the undead standing at the edge snapped their teeth at them but did not leave their group. Lucas ordered his men to position themselves on the right in a long line, forming a semicircle. He himself ran in the opposite direction to join Lejla. The air was vibrating with tension.

Lucas estimated the number of zombies in the square at five hundred. Their troops totaled a mere hundred and fifty. Only now did he notice how acrid the stench was. Backup pushed out of the ranks of the undead into the open, passed the ring of people they had been besieging, and climbed onto the roof of a car.

All eyes looked up. Two seconds passed. Into the almost absolute silence, the strange voice spoke a single word. "Fire!"

At first, nothing happened. Everyone seemed to be lost in the fascination of the moment. But a female soldier in Lejla's troop was the first to come to her senses, raised her weapon, and fired into the gray bodies. A heartbeat later, all hell broke loose.

When the first volley began to thin the ranks of my half-siblings, I got off the car and walked away. I didn't need to see the massacre that would last several minutes—it was enough for me to have initiated it. Anyway,

I knew they would not escape the hail of bullets. The troops would then follow me, so I didn't wait for them.

The remaining three hundred meters to the factories were free of surprises. At the south gate to the complex, Lejla's and Lucas's units joined me. The Newgoslavian stood next to me. Together we peered through the wire mesh gates into the empty forecourt, which must once have been a workers' parking lot.

"Can you see anything?" asked Lejla.

"No undead, if that's what you mean," I replied. "But I am receiving strange messages that I can't decipher."

"You're communicating with them," she said, more in admiration than surprise. "Did you order them to line up at that traffic circle?"

"Yes. They must be in bondage to the other anomaly. I merely made use of the authority that comes with our . . . genus."

"So what are they saying now?"

"As I said, right now I'm having a hard time understanding them. Not all zombies communicate the same way. What about your father?"

She spoke into her radio. "Stari? Lejla here. How far along are you?" Except for the salutation, she spoke in English. After what must have been a response, she whispered to me, "He's in front of the entrance to the factory compound to the north. It's all quiet there, too." Then she added, "What if we finished off all the zombies in the traffic circle? I mean, there were quite a few."

I grimaced, signaling my disagreement. "There are still plenty of them around. But I don't know where they are."

"My father wants to start storming the compound now. He's asking if we're ready."

I nodded. "Take your positions and give him the green light. It'll take Lucas another five minutes to get to the west entrance."

"And where are you going?" she asked.

"I'm going to join Lucas. The other anomaly is somewhere nearby. I can sense its presence."

"You mean you can smell their vapor?"

"Yes, if that's easier for you to understand," I replied. "You take care of the prisoners first and foremost! And I'll take care of the anomaly." With these words, I turned around and moved toward my next goal.

After a few steps, I turned left around the corner. Lucas's unit followed me at a distance of thirty meters. Since it was important for me to scout the area beyond them, I hurried ahead. The pheromone trail became more intense but also more confusing. I approached the main entrance, eager to decipher the messages. Then suddenly, several things happened at once.

The number of scent markers went through the roof.

Around a hundred meters ahead of us, I spotted ten or twelve human gunmen, who had just stepped out of the main gate onto the street. I was wondering which unit they belonged to when I recognized the second anomaly in their midst. The figure sniffed and looked in my direction. Suddenly, I understood the messages that had seemed so unclear before. I whirled around to warn Lucas, raising my left hand. They had obviously seen me because bullets whizzed past. I flinched. One bullet pierced the forearm I was signaling with. The Frenchman's unit pressed close to the wall. I did the same and let my eyes wander back to the main entrance. The figures fled across the street, disregarding the shots from Lucas's team. I looked at the wound. The white secretion was working to close it. It smelled sickeningly of decay, as it did every time. I waited a few seconds until the black bleeding stopped.

Lucas darted toward me. "Are you okay?" he asked, glancing at my arm.

"Yes, go away. Forget everything we planned. Turn around immediately and go back to Lejla! Tell Tiz to stop, too. Get out of here!"

"Huh, what?" His face was one big question mark.

"We've fallen into a trap. You can't do any more here. Save yourselves," I explained hastily, looking back to the place where the unknown group had switched to the other side of the street. There was no one to be seen. But Lucas stood rooted to the spot. "Go, you idiots!" I shouted at him and ran after the anomaly.

He had run into a street that ran westward. His scent trail was fresh and led me through alleys and deserted courtyards. Following an impulse, I stopped abruptly at a street corner.

I sniffed. Obviously, an ambush was waiting for me. I could smell the sweat of the man hiding behind a concrete wall post three meters ahead of me. Spear first, I approached him, carefully, scraping the back of the blade against the masonry. I hoped to arouse the man's curiosity by doing this, and my plan worked. First, I saw the muzzle of his submachine gun slowly curve around the corner. Then his eyes came into view. Quickly, I thrust with all my might.

He recoiled, too late. The tip of the spear slid into his eye socket. The man dropped his weapon and cried out. The blade disappeared halfway into his skull. Then he went limp. With a jerk, I pulled out the spear, took the rifle, and sprinted after the rest. I spotted them as they crossed a fence between two meadows by the river. They ran across it without bothering with the fence. The rusty wire mesh had probably been cut in advance. Everything seemed to have been planned long ago. I quickened my pace, gripping the firearm with my right hand. There were three rowboats on the shore, and they jumped into them. Only then did one of the people at the oars spot me. But it was too late for them to raise the alarm. The automatic weapon in my hands crackled repeatedly. I tried to get the anomaly, but its companions pushed their way into the line of fire. I took out three with my first volley. One of them fired from the hip and caught me in the leg. With my left hand, I hurled the spear into the middle of his chest, knocking him backward out of the boat. The others swung their weapons toward me, but I had already plunged after him. As I flew through the air, I grabbed the spear, which was sticking out of the river. Entering the water, I yanked it free. Bullets smacked down all around me. I dove under the boats, which were driving away. Only when the current took them after a few seconds did I dare return to the surface. They were now thirty meters away. I wanted to fire, but I was distracted by the sounds of the battle at the factories. My friends were in trouble, but I couldn't help them. I got out of the water and ran after the anomaly in the boat.

Lejla's team waited tensely for Lucas's unit to move into position. They heard a low droning from above them. Lejla looked up. The delta glider was approaching from the southwest. "We have a good view of you," she heard Jens say on the group channel.

She had informed him earlier by radio about the attack of the wandering corpses. He, Waltraud, and Eva had immediately hurried into the air. He reported that they had observed the events in the traffic circle and were relieved but also astonished about the outcome.

"Lejla and Tiz are in position; Lucas's company is right by the west gate. Well done, guys," Jens said on the group channel. Suddenly, he said, "Um, have any of you already gone off on your own?"

The aircraft hummed over Lejla's head. "Yes. Backup," she confirmed.

"I can see Backup from here. But a dozen more people have just appeared right by the gate. They're coming out of the hall."

"That . . . can't be us," Lejla said. At the same time, a queasy feeling flared in the pit of her stomach as it always did when trouble was brewing. She was about to ask another question when shots rang out from behind the factory.

She heard Tiz shout on the community channel. "Who the hell is shooting?"

"Backup and Lucas were just attacked," Jens replied.

"Attacked? By who?" Tiz's voice was filled with frustration.

"The people who left the hall," Jens answered.

"Let's go in now," Lejla's father announced impatiently.

She knew it was too soon, but in this situation, she didn't dare contradict him. She raised her fist to signal to her people the imminent attack. But when the doors of the factory building swung open with a squeak, she stopped. Astonished, she looked toward it—and discovered dozens, no hundreds, of zombies rushing toward her.

At the same moment, Tiz yelled, "What the hell . . ."

She and her father fired simultaneously. Lejla cursed the narrow access gate, which only gave a handful of her people a clear view of the hordes of undead. But there were so many that it would hardly have made a difference if the driveway had been ten times as wide. And the zombies were approaching with frightening speed.

Lejla moved away from the gate to consult with Tiz and Lucas.

"Guys, what's going on over there? The undead are pouring out of here en masse."

Lucas spoke first. "Backup ordered me to retreat, then ran after the group that had just attacked us. We'll come and help. But I don't know if we'll make it soon. We're also being pursued by quite a few of them."

"Oh, jeb'o te život," Lejla burst out.

"Retreat! Retreat now!" roared Tiz so loudly that Lejla almost ripped out her earpiece in fright. "They've infected everyone they've imprisoned."

Lejla blanched. If that was true, they were mercilessly outnumbered, weapons or no weapons. The prisoners numbered in the thousands. If Tiz was right, and they had been transformed . . . But where else could so many zombies have suddenly come from?

Tiz's conclusion seemed logical. The number of her own people was insignificant in comparison. She looked toward the first line of attack. The undead had arrived at the gate. "Retreat! Everyone back to the landing point!" she shouted. But the order was lost in the din of battle. *Run for your lives*, seemed a more appropriate command. She ran to the front line, pointing her weapon at the undead. "*Retreat!*" she shouted, covering her soldiers. "*Back to the landing point!*" Only now did they obey. When the last of them had turned back, she fled, too.

The zombies were advancing quickly. They were fresh and hungry, and Lejla could literally feel their anger on the back of her neck. She thought about drawing them into urban warfare, but her ammunition wouldn't last forever. She had already used a good third of it without having achieved anything. Her intended goal, the riverbank, where lifeboats, reinforcements, and more weapons were waiting, seemed infinitely far away. Nevertheless, she quickened her pace.

In the crowd of people fleeing ahead of her, she spotted Lucas, who kept looking back at her. A glance over her shoulder told her that the zombies were barely fifty meters away. The Frenchman dropped back to her.

"I contacted Dennis," he said. "Aerial reconnaissance has now informed him of our failure. They're waiting for us, ready to go at a moment's notice."

She nodded listlessly. She felt miserable. So many people had been . . . squandered—people they'd wanted to save. The whole mission had been in vain . . . At least her own losses were limited, she tried to tell herself. Immediately, she felt ashamed of her thoughts. She focused on the long road ahead.

Dennis, the leader of the Black Masks, was eager to be in a real battle again—it would be his first in a long time. Since they had wiped out the last undead in Scandinavia three years ago, he rarely had a reason to take up arms. Now he was enjoying the anticipation of the imminent fight. Leaning on the handle of his ax, tapping a confused rhythm with the index finger of his ringed right hand, he waited for the swarms of zombies advancing toward them. It wouldn't be long now. After landing, he and his squad had warmed up by going through movement sequences. He saw movement to the east.

"Asa," he said to the woman next to him, "the first of them are on their way."

Asa tilted her head as if listening for something quiet. "If that's them, they were pretty fast," she replied with a skeptical undertone.

Dennis saw the arrivals waving. He waved back. They were now within a hundred meters of them. The clothes they were wearing were the same as those of the Newgoslavians. Their weapons were also the same. He wondered why Asa was so suspicious. From experience, however, he knew that her gut feelings were rarely wrong. "Get ready to counterattack," he said over his shoulder, not taking his eyes off the approaching forces.

They opened fire at fifty meters. Being prepared for this probably saved Dennis's life. He threw himself down on his belly. Asa had bent down low, her pistol drawn, and was returning fire. The Icelandic greenhorns were stunned for a second, remaining stock-still in their positions. Three of them were hit. The rest then broke free and fired at the attackers themselves. Dennis kept an eye on the latter, waiting until they stopped shooting to reload. At that moment, he jumped up and sprinted toward them. He was under no illusion that he'd be able to take them out single-handedly. But his people would follow him every step of the way and give him support.

The adrenaline rushing through his veins seemed to skew his sense of time, making him see the details of the battle with frightening accuracy. He was just ten meters from the first attacker when they resumed fire. But it was too late to stop Dennis. He threw his ax with both hands, splitting the skull of the man who had just taken aim at him. The force knocked the gunman off his feet. The Swede drew his long knife and rolled forward, dodging the projectiles that were slamming into the ground beside him. Taking advantage of his centrifugal force, he stretched out and rammed the blade into the stomach of the second person in his way. The figure remained upright, looking at all the blood spurting out of the wound with a stunned expression on his face. Using the dying man as a shield, Dennis picked up his weapon from the ground and fired. He'd retrieve the ax as soon as the magazine was empty.

Suddenly, a silhouette appeared from the right. Dennis swung the gun, but the figure was damn fast. Ice-cold hands grasped his forearms. They squeezed mercilessly. Before he could make a sound, his bones cracked like brushwood. His hands dropped limply, and a brutal pain flashed through him. Bewildered, he looked into the face of the powerful creature that could break limbs with its bare hands. It had gray patches of skin of various sizes all over its body. One eye was a zombie-like white. The human-looking eye looked right at Dennis. *The anomaly.* He was too dismayed to react to the pain. The figure let go of him and raised a fist above his head. He knew the coming blow would break his neck—and there was nothing he could do about it. Dennis closed his eyes . . .

Something crashed into the anomaly and knocked it to the ground. He looked up. On the floor, he saw two figures wrestling with each other. Only then did Dennis's body react to the agony in his arms. Within two seconds, he lost consciousness.

I only hoped they wouldn't cross to the other side of the river, because then there was no way I'd be able to get to them. So as not to give them this idea—which might easily occur to them if they spotted me—I kept to a distance of two to three hundred meters. I limped southward. All the while, I could hear sounds of fighting coming from the city, moving in parallel with me.

The shot to my leg made it difficult to advance. The fast current helped the boats. I had to strain to keep them in sight. I shadowed them like this for the next five kilometers until they joined a larger group below a hill with a medieval ruin on it. The anomaly was moving freely through their number. Weapons and ammunition were exchanged, and the now expanded unit moved on. They disappeared from my sight in the narrow, winding alleys, so I followed their scent trail. The trail took me half a kilometer over the hill. Once at the top, I sighted them three hundred meters away down in the valley. They had come out on the riverbank not far from the spot we had chosen for landing. I saw the boats around which the northern European battalion had gathered. They outnumbered the attackers, but I remembered what a tremendous advantage a surprise attack would give them. Besides, they had the anomaly.

It walked with its escorts toward the waiting rescue party. Probably in order not to arouse suspicion, they waved at the battalion in a friendly manner, moving with a certainty that was intended to signal comradeship. I wanted to shout a warning, but the intruders had already crossed the short distance and opened fire. Heedless of my leg wound, I ran.

When I arrived at the battle site barely half a minute later, I realized the defenders were returning fire. Several had fallen in the first wave of the attack. Some of the Black Masks had rushed forward and were fighting back. One attacker became aware of me, shouted a warning, and took aim at me, but my spear entered his throat and his words ended in a gurgle. On the other side, I spotted the anomaly gripping a masked man by the forearms. Three seconds later, I jumped it from behind. We hit the ground hard, rolling and exchanging blows. It had tremendous strength, far superior to mine. I looked to gain an advantage with my speed, but the anomaly was almost as fast.

We separated and got to our feet.

[You are . . . like me,] it marked.

[No. We are not the same,] I signaled back. But something inside me fought this conviction. The long-suppressed zombie-like feelings made their way to the surface. I ignored them and attacked.

The anomaly let my hook fly by and landed a haymaker near my stomach. It yanked me into the air by my hair, leaving my feet dangling free.

[You're a half-half, too. Why are you fighting me?]

"I am not like you!" I screamed, bringing my left forearm explosively upward, shattering its wrist.

It let go of me, kicking with its legs. As it hit the ground, it broke several of my ribs with a kick. I felt them digging into my lungs. The anomaly reared up over me. Looked at me. [*Confusion.* You are like me. We are . . . like you. We are all . . . the same,] it suggested to me in amazement, as if it had stumbled upon a whole new thought. I couldn't help but sense the desperation in its signals. Its facial expression, on the other hand, was unreadable, leaving aside the fact that I could neither move nor breathe because of the pain.

[Why are you fighting us? You belong to us. There are not enough of us anyway. We are the same,] it repeated.

Its frustration was like mine. It tore me up inside to have finally found another being that might be able to understand, even share the unbearableness of this existence, our only difference being it was not able to keep the darkness in check. My eyes filled with tears.

[We can . . . not be,] I started. [Our survival . . . is not desirable. Our species has no future.]

[Wrong. Wrong. We can survive. This site . . . is the proof.]

Images of the inside of the factory appeared in my mind's eye. The tone of its statement was almost euphoric about its success with it. My stomach turned. [We are . . . death,] I marked. [We are . . . corruption.]

Unbridled rage flared up in it. [We are nothing of the sort.] A surge of pheromones roared at me. My rejection enraged it. The anomaly came at me again. Blindly, it struck. I felt my left cheekbone break. A kick tore the tendons in my knee, hammer-like punches pounded my abdomen. It took out on me all its pent-up frustration at its unrequited affection, whirling me around like an old dish towel. Through all the pain, I saw the approach of something I had longed for. Oblivion was waiting for me in the beyond, which was finally opened its gates to me. Redemption was near. I closed my swollen eyes, waiting for the blow of liberation. But the torment stopped abruptly. I looked up and saw, in a blur, the anomaly being rushed by its entourage toward the boats. Immediately, several people bent over me. Their silhouettes were familiar. I tried to smile, but my bloated face refused to obey. It was becoming more and more difficult to breathe; the injured lung was barely functioning. My belly was burning like fire, obviously due to internal bleeding. How bad my legs were, I couldn't tell, because everything below my navel was numb.

Waltraud took my hand. Joy flowed through me at her touch. I gasped and coughed up blood. The sudden pain in my chest made me wince. Eva touched me on the forehead. Warmth spread from my heart. I breathed jerkily, afraid of choking again.

Jens knelt next to me. "Gently," he whispered in a quavering voice. I wanted to say something comforting back. That they didn't need to worry, or how much good our friendship was doing me. But my strength was leaving me. One last look at their saddened faces told me they knew it all anyway and felt the same.

A black veil was closing in around my field of vision. I breathed in once more. Everything dissolved into darkness, lost all meaning. Longing and pain fizzled out, grief and fear were extinguished. I breathed out and detached myself from this world.

"Oh shit," Jens cursed in the yacht's narrow cabin. Lucas's team was engaged in a skirmish at the north gate of the zombie factory with a group that, in our estimation, shouldn't have been there in the first place. Backup was caught in the cross fire and might have been hit; I couldn't tell from this distance. High above them, we were doomed to inaction. Seconds later, droves of undead poured out of the complex into the open area where we suspected the prisoners were. On the communal channel, Lejla, Lucas, and Tiz each spoke. The Newgoslavian leader suddenly yelled at them to retreat. The wandering corpses had infected all the inmates, and they were now being unleashed on the rescuers. There were too many to stop.

I didn't doubt it for a second when I looked down from the plane.

"Where's Backup?" asked Waltraud. "All I can see are zombies."

"There," I said, pointing toward the shore to the east of the factory site. Backup was involved in a fight and had just leapt headfirst into the water.

In the city, the units began to retreat.

"And who's that?" Waltraud pointed to a larger group far away to the south.

"That . . . I don't know," the Dutchman replied. "Can't remember us putting a post there. I'll fly over it." He swung the plane southward.

A minute later, we were flying two hundred meters above them. Before anyone could say anything, we saw muzzle flashes. A few bullets hit the wings. There was a brief shower of sparks in the cockpit. There was a loud screech in my headset, then our radio went dead. Jens turned away immediately.

"They're not ours," Waltraud said.

"Oh, you think?" he replied sarcastically.

"They're only around a kilometer from the landing site," I mused. "What's to stop them running over and throwing a wrench in the works?"

"Fuck, you're right. We have to go down and help them," Jens suggested.

"It's looking bad," the Norwegian replied. "But what about air reconnaissance?"

"Fuck it. If everyone dies, it'll be no use to us anyway. I'll land at the first opportunity. We have enough weapons with us. But I don't want to decide this alone." He raised a hand to indicate his vote. Waltraud followed him seconds later. Throwing overboard my resolutions to stay out of dangerous situations, I did, too.

Jens then pointed to the spring green of the fields lying fallow to the south. "I'll take us down there. Then we'll have to walk the four or five kilometers back. How fit are you, Eva?"

"Fit enough," I replied.

He nodded.

Ten minutes later, we were running back. I was carrying four light rapid-fire rifles, my backpack full of ammunition. Waltraud and Jens carried the same. We crossed a bridge. On it, he suddenly stopped, pointed upstream to the place we had been fired on, and said, "They're gone. We have to hurry."

The Norwegian and I yelped in agreement. For the last mile and a half, we pushed hard. Soon my lungs were burning with every breath.

When we left the bend in the road behind us, we spotted the strange group. They had stormed onto the landing area and were harassing the Black Masks and my protégés. The three of us split up, attacking them from behind.

It was hard to tell friend from foe. At least I knew not to shoot at the masked men. The strangers faltered for a few moments, caught off guard by our attack. Then they split up. A handful held us off, while the others worked their way up to the boats. They captured most of them and rendered the rest useless by firing shots through them. The ranks of the Nordic unit had thinned and were falling back westward. Amid it all, I spotted a figure with blotchy skin dressed in rags, flinging a lifeless body around. Something in me tensed as I realized the body was Backup. At the same time, I realized the other being must be the anomaly Backup had been after. Four of the strangers went over to it and escorted it briskly toward the river. I fired at them, emptying half a magazine. Two of the escorts fell to the ground, but the anomaly made it to the boat. The rowers scrambled to get the boats into the current.

I rushed over to Backup, whose facial features were no longer recognizable from the impact of the massive violence. Backup's arms and legs were sticking out at unnatural angles. Blood bubbles formed on his swollen lips with each breath. We knelt, horrified at what we were seeing. Gently, we touched Backup's hands and cheeks. A cough escaped from his ravaged lungs, which probably caused even more pain. Jens lovingly whispered something I couldn't process in my state of shock. Backup seemed to smile, looked at each of us in turn—and died.

None of the three of us dared move. A few bullets whizzed by, but we didn't care. I can't say for sure how long we stayed like that. At some point, our troops returned from the city. Someone shook my shoulder and pulled Waltraud and Jens to their feet. I was almost carried away. I tried to fight it. "No! We can't leave Backup here," I said.

The young Newgoslavian appeared and assured me she would take care of Backup. I watched as she called to some members of her unit. Two of them rolled the lifeless body in a tarp and carried it away. Lejla was pulling me along by the hand. Weakly, I let her. "We have to get out of here," she said, trying to make me understand the seriousness of the situation. I heard the guttural screams of the undead close by. We fled.

After a while, I became aware of our surroundings again. We were following a road full of potholes at a light trot. Apart from meadows, there was nothing else to be seen. I left the ranks and took a side path to survey the entire company. I was shocked to find that our numbers had more than halved.

Our rear guard was running behind us at a distance of two hundred meters, firing constantly. Single shots, from which I deduced ammunition was running low. Then I looked at the time. It was only noon, and I could not understand how so much had happened in such a short time. Lejla broke away from the stream of fleeing people and joined me.

"Are you okay?" she asked gently.

I shook my head. "Not at all. What the hell happened back there?"

She sniffed. "I can't tell you until we question those two."

She pointed to two men with their hands tied behind their backs. "They didn't make it to the boats in time. So their people just left them behind."

"I want to be there for the questioning. But I'm more worried about the crowd of zombies behind us. And why are we moving so slowly?"

"We have quite a few casualties, which is dictating our pace. And frustration at the losses and the failure of our mission is diminishing the morale of the troops. We've never experienced anything on such a large scale as this. Hardly any of us have served in an army that provided coaching in this kind of psychology. We've only just been trained."

"Hmm, but if it goes on like this, the zombies will overrun us long before we reach the coast," I said, stating the obvious. I thought of Cassiopeia, who might never see her mother again.

"See that hill?" asked Lejla.

I looked southwest, following her pointing finger. "It's a long way off," I replied.

"Six kilometers," she explained, "That's where we're going to hole up. From there, we plan to send someone out to get reinforcements from the ships. The sea is just beyond it."

If the undead haven't finished us off first. Instead, I asked, "Is there still no news from the ships?"

She shook her head. I hung mine, resigned to my fate. Wordlessly, we marched on.

With each kilometer we covered, the shots became less frequent, but not because the number of undead had decreased. As we walked, I counted my cartridges. Forty-seven. Forty-six of them I would dedicate to the wandering corpses.

I didn't really expect to reach the hill in time. Lejla walked along the rows, taking the remaining ammunition from people who were looking after the wounded or were wounded themselves. I followed her toward the rear guard. She spotted me, came up to me, and held out her hand, probably assuming I was going to hand her my weapons. I shook my head. "No, I want to come with you," I explained.

"Negative! Go to the front, please. The troops need strong leadership in case something happens to us. Tiz, Lucas, and I will buy you at least enough time to get to the beach."

"And then what?"

She shrugged. At that moment, there was a flurry of activity at the back of the column. Dozens of shots rang out. Lejla and I looked over. The defenses in the last row fell silent. The undead had broken through in two places. The Newgoslavian shouted, "Every man for himself!" and charged toward them. But our remaining troops continued to maintain order. I spotted a giant carrying Backup's remains. The company dragged itself the remaining three hundred meters toward the hill. I didn't understand how they thought they could face off against the wandering corpses there. It was a bleak slope covered in grass, a few perennials, and small bushes. Our fate seemed sealed. *What a failure, this whole mission has been.*

Lejla continued to cover the rear guard. They all fled past her, revealing a bizarre picture—a single person against hundreds of undead. They were ten meters away from her when she finally turned around and took to her heels. The point of it all was still hidden to me. We were lost, no matter where we fled. In a fit of gallows humor, I ran, too, and reached the head of the column. From there I looked back briefly.

Waltraud was carrying Backup's spear. Jens snatched the sword from the hands of a wounded Scandinavian. Other uninjured fighters saw this and followed suit. They fell back to fight the fastest of the undead. On the opposite side, I was among the first to reach a spur on the hill. Fifty meters before the crest, I stopped abruptly. The ground was stonier here than in the fields. I stooped down immediately and grabbed two earth-smeared pieces of rock, larger than my fists. Quickly, I collected around twenty of them. I have never been a good thrower. Today, however, it was time to become one. I looked around. My collecting frenzy had encouraged others to follow suit. The sight did not give me hope, but it was better than nothing.

We numbered just one hundred and fifty people, a good thirty who were not fit, so we formed a human rampart in front of them. The zombies reached the slope. I still had lead left for forty-six undead. *We will fight our last battle today with the remaining cartridges, swords, axes, and stones.*

The whole situation was absurd. A few hours ago, we had wanted to free the people who were now staggering toward us and attacking. This time I fired slowly and carefully, not wasting a bullet. I had to let them get much closer than I would have liked. The defenders shot the remaining ammunition. The attack wave drew inexorably closer. Fifty meters became forty. My magazine was almost empty. Thirty meters. I inserted the single cartridge into the gun and loaded it. Then I bent down and started throwing rocks. Twenty meters. This bore little fruit because the rocks mostly sailed harmlessly past their targets. Ten meters. The last stone flew out of my hand. Ironically, this final throw caught a zombie in the forehead, and it stumbled backward, taking two more with it. I reached for the gun. My index finger found the trigger. The cold muzzle touched my temple—I closed my eyes. *Cassiopeia, my dearest daughter, I am sorry. I am so infinitely sorry.* My fist tightened, and I squee—

A piercing call rang out, high and powerful at the same time. It was a sound I had never heard before, with a tremolo in it that flattened out toward the end and made my blood run cold. I faltered on the spot. Opened my eyes. Everything around me froze. All eyes were glued on the crest of the hill where the sound had seemed to come from. Even the undead looked surprised. I peered upward as well, to the spot where dozens of silhouettes had just appeared. The ship's crews, I rejoiced, until I remembered they weren't armed with compound bows. But those were exactly what the figures were carrying, looking down at us from the ridge. Some of them had long pitch-black hair that was blowing in the breeze.

The panic that had almost driven me to suicide just five seconds before gave way to total incomprehension. Once again, the call echoed out. I saw a figure who was presumably the leader raise its arm, and the bows were pointed toward the sky. The strings of the war tools tightened. With a jerk, the commander's arm came down. A shower of arrows whirred into the sky. Even before the projectiles reached the apex of their ballistic curve, they were followed by a second volley. Those of our squad who were in close combat with the undead broke away from their enemies, who reacted a second too late. We ran up toward the fire, dragging the wounded behind us. The first salvo caught a wide sweep of zombies. While the second was still hanging in the air, I saw the shooters lay down their weapons.

At that moment, a single figure ran down the hill. She was armed with some kind of ax, but instead of a metal edge, the ax-head had been replaced with an oval white stone. A black band ran like a painted blindfold around her head, which was clean-shaven at the sides. She gained speed with every step, and just as the arrows found their targets again, she lunged at the undead, slashing left and right as if fighting her way through a dense jungle. I knew this fighting style and knew exactly what was coming next. The battle cry rang out from above once more, but this time from dozens of mouths.

I couldn't take my tear-filled eyes off the fury in human form, so I didn't see her entourage until they had rushed past me. Franca was freeing Lejla and Tiz from a tangle of undead, and even Lucas was now visible. I hoped they were unharmed, but I had no time to pursue the thought. Suddenly, the will to survive and the desire to fight were rekindled within us. We fought back with everything we had: stones, sticks, and knives. Some used their firearms like clubs. Waltraud and Jens were blazing with bloodlust. Tiz had gone into a berserk rage to match his temperament. With whom Lejla and Lucas were fighting I couldn't see, but they kept the pack at bay until our allies advanced on them down the hill.

What happened from then until the end of the fight is not clear in my memory. At any rate, the battle continued until all the undead had been defeated. This was achieved mainly with tomahawks and knives, but also with spears and baseball bats. Our allies seemed to be immune to the zombie plague—the bleeding bites and scratch marks they suffered did not cause them to turn. As soon as I had caught my breath, I kept an eye out for my old friend. I found her hugging Waltraud. Next to her was Jens, who was looking around searchingly. As soon as he caught sight of me, he exclaimed joyfully, "There she is!" and led me over to the two women.

"How . . . What the hell are you doing here?" I stammered.

Franca seemed happy—quite different from the way I remembered her.

She had acquired a strong North American accent. "Aren't you even happy we saved your lives?" Since I couldn't bring myself to say anything, she explained, "Cas told us where you were."

"Cas? My Cassiopeia?" The words shot out of me.

"Yeah, that's the one."

Panic seized me. "Where is she? Is she all right?"

Franca pressed on. "Well . . . she's fine. She's doing amazing," she added quickly, holding her palms placatingly in my direction. "She's"—she pointed her thumb over her shoulder eastward, toward the sea—"on our ship."

"Cas is here? *On your ship?*"

"Easy, Eva. I can explain everything. It's a long story. The main thing is that everyone is okay." She looked at us in turn. "It's good to see you guys! All that's missing now is Backup," she said to the group with a grin.

Seeing us fall silent and look away, she asked aggressively, "What?"

I turned away and began to search the ground. Waltraud, Jens, and Franca followed me. The bystanders had fallen silent and were watching us. After two minutes, I found the tarp. I knelt next to it. With trembling fingers, I tried to unroll it but was unsuccessful. The Norwegian woman gave me a hand, and Backup's stiffened body became visible. At the sight, I was once again seized with overwhelming sadness. Not even the victory we had won could outweigh the loss of the person with whom I had been friends for so many years.

CHAPTER 10

INFERNO

Distraught, Jens stands over Backup's motionless body. Next to him squats Franca, holding their friend's limp gray hand. Eva and Waltraud are crouched beside her, their faces petrified with horror. Jens's chin trembles. The sounds of the crowd around him blur into a mush that is muffled in his mind. He is in shock.

Tiz, who is standing opposite him, raises his head. Jens looks at him. In the Newgoslavian's face, he sees undisguised rage and endless hatred. His state of shock subsides, and he wonders if fate is holding a mirror up to him.

"You!" says Tiz, turning to him. "Where's your plane?"

Jens explains.

The Newgoslavian then goes through the ranks of his men, taking their HKs and spare magazines if they still have any. More than a dozen hand grenades go into the backpack he has also snatched. Then he looks back at Jens. "Let's go! Take me there!" he orders, as if Jens were one of his subordinates.

"What are you planning?" he inquires.

Some of those present are now following their conversation.

"What am I going to do?" his interlocutor spits out punctiliously. "I want to bring those responsible for this to justice once and for all."

Waltraud slowly gets to her feet, watching what's going on around her. Jens catches her eye. She reloads her Kalashnikov and nods at him. Looking sideways at Tiz, she says, "Let's go, then," and she sprints off down the hill.

Shouldering the backpack full of weapons and explosives, the Balkan warrior runs after her. His daughter calls out to him, but he waves her off without so much as glancing at her. A second later, Jens is hot on their heels. He doesn't have to turn around to know that Franca is following them.

On the way, no one says a word. After an hour, they reach the plane. To reduce its weight, they throw out everything that is not a weapon and take off. Jens, who is piloting the plane, hears Tiz breathing agitatedly at his back. Once they are airborne, he frantically inquires, "Where are they? Does anyone see them?"

The sea comes into view. They see their own ships in the places where they left them. Almost all of them are smoking slightly because the water used to put out the fires is evaporating from the still-glowing planks of wood.

But the boat with the huge spinnaker has disappeared.

"Someone wanted to be sure they couldn't be followed," says Waltraud.

Jens turns the plane on a northward course. "I'm going to climb higher," he explains. "Maybe that'll help us spot them quicker."

The temperature in the cabin drops rapidly, but the tension doesn't. After ten minutes, he murmurs, "Hmm, if they haven't gone south, we should see them by now."

The plane makes a long, extended turn. They glide southward at maximum speed until Jens spots a white dot on the horizon thirty minutes later. "That might be them," he exclaims. Tiz and Franca lean forward, their gazes following his outstretched finger.

"Yes, it can only be them," confirms Tiz. "And now I know what they're up to!" he blurts out. "They want to go to Corfu, to resume their trade. Because there are still enough human resources there for them to draw on."

Whether this is true or a figment of the Newgoslavian's imagination is of little concern to Jens. He wants to see them all dead, no matter what their immediate plans are. Behind him, he hears Tiz loading the weapons and releasing the safety catches. A metallic clatter tells him that someone has also reached for hand grenades.

"What's the plan?" asks Waltraud.

"So," Tiz replies, "here's what we're going to do."

Dalibor spits into the sea. In his ears, the sound of the wind in the rigging mixes with the glide of the hull through the salt water. Leaning over the railing, he stares westward. He is blinded by the sun, which only worsens his mood after the mission didn't go entirely to plan. Lately, too many people seem to be interfering in his affairs anyway.

Like the Frenchman who stopped him from ripping out the guts of that brat in Zadar. Dalibor's breathing is still impaired by his broken nose. But at least they now have an anomaly, which they got out of Shkodër alive at the very last moment. He shakes his head as he recalls the effort required to track it down. Convincing it to flee the approaching invasion had cost him twenty-five of his comrades.

But the story had begun six months ago. Someone had approached him back then with a request to smuggle a group that had fled Germany into the safe areas inside Newgoslavia. It was good money. Dalibor hadn't asked any questions. Within three weeks, he had mobilized a team of seasoned zombie war veterans. They were all men he could trust.

Overrunning the Kresnice crossing, which was only guarded by twelve border guards, was a standard operation, and which they accomplished without casualties. The orders then were to pick up the convoy that was waiting five kilometers from the border and escort it along the long-forgotten roads to Banja Luka. Dalibor had quickly realized why they had chosen a city that had been wiped out in the apocalypse. Nobody would look for them there.

The trip had taken two weeks. He had initially wondered about the nature of some of the containers being pulled by electric cars. He counted seven of them, all with massively reinforced doors. There were also vehicles pulling traditional caravans. All of them had grilles fixed to their windowpanes, which were darkened from the inside. The occupants had always eluded his gaze, and he did not inquire what they were up to in his country. Dalibor's mercenary force escorted the caravan to its destination without incident. He was already thinking he had fulfilled the order and completed the mission.

But he was wrong. His assignment was extended indefinitely. First, he had to shield the arrivals, who had settled in the former university hospital, from the surrounding area. For the money he was offered, he was more than happy to do so. Since no one lived in the area, and hardly anyone ever went there, there wasn't much for him to do. Three months and an eternity of absolute boredom later, the monotonous routine changed. One morning, they left for Bihać. Dalibor and his unit were to mingle with the population near the town hall without attracting attention while the delegation he had accompanied stopped in for a discussion with Tiz. After half an hour, the delegation came out without having achieved anything. Even though Dalibor couldn't see much of the cloaked figures and so couldn't read their expressions, he could tell from their stiff posture that the meeting had not gone as they had expected. It was rumored within the unit that the Newgoslavian troop leader had responded to their request with a resounding refusal, which reinforced his impression. The fact that two days later they commissioned him to locate and kill Tiz's daughter confirmed that his suspicions were correct.

He then set out with two of his men to find Lejla. It took them six weeks to locate the woman. They had questioned several people as inconspicuously as possible, but they got more information from listening to radio messages. So four weeks ago, they had gone to Zadar, where they waited five more days for the *Sinji Galeb*.

I should have finished her off right there at the diner, Dalibor cursed the night after the unsuccessful attack. Still, he knew it wouldn't have been a good idea to go after her at Sweet Chili. There were too many people around. He didn't want to take the risk of being stopped and possibly arrested. So they had followed her to the sea organ. In retrospect, Dalibor chided himself for underestimating the young Frenchman.

With his swollen nose, he was heading toward Lika to stage an ambush. His orders after the botched attack were to fell a tree at a certain spot outside Bihać and disappear until dawn. Dalibor had dutifully completed the first order. But then he had stayed put in a hiding place to observe what happened next.

A truck emerged from the twilight—one he recognized from Banja Luka. Not far from the felled trunk, behind which a shrouded crew set to work, a container had been placed deep in the forest, and then camouflaged with ferns and branches.

Once they had left, Dalibor inspected the container. But it was either empty or so well soundproofed that he couldn't hear any noise from the inside. The radio-controlled locking system on the door made him wonder.

He went back to the tree and discovered a flashing plastic box on it. Dalibor was neither a physicist, nor a chemist. He didn't even do DIY projects, so he didn't understand how the box worked. But he wasn't stupid, either. He could well imagine it had a built-in sensor that was connected to the lock on the container. As soon as the tree was moved, the door would spring open, and whatever was behind it would come out, Dalibor guessed. His instincts told him he didn't want to be on the scene when this happened.

He returned to Banja Luka without any detours. Along the way, he began to get interested in the work of the enlisted men. As they drove, his two comrades-in-arms fed him unconfirmed information that a process had been developed that made it possible to create a special species of zombie. The substance required for this, it was whispered, had been isolated from the tissue of an infected human who had supposedly survived the infection. Dalibor usually stayed away from the rumor mill. However, the widespread secrecy that was being insisted on and the incident with the container in the forest had now made him curious.

On his return, he finally realized that there was much more to the stories than he had initially been inclined to admit. No sooner had he made his report than he was condemned to set off for the southern Balkans. Thanks to the information he had received from his informer in Bihać, Dalibor was now not only aware of the possible existence of an anomaly, but also that a rescue mission had been planned for Shkodër. He now had an inkling, even before he had received the strangest of his directives, of what his actual mission would be—to locate the anomaly and get it out of there. By force, if necessary, as it turned out to be. But if it was dead, it was worthless. So he should take care to bring it safely to his clients.

Dalibor worked out a plan to enable him to comply with the request. He had enough subordinates who would follow him to Shkodër. They had enough weapons. A ship would get them there within a week.

So resources were not a problem.

All he lacked to put a plan into action was time. The Bihać units and the teams from northern Europe were about to launch an invasion themselves. Dalibor was under pressure, but he had resolved to turn this to his advantage. And he was already thinking about how to do this.

Within a week, he set off. The ship and its crew arrived off what had once been the coast of Montenegro, just a few kilometers north of the former Albanian border, a mere three days after Tiz. They went ashore at Petrovac. In order not to run into the northern European rescue forces farther south, they chose the northern route around Lake Skudari. At the gates of Shkodër, they split into two groups. One unit went to the south of the city to provide cover for their retreat.

With fifty of his men, Dalibor set out for the factory. For four days, they scouted the area from the upper floors of the surrounding buildings until they spotted the anomaly. Even from a distance, it was different from the undead, because it moved like a normal human being. In the zoomed-in image on his remote control, Dalibor recognized the zombie-like gray areas of skin on its neck and face. Only one of the eyes had remained human. When it spoke to the collabs, its lips moved as he had expected. But to communicate with the undead, this was probably not necessary. Dalibor remembered that the zombies communicated by scents, which they could selectively secrete. Now they only had to wait for the right opportunity to strike.

For forty-eight hours, they had watched her in secret. But when they received word by radio that the invasion had begun, they were forced to improvise.

They went to the factory at dawn. Dalibor lost most of his people on the way there. However, the rest of them managed to get ahold of the anomaly so that he could try to have a conversation with it. The enormous agitation he felt had sharpened his memory so much that he could remember with absolute clarity the terrifying impression it had made on him. At first, it was like a caged animal, knowing full well that the armed men around it could take its life at any moment. After several attempts, they created a kind of communication that allowed him to put his proposal to the anomaly. Of course he had expected it to reject it. Even his warnings didn't get him any further.

But in the end, it was the invasion that had helped persuade it to flee. His gamble had paid off. When shots rang out in the city, reinforcing his warning to the anomaly about its impending doom, it had grudgingly agreed to go with him. However, not before it had spent half an hour directing the zombies remaining in the area toward the prisoners.

Almost too late, they had stepped out of the factory. The numerous invaders had got to within a hundred meters of them. They narrowly escaped them and a figure who had fearlessly pursued his unit to the river. The same person caught up with them boarding the boats five kilometers downstream.

Only the anomaly saved his team from defeat. Which was when Dalibor saw what it was capable of in battle. The respect he had developed for it had quickly mutated into fear. He'd had to force himself to lead it away from the battlefield and not to leave it to the hail of bullets heading in its direction.

In the meantime, his mercenaries had overrun the rescue forces' vessels. Under cover of darkness, they rowed to the vehicles that had been left with a minimum of guards. They eliminated the opposition, destroyed all the radios, and set fire to the sails. They took the largest one, which also had an enormous cache of weapons in its hull. Then they intercepted Dalibor and the anomaly at the Drin delta.

The injured anomaly was immediately taken below deck to the New-goslavian three-master's captain's cabin. The tissue had quickly closed around its wounds. When Dalibor saw this, he wondered if he'd ever stop being amazed. It took a long time, but he did. His new directive was to set out immediately for Corfu, not to return to Banja Luka as planned. Once again Dalibor followed orders, and they set sail southward.

Now, five hours later and standing at the railing of the fleeing three-master, he wonders what his clients are hoping to achieve by creating strange zombie breeds from the anomaly's cell tissue. Within his ranks, people have been saying they wanted to make their mark on world events, or at least on what was left of the world. Dalibor snorts contemptuously.

What do they want to do, rule the world? As if there's anything left out there to conquer. Even in his thoughts, his voice is full of sarcasm. But his clients seem to be obsessed. He can't get excited about the idea of wasting so much energy on something so pointless. Then he reminds himself that their motives should all be the same to him personally. He is a mercenary who enjoys his job, even if the pay is not always lavish. Dalibor lives for the thrill that comes with the assignments, which have become rarer in recent years because there have been fewer undead to eliminate. That's why this assignment came at just the right time for him. And on top of that, he would be well paid this time.

He blinks. The sun's damned rays bring tears to his eyes. Dalibor wipes the tears away with the back of his hand. When he looks up again, he spots a narrow, horizontal shadow right in front of the sun. His curiosity is immediately aroused. He forces himself not to look away. The object can't be more than a hundred meters away. Moreover, it seems to be approaching rapidly.

Dalibor's survival instincts quickly kick in. He starts to run. "Take cover! Everybody, take cover!" he yells. Volleys of machine gun fire ring out from the sky behind him. Almost instantly, bullets whizz past him, close by. Three of the crew members are hit and fall to the ground. Somewhere, someone cries out in pain. Dalibor curses himself for having put down his rifle. He sprints through a hail of bullets to retrieve it from the cabin. But suddenly his neck bursts open in a wave of heat. In a split second, he loses connection with the rest of his body. His head seems to race toward the planks as if detached from his body. Even before he realizes what has happened to him, his world darkens forever.

They approach the huge sailing ship. The sun at their backs makes its white spinnaker shine. Jens steers the plane straight toward it, adjusting the direction over and over again. Waltraud, Franca, and Tiz are already waiting with guns drawn.

"A hundred meters," says Jens.

Behind him, hand grenades knock together on someone's lap. Windows are pushed open. The driving wind rushes loudly through the small cabin. Jens looks briefly over his left shoulder and sees the Norwegian woman leaning her upper body out into the open, the muzzle of her HK pointing at the three-master. Instinctively, he knows Tiz is doing the same on the right-hand side. Meanwhile, Jens can clearly make out people in the rigging and on deck.

"Fifty meters."

Suddenly, a figure on board is moving frantically, waving its arms. Apparently, they have been spotted.

"Now!" shouts Waltraud. At the same time, she fires. Tiz fires, too. Jens watches as dozens of bullets smash into the hull, piercing the sails and sweeping crew members off their feet. They replace their empty magazines in seconds. The two shooters fire without ceasing. Just before they fly over the ship, Jens looks over his shoulder at Franca, who pulls the pins of four grenades and tosses them onto the deck in pairs. The shock waves from the explosions make the plane shake. Jens pulls the rudder first to the right, giving Waltraud a clear sightline to the port of the ship's stern. A few moments later, he switches direction again. Their bombardment falls silent. In order to turn quickly, Jens goes full throttle.

The starboard wingtips dip down toward the sea.

They can now hear sporadic return fire from the ship. The plane shakes slightly each time bullets catch its wings. Jens straightens it up, this time giving Tiz a clear sightline. His short volleys are a storm of lead.

Jens contemplates the extent of the devastation below him. Dead bodies are strewn across the deck. But although the huge three-master is on fire in two places, it doesn't look seriously damaged. Franca drops grenades again. Two of them land in the sea instead of reaching their intended target. Jens heads for the sun, bringing the plane out of the danger zone.

"Damn! That's not good enough. It's just not enough," Tiz exclaims, hammering his fist on his seat.

No one disagrees. Once the fires were extinguished, the boat would be able to sail again. Damaged, but maneuverable.

"That's not the only bad news," Waltraud says. "One of the bullets must have damaged our system. We're now flying purely on solar power."

"We can't switch back to the batteries?" Jens inquires.

"Nope. Either the cables or one of the batteries itself were hit. The cables could be repaired on land, but we should turn back immediately to be back before sunset."

"I can't let them get away with it," Tiz interjects.

"There's nothing I can do about it now," Waltraud defends herself.

"You can always do something," he counters. Jens senses Tiz's frustration and feels the same way himself.

"How many shells do we have left?" inquires the Newgoslavian.

"Three," Franca replies.

He then rummages in his backpack before turning to Jens. "I need your help again." His voice sounds strangely calm. The usual irritable tone has vanished.

"What do you want me to do?" asks the Dutchman.

"Make one more pass over it. After that, you can head back. I'll do the rest."

Jens looks at him over his shoulder, uncomprehending. Tiz sighs and explains what he intends to do next.

This time they fly toward the three-master head-on. Tiz's hope is that the spinnaker will hide the plane until he can put his plan into action. He firmly rejects the objections and concerns of the rest of the crew.

"If they reach Corfu, it'll be over for the people there," he says, speculating that no one will disagree with this argument.

"But what about your daughter?" asks Waltraud. "Shouldn't you be thinking about her, too?"

This makes him laugh bitterly. "What do you think has been my greatest driving force over the years?" When no one responds, he continues,

"Making sure she doesn't have to be afraid when she leaves the house. We were so close to achieving that goal—until those monsters down there showed up." Tiz points to the ship below them. "If they get their way, it will all have been for nothing."

Waltraud looks aside, clearly embarrassed.

"You may think I don't know how my antics come across in public," he adds. "Even if it doesn't necessarily look like it, I am capable of self-awareness. But I'm not capable of change, unfortunately—I don't have the strength or motivation for that. Too much of me was broken during the civil war. Perhaps my traumas could have been treated in one of the rich countries of the West, but, unfortunately, I had no way of accessing them. And then the pandemic came, and now there's no one who can help me, either here or in the West." Tiz hangs his head. An awkward silence follows his words. "My head's so messed up now. I can't cope with it anymore," he adds quietly. "I haven't been able to for years. I just want Lejla to have some good memories of me. Not the image of an angry man who's gone mad and can't commit."

There is silence for a moment and then Jens finally answers. "Okay, get ready, Tiz. I'll adjust the course."

He stows the remaining eight clips in the cargo pockets of his pants. He hangs the two MP5s crosswise around his neck. The remaining hand grenades go into his vest pockets. Finally, he takes a knife out of his right boot.

The white sail is almost within reach. It is blocking their view of the deck. Tiz takes a deep breath. He feels strangely detached and is highly focused at the same time. All that matters now is putting a stop to the people on the ship.

"You have twenty seconds," the pilot announces. "But I'm afraid I can't fly lower than fifteen meters."

Tiz nods. Jens's countdown sounds like it's coming to him through a waterfall.

Despite the adrenaline, he remains calm. He has to brace himself against the door, which can only be opened with difficulty at a hundred and ten kilometers per hour, as if the plane wants to keep him in the cabin. Jens has just finished counting. *Soon it will all be over*, thinks Tiz. He plunges out feet first.

The free fall at high speed takes his breath away. Tiz hurtles toward the ship at a forty-five degree angle. He clasps the knife pommel with both hands. At the last second, he yanks the blade over his head before landing on the inflated sail as if it's a giant airbag. The force of the collision with the spinnaker drives the remaining air out of his lungs. His arsenal of weapons bores into his torso. With all his might, he pushes the knife through the heavy cloth. Then he slides down. The canvas gives way more and more and he cuts a larger and larger hole in it as he descends.

On deck, someone gives a yell. Rapid-fire weapons ring out. The shots flying close by Tiz shred the sail. One grazes his forearm. He drops the last three meters, comes up at an angle, and twists his left ankle. He drops onto one knee. Before he can fire, a bullet hits him in the shoulder. The force of the impact spins him around. Ignoring the pain, he reaches for the submachine guns again. Fires. Swinging the muzzles from side to side at stomach level. The crew he hit scream out, his double salvo ripping holes in their ranks. Tiz reaches into his vest pocket, unlocks, and tosses a hand grenade toward the stern. He immediately takes cover at the base of the mast in front of him. The explosion causes wood and metal to burst, followed by more cries of pain.

His ears are ringing. His magazines full, Tiz tries to stand up, but his body isn't functioning as usual. His damaged ankle is swollen. It takes him a huge amount of effort to fire with the hand of the arm that was hit. Staggering, he approaches the center of the ship where the entrance to the lower deck gapes open. Two bullets burn into his stomach, yanking him around. Tiz spots the likely shooter among the clouds of smoke and responds with a long lead salvo. He doesn't care whether he's hit him, but the firing stops. His target is directly below him. He fires blindly through the opening. His eyelids flicker. Tiz feels his reserves of strength dwindling. The rage and hatred blazing inside him are all that are driving him on.

Fear-filled screams force their way out the bowels of the sailing ship. He welcomes them. Smiling, he shuffles to the stairs. Coughing, he descends them. Ahead of him he hears frantic footsteps. On the off chance, he shoots in their direction, misses a step, and falls headlong to the ground. His face lands in a sticky puddle that tastes of blood. He rests for a couple of heartbeats before crawling on with the last of his strength. On deck, he hears footsteps and panicked shouts. They are looking for him, he registers with some satisfaction. But his life force is fading with every breath. His vision is darkening; everything seems blurred. Nevertheless, he continues to crawl along the narrow corridor to the storage room. His head bumps against something hard. Tiz looks up. Through his veil of exhaustion, he spots a green wooden crate with white lettering, the kind he knows well. Behind it and above it, dozens of the same boxes are piled up. He has arrived at his destination. Trembling, he fishes out the last hand grenade.

He removes the pin with his teeth. His arm goes limp. The explosive device rolls out of his hand and clatters against the chest. Tiz rolls onto his back, smiles, and exhales one last time.

Jens keeps looking out the window over his shoulder in the vague hope of finding out what is happening on the three-master. All the while, he hears gunshots and screams.

Suddenly, a glaring ball of light appears at the spot where fractions of a second before the ship damaged by their air attack was smoking away. The huge explosion blows it into thousands and thousands of pieces and sends out a shock wave that reaches the plane seconds later, shaking it to its core.

Then it's all over. Jens repeatedly checks the panel displays. He feels devoid of all emotion. Tiredly, he asks himself whether he will ever learn to deal with the losses he has suffered. Within a few hours, he has seen two people die, each of whom had grown close to his heart in their own ways.

His hand moves to Waltraud's, which squeezes his tightly. The look in her eyes tells him that she is suffering, too. But he sees no tears.

In the back seat, Franca looks emotionlessly out the window. He knows well this tough aura she tries to hide her painful feelings behind. He probably seems just as emotionless now.

Have we all become like Franca, unable to deal with the ups and downs of our emotions? Unable to laugh when we feel joy and cry when it hurts? To surrender to love?

That's probably what happens to people who have to fight for survival every day for ten years in an apocalypse. The means of expression that allow us to process these feelings just atrophy.

So how are we any different from the zombies we're desperately trying not to become?

When he can't come up with a satisfactory answer, Jens looks at the display again. He is gradually becoming convinced that several of the solar panels are defective because the energy yield has dropped significantly. But there'll be enough to get them all back to Shkodër, he notes indifferently.

In the silence of the cockpit, he checks once again that they are on the right course. Then he accelerates, agonizingly certain that he cannot escape his grief.

CHAPTER 11

RETURN

Cassiopeia is sleeping. I am dog-tired, but I can't stop looking at her. On the other hand, I want to finish the chronicle of my adventures with the people dearest to me before the memories begin to fade. Or the pain overwhelms me.

Now I'm sitting at my desk in the cabin as we sail past Sicily on the same latitude as Malta. After every sentence I write, my gaze is drawn to Cas, who seems unmoved by all the chaos of the past weeks. My displeasure at her reckless odyssey has long since faded. The blanket she's lying under is rising and falling in time with her breathing. Her features look soft in the cool light of the LED lamp and are in sharp contrast with the pronounced lines of her eyelids and lips. Right now, she embodies the calmness, serenity, and the confidence that the future may bring the good things that I have been longing for. My hopes of ever reaching this state seem to have been extinguished for a long time. *Losing all hope is freedom.* I remember hearing someone say that once, an eternity ago. Back then, the deeper meaning of the words had escaped me, but today, with the certainty of having lost something fundamental, forever, and irretrievably, they seem like my final salvation. To entrust myself to the limbo of uncertainty in order to reach a state approximating to tranquility or even contentment seems impossible.

But I digress. The events of the last few weeks, which are directly linked to events of nearly ten years ago, are what I intend to write about. Our troops had headed out to help people in need. We had failed spectacularly, and we could have considered ourselves lucky that anyone at all from the original crew had returned home. And with that, our story could have come to an end. But there's a lot more that deserves to be mentioned.

When the battle of Shkodër was over, there were huge gaps in the ranks of my unit. If my greenhorns had not been mixed with the Black Masks, who had probably saved them from total extinction, I might have had to set off for Iceland alone. The sometimes disturbed looks on their faces told me that they were trying to process their appalling experiences. But I wasn't worried about this because I knew exactly what quality of psychological treatment would be waiting for them when they got back to Reykjavík. They'd ultimately be able to cope.

After the battle, we tended to the wounded. We weren't able to save many. The last of the zombies floundering on the field were unceremoniously liberated. We tied the two traitors we had captured back-to-back with each other. A guard was posted, even though neither of them seemed particularly eager to incur further wrath by trying to escape.

In the late afternoon, Waltraud and Jens returned with Franca. After a bumpy landing in the fields below the hill, they got out. Tiz wasn't with them. I looked for Lejla and found her in the crowd of onlookers. The young Newgoslavian broke away from the ranks as if in a trance and ran to meet the party from the plane.

Her steps became slower the closer she got. From where I was standing, it looked as if Waltraud was trying to make eye contact with her. As soon as she shook her head, indicating the outcome of the mission, Lejla fell to her knees and began to cry. It almost strangled me. Even though I wasn't close to her in the crowd, I went over to the young woman to offer her some comfort. She hardly noticed our condolences. She went to the *Sinji Galeb* to mourn. Only Lucas was allowed to stay with her, and he gave us regular updates on how she was doing.

In the evening, finally, I saw Cassiopeia. She immediately wanted to be close to me. After that, she did not leave my side. Whenever I went to the bathroom or showered, she would sit by the door, waiting for me to come out. At first, I raged at her recklessness, which she was unable to understand. "I wanted to be with you," she said in response to each of my tantrums, which admittedly were limited. As she said it, she looked at me so pitifully that it almost broke my heart. Trying to elicit further details about her escape was a waste of effort. Since I'd find out all about it from Franca sooner or later anyway, I left the child alone.

The time came on the second day after battle. My long-lost friend joined us for breakfast, which the rest of the crew ate under the late spring sun. Despite the friendly weather, the mood was low. We had lost so many people that it was reasonable to question the whole point of undertaking the rescue mission. Except for half a dozen sentries, everyone found a place on the deck of our yacht. Franca brought only Silent Star for company, and her presence provided some distraction from the gloomy thoughts that tormented the crews.

I kept thinking about Backup.

After Waltraud, Jens, Franca, and I, with heavy hearts, had told the remaining rescuers about our history with Backup, we listened for hours to the Italian woman's account of the odyssey that had taken her twice across the Atlantic Ocean. But giving all the details in these pages would go beyond the scope of this memoir. So I will only report the relevant part, about her return.

"As I said," she said after finishing a long narrative, "I escaped from GenLaboratories, where I was subjected to various tests because of my zombie fungus immunity. I then teamed up with the survivors who saved my life. Together, we searched for a spot to settle down to make a fresh start. But that was not . . . feasible. As a result of the nuclear strikes in the big cities, which the American government was intending to use to fight the plague, whole areas were contaminated. The electromagnetic pulses generated in the process had also destroyed all electrical equipment," she explained. "All over the continent. We couldn't contact anyone even to find out what was happening in the other parts of the world. After six years of finding nowhere to settle in the United States, we were forced to take the last survivors somewhere it might be possible to build a new life. Because the undead there are far more agile and stronger than their European counterparts. The mutation might have been cause by the radioactive radiation."

She hung her head. I knew that feeling of helplessness that the memory stirred in her. "I know there were attempts to get to the bottom of the phenomenon," she continued. "But all of them had failed. And after six years, we had to admit to ourselves that we'd be doomed if we didn't get away in time.

We then captured ships, of which there was no shortage in the port of Wilmington, and set off northward, hoping to find at least the Canadian wilderness free of the undead. That was about a year ago. But there, too, hordes of extremely aggressive zombies were waiting for us. On top of that, it seemed that during the winter months, the polar cold had an invigorating effect on them."

"Hey, this is something I've been racking my brain about for years," interjected an audience member. "I mean, why don't low temperatures bother them? How do they cope with hypothermia?"

The expression on Franca's face took on a fatalistic quality.

Nevertheless, she smiled. "Does the term *Iceman* mean anything to anyone? From before the apocalypse?"

We looked at each other and shook our heads.

The Italian sighed. "While I was at the GenLaboratories complex, I met Dr. Brian McTiernan. He was the project leader that aimed to develop a vaccine against the zombie plague."

"Wait a minute," I interrupted her. "Backup said the Germans already had one."

"Yeah, right. But GenLaboratories wanted to develop one of their own," she pointed out. "All the same, Brian was one of the few people who still treated me like a human being and not just as a test subject. Because of my experiences, he'd often ask me for advice. Like when we had wondered during the first winter why the zombies were immune to the cold. We discovered the answer to that much later, after going through Ethan Boileau's file for the hundredth time. In the first weeks of the pandemic, they had compiled all the information about him that ever existed. From his birth certificate and his bank account activity to his Facebook account."

"Patient zero," Waltraud said in surprise.

Franca nodded. "Correctomundo. In retrospect, I could have slapped myself for not thinking of it sooner. But no one thought for a second that it'd be found among all the info on social media."

"And what does all this have to do with Iceman?" someone asked impatiently.

Franca smiled almost benignly. "Iceman was a Dutchman back then, who had developed his own method for freeing himself from the depression he had fallen into after events in his private life. Meditation and breathing exercises were parts of this practice, but learning to survive in extremely low temperatures was the main focus. After perfecting his technique, Iceman was able to spend hours covered in ice without freezing to death," she explained, ignoring the skeptical looks. "He swam among the Arctic ice floes and dove under meters of ice layers on frozen lakes—clad only in a bathing suit. His practice had no esoteric or religious frills. The philosophy dispensed with dogma. And the health benefits of his method were undeniable. When even science began to take an interest in it, there was real hype around the Iceman. You could attend a workshop anywhere around the globe, or get the knowledge via an app. His followers worshipped him like a rock star."

"Ooh," said someone for whom the proverbial lightbulb went on.

Franca nodded at him. "Ethan was a member of a number of groups on social media whose members celebrated the method developed by Iceman. Apparently, he also practiced it regularly himself."

She paused. "The ability of the undead to withstand the cold is most likely due to this."

"Fucking Iceman, eh," said the Canadian at Franca's side.

"Indeed," the latter confirmed, taking a sip of water.

"What happened farther north in Canada, when you were looking for a new place to stay?" inquired Jens.

"That's right; that's actually what we were talking about," the Italian replied.

"Well, the undead gave us a run for our money there, too. They were even there to greet us in Newfoundland. As a result, I advised everyone to sail for Europe." Franca took a full lungful of air. It was a gesture that had burned itself into my memory years ago. She had often used it before getting on to something significant. "I remembered that Eva and Patrick had left for Iceland. Honestly, after all these years, I had no hope of ever running in to any of you again. But I needed a straw to clutch at. One that would save me from abandoning myself completely to fate. But at first, they ignored my suggestion. The elders of the Indigenous communities could not be convinced that we would find landscapes in Europe like those they had once inhabited on the North American continent. If they felt compelled to uproot, they at least wanted to settle in a similar environment where they could continue to live according to their customs and traditions." A bitter smile played around her lips. "On top of that, we didn't even know what the zombie population was like in Europe by now. We continued to try our luck with smaller hunting and scavenging excursions in Canada, but we were increasingly unsuccessful. Food supplies dwindled, the situation became more desperate—until the elders realized that everyone would die if we didn't strike out in a new direction, familiar landscapes or not. So, we finally set out for Iceland.

The decision seemed to fire up the last remaining survivors, but I could tell by looking at them that another disappointment would be fatal. It would break their spirit. So everyone was all the happier when a fishing fleet sailed toward us about twenty nautical miles from Reykjavík. Okay, at first, they were very wary and skeptical of us, but from the moment I asked if they had heard of a German couple named Eva and Patrick, they were thunderstruck. How could I have known how big Iceland is? In my mind, it was an island where everyone knew each other." Franca grinned at me. "The fishermen first questioned me about how I had heard of you. I gave them a long answer, and they told me a story. The legend of the massacre of Vágur."

So the circle had been closed. I smiled back wistfully.

"The news of Patrick's death hit me hard. But you seemed to be notorious." She smiled graciously.

"Yeah, I heard that too," I said, far less enthusiastically.

Franca shrugged. "On the ship, everyone knew who you were, what part of the island you lived in. Even that you had an eight-year-old daughter. They were seriously impressed when I said I was friends with you. At first, they wouldn't believe a word I said—I guess sailors assume everyone is spinning a yarn. But how could I have found out about you in America? My description of you, however, tallied with those of them who had supposedly met you. In the end, they had to believe me. And then we set out to find you."

"I don't suppose you sailed directly to Holmsberg?"

"How do you think we came across Cassiopeia?" said Franca. "As soon as we got the info on your location, we headed there. I went there with Star"—she pointed to the Canadian at her side—"and a handful of others in one small boat. Cas was sitting in the grass as if she had been waiting for us. She was leafing through your journals. She was quite startled by our arrival. I immediately introduced myself and asked if she knew an Eva who apparently lived around there. Long story short, Cas simply said, after she had recovered from her fright, *Yes, she's my mother*. We then took her back to her grandparents. But while we were talking to them about sailing after you as soon as possible, she stole out and hid on our ship. Three days later, we caught her stealing food from the galley."

"Good thing you didn't turn around to take her back," I said, trying hard not to sound cynical. "You rescued us at literally the last second."

Franca shrugged. "If we hadn't sailed on with the same ship, those who stayed would have dropped Cas off in Reykjavik. Some wanted to see if Iceland was suitable to settle in—and if they were even welcome there. But I sailed right after you. Cas was on my ship, so we took her along without further ado. From your diaries and the transcript of the first message from Sweden, we learned exactly where you would be." Franca took another sip. Her expression darkened. "The column of smoke from that burning armada was visible for miles around when we arrived. I was afraid I was already too late. Nevertheless, we rushed to help. While the fire was still being put out, I asked about you and learned you were in big trouble on land." Her tone became a shade darker still. "If only we'd been on the scene faster, we might have saved Backup."

"No," said Waltraud shaking her head, "you're looking at it wrong. Backup wasn't the Backup we used to know. The person who was inhabiting Backup's body had long since chosen a different path. One that we may never understand."

A silence followed her words. I tried to imagine what it must have meant for Backup to lead such a life and kept coming back to the realization that Waltraud was right.

"So what's next for you guys?" I asked Silent Star, trying to distract from what was, for some of us, a painful topic.

She looked uncertain. "I have no idea," she replied, shaking her head.

"Excuse me for butting in," a Newgoslavian woman four seats to my left called out, "but I might have an idea." We looked at her. It bothered her to suddenly be at the center of the discussion. Stammering, she looked at the Canadian. "I . . . know a patch of land—similar to the prairie . . . just three or four days' sail from here. There are forests, rivers, and lakes all around it, too. It might be just the thing." She shrugged. "Or it'd at least be worth checking out now that you're in the area anyway."

Star leaned forward. "Tell me more," she replied curiously.

"And don't forget to mention the wild horses of Livno!" someone else interjected.

And so the conversation continued late into the night. Plans were made, new alliances formed, and old ones renewed.

"What are you going to do?" I asked Franca. "If you want, you'd be welcome to come to Iceland with us."

"That's a good suggestion. Maybe I'll come back to it, too. But for now, I'd like to go back to Florence, visit my old home."

"There's nothing there," I interjected. "The population of northern Italy was wiped out."

She shook her head as if to contradict my words. I saw a deep sadness in her brown eyes. "Yes, maybe," she said, "but I have to go there at least once, to stand there and see it for myself. Since the apocalypse broke out, all I've done is travel. Majorca, Germany, North America—and there I crossed almost the entire continent. I'm tired, Eva. My soul feels . . . uprooted. When I've made sure there's nothing waiting for me in Florence, I'll be able to let go better . . . at least I hope so . . . and look for a new home. Maybe Iceland, too. It's supposed to be beautiful there. But right now, part of me just wants to go home. I hope you can understand that. But if you don't, who will?" She laughed.

"Oh, you bet I understand you. If you don't find what you're looking for, my door is always open. Maybe we can start a retirement community with Waltraud and Jens."

We laughed. Tears of joy and melancholy ran down our cheeks.

"I'll talk to them," Franca said. "Those two are going to come with me anyway. Star, the young Frenchman—what's-his-name—they want to come, too, and a few others."

"Ah, you mean Lucas," I replied. "Then you're in the best company. When are you leaving?"

"Tomorrow. Lejla's people will take us to Rimini. Faster than sailing all the way around. And you?"

I nodded. "Tomorrow, too. There's nothing to keep us here."

"Let's get everything ready so we can have a relaxed last evening together," she suggested. She then paddled over to her ship to pack and say good-bye to the members of her old crew who wouldn't be accompanying her.

She was back on board as the last rays of light were gleaming in the sky. In the meantime, we had prepared our yacht so that we could leave at dawn without further ado. Sixteen people who had followed Franca to the Adriatic expressed the desire to sail to Iceland. They wanted to tell their compatriots there about the land they might be able to settle.

They'd make their way back with any who were interested. We had an abundance of empty cabins, so we agreed. The North American refugees agreed the following day to explore the area between Zadar and Bihać. The rest were welcome to settle in one of the two towns.

The inner struggle of the Newgoslavians after Tiz's death was plain to see. It seemed as if the shock was preventing them from making any decisions. At first, they gathered around Lejla, asking her to lead them. In a quiet minute, I asked the young woman why she had shaken her head and refused every request and what she had advised them to do.

"Government? That's not my thing," she replied. "Besides, Tiz wouldn't have wanted the population to hand over responsibility for their lives into the hands of some leader or other again. If history's taught us anything, it's that this never ends happily for us southern Slavs. He'd have preferred them to manage without authorities."

"You want them to continue in anarchy?" I bristled.

Lejla shrugged. "Why not? It doesn't mean everywhere will immediately descend into chaos. They have to find a way for everyone to respect certain social standards. That's a lot of personal responsibility for each individual, but at least it'll be difficult to turn people against each other again."

"And what are you going to do?" I asked.

"I don't know. There is nothing keeping me in Newgoslavia. I'd gradually like to see more of the world. Maybe I'll go with Franca, Lucas, and Lena. We'll see what happens . . ."

And that's what she did. Secretly, I believed Lejla was following the call of her heart rather than the call of adventure. Who would have blamed her? Lena was a likeable woman for whom hardly any path was too long or too arduous to follow for love.

We spent the last night under the open sky together. Cas had fallen asleep in my arms. Someone brought a blanket and covered her. At dawn, we got up. Our good-byes were brief and painless, as if to signal that we'd see each other again soon. Cas and I watched and waved after them as they rowed over to their sailboats. With the first rays of sunshine, we unfurled the sails. A breeze came up, rippling the surface of the sea, stretching the lines, and tearing apart the threads of our friendship one more time.

It's cool outside. The sea is calm. Our ship is gliding steadily toward . . . home? Is Iceland home just because there's a house and a bed waiting for me there? Can a foreign piece of land that shelters you from death seriously be home?

Can anything be home for a human being after they have been uprooted along with their roots and, on top of that, robbed of their heart? Or is it relationships with others, if they make us feel safe, that we've arrived, that are home?

Once I would have answered at least one of those two questions in the affirmative. But life has made me cynical, so I say no.

My gaze falls on Cas, and joy flutters in my chest. *Here! This is everything you need*, says my broken heart submissively. For a split second, I'm inclined to fall for it. But I pull myself together. Children are not home. You can't force them to become a surrogate home for adults. They may always be the most important thing in life, at least for certain parents.

But children eventually leave to seek their own homes. They have to. What form Cassiopeia's home will take—and whether she will find one at all—is written in the stars. But it is not up to me to determine this. I must leave this question with me, not burden Cas with it. It is my duty to go in search of my own home in this present time.

For the demons do not like being uprooted. At the moment, they are slumbering, fed up with the war. I don't want to give them an excuse to rise again. And I'm just as reluctant to deny what remains of my heart the motivation for my own existence. Otherwise, I might have gone and lain down in the fields outside Shkodër. Then I think of my daughter, and the task is crystal clear in my mind's eye.

I have to be the home Cassiopeia needs until she has grown enough to break away. The thought of the time after that is frightening because that's when—at the latest—I will be forced to confront my fears.

It's late. My wristwatch tells me it is dawn. I want to sleep, but the fear of finding a bigger emptiness inside me in the morning is paralyzing. Even the words are leaving me. Once again, I stroke the old diary lying on the table. I pick it up with my left hand and bring it to my heart. The memories immortalized in it are unspeakably painful. But they also hold comfort, which gives me the strength finally to go to bed.

ABOUT THE AUTHOR

Dinko Skopljak is the Yugoslavia-born author of the Anno Initium trilogy, which launched with his debut novel, *The Stranded*. Prior to becoming a writer, Skopljak worked variously as a dental technician, a photographer, and a web designer. A lover of science fiction and fantasy, cinema, and nature, he lives in Würzburg, Germany, with his two daughters.